Norcliff

K.A. Connolly

For Rey, who helped me to pick myself up,
dust myself off, and start anew.

Preface

THIS NOVEL CONTAINS some scenes involving graphic violence, as well as one scene of sexual harassment and minor assault. If this troubles you, please either refrain from reading or proceed with caution.

Prologue
A Change in Occupation

A LORD IN a silver hauberk brought his chestnut brown horse to a halt before the beggar by the side of the dusty country road. Though his retinue of guards drew in close with suspicious frowns, the lord on the horse smiled with the ease of one whose face seemed built for joy, and his blond hair gleamed in the sun. "What brings you to the side of the road in such a sorry state, my good man?" he asked.

The beggar stared up from beneath the hood of his cloak but didn't reply. Everything about him seemed worn, from his dirty brown hair, to his dim brown eyes, to the faded scars on his face. The guard riding closest to the lord gave the beggar a stern look. "You will answer the question Lord Hart has asked of you, or you will suffer the consequences for your impertinence."

"Peace, Hayward, such force isn't necessary in so trivial a matter." The beggar watched with deadened eyes as the lord dismounted to stand before him with a kind smile. "However, I must admit to a growing curiosity about you, stranger. Will you not tell me about yourself? What's your occupation?"

The beggar looked away into the distance with a grim cast to his face. "My occupation is death."

The lord's face fell into a more serious expression, and his smile grew sad. "There's no future in death."

The beggar pulled his cloak more tightly shut around his shoulders. "There's no future for me, either."

Lord Hart gave a great sigh and straightened to his full height. "That settles it. If you have no future, then you won't be too busy for a visit to my home."

"My lord -" Hayward cut himself off as Lord Hart gave a slight shake of his head to waylay objections.

Lord Hart gave the beggar a questioning look. "Did you have other plans for this evening?"

The beggar's mouth tilted sideways in wry amusement. "I have no plans."

Lord Hart clapped his hands together. "Excellent. Come along, then. You may dine with my family tonight." The lord mounted his horse with a cheerful laugh. "Though you may find the journey to my home tiresome. We have many more stops to make along the way."

Hayward reluctantly loaned the beggar the use of one of the spare pack horses, and the procession rode off with one new member. Lord Hart was true to his word and stopped off at every cluster of homes they passed to speak with the villagers, who greeted them with good cheer. Each town they visited held a brief greeting ceremony followed by a discussion and an offering of the yearly tax. The beggar watched as Lord Hart made time to greet each community leader and merchant in his path with patience and genuine enjoyment. After a few of these breaks in their journey, Lord Hart turned to the beggar with a wide grin.

"One more stop, my new friend, and then we shall have the chance to get to know each other better. But first, what's your name?"

The beggar hesitated, then gave a resigned shrug. "Jax will do."

The lord smiled widely. "Jax it is, then. Well met, Jax! You may call me Finley." Hayward harrumphed from his post to the right and a little back from the lord, where he had spent the day shooting dark looks at Jax and muttering under his breath.

"Thank you, my lord." Jax dipped his head.

"Not another one." Lord Hart laughed. "I'm surrounded by so many people who refuse to call me by my name that I fear I shall forget it! What will become of me, when I grow old and forgetful and think my first name is Lord?"

"Your strength of mind and memory is unquestionable, my lord,"

Hayward said, puffing himself up as though offended by the very idea of his lord forgetting something.

"That's kind of you to say, Hayward, but we both know I am no more intelligent than any other man, and a great deal less intelligent than many." Finley grinned at Jax. "Mark my words, Jax, I will have you call me by my first name sooner or later."

Jax's mouth twitched. "We'll see."

Their conversation drew to a close as they rode into a town that was larger than the others they had visited that day. They stopped outside the elegantly arched doors of a cathedral. "I say." Finley paused on his climb up the cathedral steps to look at a bundle of cloth to the side of the entrance. "Pastor McCleary usually runs a tidier ship." He knelt to pick up the bundle of cloth, and a wail started up from under the pile of ragged blankets.

"My lord!" Hayward rushed up next to Finley, who pulled back the blankets to reveal the tearstained face of a baby. "Let me take it, my lord. It could be carrying all manner of disease." Hayward held out his hands, and the baby's crying intensified.

"Really, Hayward. You're frightening the poor thing." Finley held the baby against his chest and swayed from side to side. The baby quieted, and Finley grinned. "Best leave the little one to me."

Hayward sighed, and a few of the guards chuckled. "Very well." He climbed the rest of the stairs to knock on the cathedral door.

A round-faced, amiable looking man with thinning white hair and wire-rimmed glasses perched on his nose opened the door. "Lord Hart, there you are! Welcome, welcome, do come in."

"Pastor McCleary, how good to see you again," Finley said as they followed the pastor into the cathedral.

"A joyous occasion indeed! How is your family?" The pastor rummaged through a wooden chest resting on a bench in the entryway. "I have gifts for your daughter."

"Wonderful!" Finley turned to Jax with a beaming grin. "Hold this, will you," he said, and Jax reflexively reached out to receive an armful of cloth and infant. Jax and the baby stared at each other in mutual shock. Then the baby waved a fist in the air and giggled. "Excellent, the little one likes you." Finley turned away to receive the gifts, and another ceremony began as a line of nuns and monks greeted the lord in the main hall. Jax hung at the back of the crowd, unable to look away from the baby, whose eyelids began to droop sleepily. He rocked slightly from side to side and watched the baby drift off to sleep. The ceremony moved off deeper into the cathedral, and Jax sat in one of the ornate wooden chairs by the entryway to watch the baby rest. There was little noise except for the tiny inhalations and exhalations from the baby and the sound of Jax's own breaths, louder and slower. A slight rustle reached his ears, all that came from the wind blowing outside, and something creaked gently in the ceiling overhead. Jax felt the muscles in his shoulders and neck uncoil, and an ever present discomfort in his mind eased. The lifted weight of discomfort was one he'd carried for so long that he'd forgotten what it was like to live without it. This, sitting here, watching over the orphaned child, felt right in a way very little had in his life. Jax felt his own eyelids begin to droop.

"Ahem."

Jax looked up to find Hayward coughing into his fist with a scowl and, behind him, Finley watching with an amused expression. "I see you've made friends," Finley said.

"I'm not well suited for friendship, my lord." Jax rose and made to hand the baby back to him, but Finley waved him off with a smile.

"On the contrary, I've found children to be excellent judges of character. Keep the baby. You may help us by watching over the little one until we reach Norcliff."

Jax held the baby closer. "Yes, my lord."

The ride to Finley's home was swift after that. The last village lay just outside the walls of the lord's keep. They rode over a moat and through sections of town separated by walls that ringed around a central keep in a pattern meant for defense against invaders and prevention of fires. The walls were hewn out of a tough, gray stone that matched the cliffs the keep was partially carved into, and most of the buildings were made of the same material, especially as they neared the keep. Finally, they stopped outside the metal double doors that led into the keep itself. Finley drew his horse up to the front steps. A groom took hold of the horse's reins, and Finley jumped to the ground to bound through the doors as a pair of servants opened them.

"Finley, welcome home!" A smiling woman with dark red hair in a long braid walked into the entryway to greet him, and Finley swept her up into a hug and swung her in a circle, laughing. When he set her back on her feet, she shook her head at him, though she smiled widely. "Lovely to have you back, my dear, but was that really necessary?"

"Very necessary." Finley turned to find Jax waiting at the base of the front steps, baby still held in his arms close to his chest. "I've found us some company for dinner. Jax, this is my wife, Evelyn Hart."

Evelyn regarded Jax and the baby with a carefully neutral expression. The baby twitched and turned in its sleep, and Jax rocked from side to side in response. At the sight, the smile returned to Evelyn's face. "Well met, Jax."

Jax bowed slightly, careful not to upset the baby. "My lady."

Evelyn looked at the baby in Jax's arms. "I see you've brought home not one but two new friends, Finley." She called for a nurse to take care of the baby. She then arranged for a bath and new set of clothes for Jax, waving off his thanks with a gaily, "It's what any good host should do."

Jax took the time to soak in the bath, despite knowing he was delaying dinner. He had not had warm water to wash with in a long time. The clothing they gave him was in good repair and fit him well. He put it on with some hesitation. He didn't like the burden of good clothing, didn't want to have to worry about losing or damaging it when he was back out on the road. The outfit suited him well, though, and it would be rude to refuse the hospitality of these kind people. So he bore the weight of respectable clothing once more, uneasy but resolved to make the effort for his hosts.

Once the three of them were settled at the dinner table, Finley began to make a case for adopting the baby. "It would be good for Erin to have a companion, growing up," Finley said to his wife, who smiled faintly.

"Yes, husband, but please don't bring more orphaned children home before consulting with me first."

Jax concentrated on eating his soup slowly enough to not make a mess, though his stomach ached with hunger, and he didn't mention that he had been an orphan, too.

Finley reached over the table to bring his wife's hand to his lips for a kiss, to Evelyn's amusement. "You're as kind as you are generous, darling."

"Yes, yes. I suppose you'll want us to keep Jax around as well."

"You've read my mind."

"How did I ever guess?" Evelyn smiled wryly at her husband, who looked at her with eyes that twinkled merrily. She turned to Jax. "Have you an occupation, sir?"

"I…" Jax didn't want to answer the way he had earlier that day and watch the lady's face fall.

"He's currently unoccupied, my dear," Finley said cheerfully, as though this was a great discovery on his part. "I've brought him here because I can recognize great potential when I see it. Did you not say you were looking to hire more staff?"

"Yes, to watch Erin," Evelyn said thoughtfully. "And now, to watch the new one as well. Is it a boy or a girl, by the way?" Jax blinked at Finley, who shrugged back. "Was there a name sewn into the baby's blankets?" Finley shrugged again, and Evelyn gave a heavy sigh. "Men." She signaled for one of the waitstaff to come closer. "Gerry, go and ask Marie the gender of the baby and see if there's a name anywhere on the baby's belongings."

"Yes, ma'am." Gerry bowed and left the dining room.

Finley grinned at Evelyn. "I would be lost without you."

"Yes." Evelyn raised her eyebrows and huffed out a soft laugh. "You would." She took a sip of her wine, and then Gerry was back.

"A girl, ma'am. There was no name to be found."

Evelyn smiled. "A sister for Erin. How wonderful. I always wanted to have a sister myself, you know."

"I do know." Finley straightened in his seat like a hound scenting its prey. "They'll run circles around me, if they're anything like you."

"Liana," Evelyn said. "Liana is a good, strong name. What do you think?"

Finley bowed his head. "You're as wise as you are beautiful, wife."

"You're a flattering fool, husband, but I love you anyway."

"I am speechless in the face of your good charity," Finley said in a dry voice.

"Oh, all right." Evelyn started cutting up her meat with some force.

"We'll keep her." She mock scowled at Finley. "And I may as well keep you too, husband, while I'm at it."

"Excellent!" Finley clapped his hands together. "I have just the occupation for you, Jax."

Jax froze, spoon halfway to his mouth. "Have you?"

"My daughter will need a companion and lady's maid. You can raise this girl and teach her to do the job."

"I know nothing about lady's maids, my lord, and even less about babies."

"Then you have much to learn," Finley said, seeming unbothered by Jax's complete lack of experience. "In return for your service, I'll give you room and board with a small salary besides. What do you say?"

Jax stared down at his plate. Earlier that day, he had been certain he had nothing more to say.

Evelyn met Finley's eyes and set down her fork and knife to look at Jax in concern. "Do you have some obligation that would keep you from these duties?"

"No, my lady." Jax looked up at the lord and lady, stunned by the offer they had just made.

"Then it's settled." Evelyn nodded. "This will make my life easier as well, since I no longer have to search for someone to hire. Welcome to your new home, Jax. Thank you for tolerating my husband's intrusions into your life, and I hope you decide to remain here long after Liana has grown."

There weren't words to express Jax's gratitude. He settled on the conventional response of, "Thank you, my lady," but it still felt inadequate.

With arrangements made for Jax and Liana, the dinner went on without a fuss. Evelyn and Finley caught each other up on what they had done while apart, sometimes asking Jax a question or two, but mostly allowing him to listen in silence while he carefully, slowly ate his first good meal in weeks.

Jax found proof of the Hart family's generosity and good nature in the easy stride and content faces of the soldiers and servants he passed in the halls, though he didn't truly need more proof of that. He spent an uneasy two weeks in the servants' quarters on a bed that was too soft, next to people who made too much noise, before he requested to move to the empty room in the back of the armory. The head butler approved his request, and Jax moved the day he got the approval. He then found himself, for the first time in his life, in a place that felt almost like a home, or what he had imagined a home might feel like, when he was a boy. He was at ease among the well-ordered weapons and spartan furniture. Jax spent his time by the baby's bassinet in the nursery set aside for the staff's children and passed the empty hours away from the nursery maintaining the weapons all around him, soothed by the mindless repetition of the work. Most of his job caring for Liana centered around feeding her, keeping her clean, and putting her to sleep. The other nursemaids helped him with the feeding and cleaning, but they were occupied with charges of their own for the arduous task of soothing a restless infant to sleep. He didn't know nursery rhymes or songs, so on his first day, at a loss in the face of Liana's recalcitrance, he recited fighting strategies and poisons instead. He found, to his relief, that they did the trick just as well.

Finley would sometimes stop in to see how Jax fared, leaning against the doorway to listen to the improvised lullabies with amusement or visiting the armory to admire Jax's skill with weaponry. After a few months of intermittent visits, he brought his lady wife along with him. Jax stood to attention when he saw her enter the armory.

Evelyn took in the sight of the neatly organized weaponry and armor, the well swept floors, and the dust-free windows and nodded approvingly at Jax. "The armory suits you well, I think."

Jax bowed. "Yes, milady."

"We've found a new task for you, Jax, and we hope you'll agree to do it," Finley said.

"I'm at your service, milord," Jax said.

Finley held up a hand with a smile. "Hear us out first, please, for this is no small responsibility."

"We want you to train our daughter, Erin, in combat, so that she knows how to defend herself. We'd also like you to train Liana as a guard, as well as a companion." Evelyn looked at Jax appraisingly. "We'd appreciate it if you didn't make this training public knowledge."

Jax tilted his head to the side, surprised. The nobles he knew of didn't train their daughters to fight. Perhaps they all kept it a secret, he thought, but it didn't seem likely.

Finley shifted his weight from one foot to the other. "Do you think you're up to the task?"

Jax crossed his arms and thought it over. He was certainly skilled at killing, but he had never had the opportunity or inclination to pass on his knowledge. He wasn't sure he wanted to introduce Erin and Liana to that aspect of life, but when he thought about who might teach them in his place, he couldn't think of anyone good enough to satisfy him. He nodded once, then met Finley's eyes and said, "Yes. I'll train them."

"Thank you," Finley said, and he and Evelyn seemed relieved at his reply, as if they had been worried he would refuse them. Didn't they realize, he wondered, that there was very little in the world he would refuse to do for them, if they asked it of him?

"It's long past time for you to meet Erin, if you're going to be teaching her," Evelyn said, and she led them to Erin's nursery, a place Jax had been careful to steer clear of in an effort to respect the family's privacy. Erin was two years old and completely outside of the realm of Jax's experience in life. He had spent very little time around toddlers, though he now had some skill with babies. He didn't know what to say to a child that might understand him, didn't know how to communicate with a young mind. He stared down at the little toddler, who stared back up at him with her halo of red-orange hair puffing out around her face and her wide hazel eyes.

Finley knelt to wrap an arm around Erin's shoulders. He pointed up at Jax. "This is Jax, Erin. He'll be your teacher."

Erin dipped into a wobbling curtsy with a solemn face, and Jax felt his chest shake in silent amusement. Evelyn and Finley watched Jax kneel on the floor to bow in return to their daughter with a rusty laugh.

"You laugh at last!" Finley clapped Jax on the back. "I think you've found a favorite today." Finley tucked his wife's hand into the crook of his arm with great satisfaction. "Now that we've settled that, let's get something to eat. I hear the cook's roasting duck tonight!"

Jax climbed up to his feet and bowed his head before following them to dinner. He felt his lips twitch upward and wondered at it, unable to remember the last time he'd smiled. He'd forgotten how good it was to laugh. He would find cause for much more laughter in the years to come.

1

A Future Lost

18 years later

THE DAY OF Erin Hart's wedding dawned bright and warm with the first blush of summer. A thin mist rose from the dew-laden scrub and the hardy grass that grew out of the rocky soil. Hart Keep was unusually busy for the early hour, with people rushing to and fro along the paths carved into the face of the cliff around the keep and the surrounding mountains. A white carriage decorated with swirls of silver clattered and jounced along the bridge that led out of the keep and over the narrow river that served as a moat. The swift current sent up a white froth that disrupted the icy, clear waters, and Erin leaned out of the carriage window to look down at the turbulent surface below.

Erin would be moving to a new home after the wedding, and it was with a bittersweet smile that she watched her family's keep pass out of sight, obscured by the close growing evergreens of the forest. She leaned against the window frame of her carriage and listened to the birds of the forest sing their greetings to the new day. The farther they traveled into the forest, the louder the birdsong grew.

"Not long now," Liana said from her seat across from Erin. Liana's black hair was swept back into a severe bun that exacerbated the forbidding nature of her sharp featured face, and her dark brown eyes seemed made of shadow. Her grin only accentuated the sharpness of her eyeteeth, making her resemble a mercurial sprite baring its fangs.

She held herself with the exacting poise befitting a lady's maid, though this was a title recently cast upon her by Erin's mother to give Erin a companion away from home. Jax often said that the two were a matched set of blades, but that Erin made the effort to drape her sharp edges in velvet, as a lady should.

"Not long at all." Erin sat back and traced the ivory colored embroidery on her white wedding gown. Her family's seamstress had taken months to finish it, and the weight of the embroidered cloth had surprised her each time she had put it on for a fitting. She ran her fingers over the geometric patterns that stood for health and harmony. A stag, like the one on her family's crest, ran through the patterns on her sleeve, with a mongoose, the animal on her fiance's family crest, rampant underfoot.

"Nervous?" Liana tilted her head. "If I were in your shoes, I think I'd drive myself wild with worry about all the ways today could go wrong."

Erin took a deep breath and looked down at the mongoose sewn into her clothing. Her red-orange hair tumbled over her shoulder, curls let down from her customary bun with only a few small braids to hold them away from her face in a concession to propriety for her wedding. She would become a Clairmaud and stand under the seal of the mongoose after today, as countless ancestors before her had become, as her family had planned from her betrothal at birth, to further cement the ties that had bound the Harts and Clairmauds together for centuries. She was sad to leave her home, but the sadness was eclipsed by a larger joy at the fulfillment of a rite of passage she and her fiancé had prepared for their entire lives as they grew up together and learned each other's ways. "There is nothing to fear," she said. "Marc and I know each other so well, we might as well be married already."

"And miss out on a great excuse for a party? No way." Liana grinned. "And there is the small detail of the wedding night."

Erin's stomach twinged with nerves. "I am a little nervous about that," she admitted, and her face heated at the thought of the final, physical barrier that stood between them, the only part of Marc's life that she had yet to learn.

Liana leaned over to pat Erin's shoulder. "Don't worry. Marc adores you. He'll treat you well."

Erin smiled. She knew that much for certain. "Yes." She thought of how he might look at the altar. He would braid his thin blond hair out of his face as well for the occasion, and the servants had gossiped that his mother had ordered golden fabric for his wedding clothes. She patted at the pearls pinned into her hair and the delicate white veil that draped down her back. White and gold would go well together. They already went well together as a pairing built out of carefully planned years of loving friendship.

A knock sounded from the carriage door, and Jax rode up next to Erin's window. "We've passed into the Greenway," he said in his gruff voice.

The Greenway was a narrow strip of meadowland shared by the Harts and Clairmauds as a gesture of friendship and used for gatherings between the two families. Erin took a deep breath and straightened the skirts of her wedding dress. She felt her eyes grow large with worry and her stomach churn with nerves. "Now that we're almost there, I find myself somewhat frightened after all."

Liana moved to sit next to Erin and wrapped an arm around her shoulders. "Perfectly natural."

Erin nodded jerkily and stared out the window, straining to pick out the first signs of the festivities. The sound of birdsong faded away, to be replaced by a great metal clattering. Erin peered out the carriage window. "Is that...fighting? What could possibly-"

"Halt the carriage! Halt!" Jax rode up alongside Erin. "Quickly, turn around!" The carriage swerved back around, and Jax pulled open Erin's door. "With me, Erin! Liana, meet us at the rendezvous point!"

Erin grabbed onto Jax's waist and jumped onto the back of his horse, her dress fluttering about her ankles in the breeze. "What's happening?" she cried, but Jax didn't answer.

They galloped swiftly back into the forest. After a few minutes of racing between the trees, Jax steered the horse into a shallow stream, and they slowed to allow the horse to keep its footing. Jax pulled a pair of sheathed knives out of his boots and handed them back to Erin.

"We'll meet with Liana at the caves up ahead. You two can hide there while I scout out the situation."

"All right." Erin tucked one knife into the bodice of her dress and hid the other beneath a sleeve. She twisted to look behind her but could see no sign of followers. "What happened back there?"

"Didn't get a clear read on it." Erin waited for Jax to elaborate, but with a twitch of the reins, he steered the horse back onto dry land and into a gallop. There was no more room for talking until Jax drew the horse to a halt in front of a wall of climbing ivy. "Here we are." They dismounted, and Jax pulled the ivy to the side to reveal the shadowy entrance to a cave. "After you." Erin warily stepped inside with arms outstretched into the darkness ahead of her. Jax followed, leading his horse behind him. There was very little noise except for their footsteps and the soft clinking of Jax's chain mail. Something dripped far away, and the sound echoed against the rough stone walls. They walked a little ways in, and then Jax tapped her on the shoulder.

"We can stop here." He tied his horse to a rocky outcropping, and they sat against the cold stone walls. Erin held her knees to her chest and waited for her eyes to adjust to the dark, while Jax began to methodically sharpen and test the edges of his blades.

Erin fidgeted. "Do you think everyone's okay?"

Jax grunted but didn't say anything.

"Yeah," Erin said softly and drew her knees up to her chin. "Me neither."

The thudding of hoofbeats outside drew them both into wary crouches. "Jax, it's me," Liana whispered from the other side of the covered entrance.

"Stay here," Jax said to Erin before leading his horse back out of the cave. Erin sat, hugged her knees, and peered into the dark. It was still difficult for her to see more than indistinct shapes. Jax and Liana murmured outside, but she couldn't make out what they were saying. Eventually, they fell quiet, and Erin heard Jax ride away. Liana joined her in the cave and hunched across from her, but it was too dark for Erin to read whatever expression might have been on Liana's face.

"How did you fare on your way here?" Erin asked, taking care to keep her voice low.

"I was followed at the start but managed to lose them in the forest."

"Who were they? Why did they attack?"

"Haven't the faintest idea," Liana said with artificial cheer.

"I need to know."

"We need to wait until Jax gets back."

"Yeah." Erin buried her face in her arms. "Yeah, all right."

The wait was interminable, made worse by the way Erin's emotions cycled through fear to exhausted anxiety and back to fear at the slightest hint of a sound that could be an enemy approaching. Liana bit at her fingernails, a habit from childhood that she had mostly stopped, and the sound grated on Erin's nerves. Finally, it was too much for Erin to bear. She sat up and said, "What if Jax doesn't come back?"

She could see the blurry outline of Liana pause in thought. Silence fell, until Liana said, "I don't know."

"We can't wait forever."

"No," Liana said slowly.

"I can't wait any longer." Erin heaved herself to her feet and walked out of the cave, unsteady on legs that had been inactive too long.

"Hey-" Erin could hear Liana scramble to her feet behind her. "Erin! Wait for me." Liana ran to grab her arm. "Come back," she said with an exasperated laugh. "We can take my horse."

"All right." Erin gave Liana a tight smile, all that she could force through her fear. "Thanks, Liana."

"Don't mention it." Liana shook her head. "Please don't mention it, especially not to Jax." She got onto her horse and extended a hand to help Erin. "This is a terrible idea."

"It's all I've got." Erin grunted with annoyance as she struggled to get onto the horse in her wedding gown. They rode at a cautious pace that Liana set despite Erin's urgings to go faster. It was disconcerting to ride along a path so familiar to Erin, in a place meant to signify peace and harmony, and to fear what might appear behind each tree and around every bend in the road. The routine sounds of the forest soon faded to a heavy silence that blanketed the edge of the woods and the gently rolling hills of the meadow beyond.

"It's too quiet," Liana muttered. She slowed the horse to lessen the sound of hoof beats. They rode farther into the meadow, and Erin heard a faint clash of metal against metal. It reminded her of the sound of sparring sessions with Jax and Liana. They traveled a little farther, and Erin started to hear shouting and ragged screaming. Liana stopped the horse and swiveled in her seat to look back at Erin. "I think we've heard enough. Let's go back."

Erin looked toward the source of the noise and saw someone in the Clairmaud colors run over the top of a hill into her sight. A man in black and red colors ran after him. "Is that -" Erin cut herself off in shock as the man in black and red raised a broadsword to begin what she recognized as a killing stroke.

"The Mortons," Liana hissed. She pulled on the reins to turn the horse back to the forest. "That's it, we're leaving."

Erin slid from the back of the horse onto the grassy meadow without taking her eyes away from the sight of the two men fighting on the hilltop. "No," she whispered, and she began to run to the fight.

"Erin!" Liana shouted, but Erin didn't turn back, couldn't. In front of her, the Morton man struck down the other with a decisive slash to the throat, and Erin screamed with fury as she unsheathed her daggers. The man looked up, eyes wide with surprise, but by then she was on him, stabbing him with swift fury in the gaps between his armor and cutting at the side of his neck. Blood sprayed onto her wedding gown as he fell to the ground with a wet gurgle of a gasp. She ran over the crest of the hill, and the battlefield came into sight on the other side. Pockets of guards and soldiers fought in messy clumps, and dead bodies littered the once green meadow, now churned into a muddy slurry tinged with red from the blood of the dead.

Erin gave a strangled yell of horror, then ran, heedless of the fighting to either side of her, to frantically search the overturned seats and dead bodies strewn on the ground for the faces of her parents and fiancé. She caught sight of blond hair, matted and pressed into a muddy bootprint, and she stumbled, tripping over the hem of her wedding gown to kneel by Marc's corpse. Sobbing, she hunched over his back and rested her hands on the torn cloth of his wedding suit where gold threads frayed and clotted up with blood from the wounds beneath. Blood crept up the skirt of Erin's dress in uneven rings of red mixed with green and brown stains from the churned up grass and mud. The clash of swords still rang in the distance, but she couldn't bring herself to leave Marc where he lay with his limbs askew, sword still loosely gripped in his left hand. Wiping at her eyes, she rolled him onto his back and brushed his hair out of his blood spattered, dirt-encrusted face. She rubbed his skin clean with her sleeve and tugged at his cream and gold brocade tunic to hide the jagged red cut parting the skin over his heart.

The metal feet of a fully armored soldier stepped into view, but Erin was too numb to do anything but stare. He bent forward and grabbed at the fabric on Marc's shoulders with gauntleted hands, and the metal tore through the cloth. He began to pull, and Erin startled into motion.

"Stop!" She grabbed at Marc's arms. "Leave him alone!"

The soldier growled and raised his sword to strike at her. She didn't bother to get out her knives to parry, feeling nothing but the faint hope that she might get to see Marc again in the afterlife.

"No!" A hand marbled with drying blood halted the descent of the sword toward Erin's throat. She barely flinched at the sudden movement. "This one lives."

The soldier scoffed but withdrew his blade. He aimed a kick at Erin's ribs, only to get pushed away. Erin stared at the warrior protecting her, confused by his gray colors and the sight of her family crest embroidered into his hauberk. He looked down at her, then heaved a sigh and raised his faceplate. Erin blinked, distantly shocked by the familiar face. "Hayward?"

Hayward bowed, proper as always. "Lady Erin."

Erin felt all the breath rush out of her, as if he had punched her in the gut. "Why?" she gasped.

Hayward looked away to watch the Morton soldiers beginning to stack bodies into a pile. "Don't be afraid, milady." He gave her an absent smile. "I've made arrangements for your well-being."

A few yards away, soldiers threw tinder and oil on top of a heap of bodies. Erin watched with her sight blurred by her tears. The many familiar faces of family and friends were terrifyingly strange to her in their stillness, but she forced herself to keep looking in search of her parents. The soldiers set the pile ablaze, and Erin sobbed from where she sat in the bloody mud, her clothes the color of rust. There were too many dead and not enough time to identify them all. Hayward pulled her up and dragged her to a safer distance away from the growing blaze, and she stared, transfixed, as the bodies vanished from sight beneath the roiling flames and billowing smoke.

"I have a message for you, milady." Hayward rummaged through the satchel he carried slung over one shoulder and took out a roll of parchment with a red wax seal. He held it out to her, but she didn't move to take it. Clicking his tongue in disapproval, Hayward broke the seal and unrolled the parchment for her to read:

"Lady Erin,

I can no longer tolerate the competition of other, less worthy suitors. I hope my actions today stand as proof of the unwavering zeal of my affection for you. Please accept my proposal of marriage. I await your reply with bated breath. Should I not hear back in a fortnight, I do hope you will excuse the rash actions I will feel compelled to take to capture your undivided attention.

Steadfastly yours,

Ardent Morton."

Hayward rolled the parchment up and held it out to Erin again. She blinked at it, and Hayward leaned down to grasp her hand and curl her nerveless fingers around the message. "I hope you reply favorably, milady." Hayward straightened and stepped back. "You know I have always wanted the best for your family."

Erin barely heard him over the roaring in her ears. They were the only two left so close to the pile of corpses. The other soldiers had long since departed, having looted and burned all that they came to destroy. Hayward waited for her to speak with barely concealed impatience, then shrugged slightly at Erin's continued silence and walked away. Erin remained kneeling, alone in her horrific vigil, and watched the bonfire of bodies slowly turn to ash.

2
Gray Tidings

ERIN HAD NO sense of how much time passed in her stupor in front of the fires. All she could do was sit, keep watch, and try to honor the last rites of her loved ones, though she had no way of knowing which loved ones, exactly, were being burned away. A hand on her shoulder jolted her out of her reverie, and she twisted around to see Liana, soot streaked, with a new cut down her forearm that bled sluggishly.

"There you are!" Liana fell to her knees and swept Erin up into a hug. "I had almost given up hope of finding you." She pulled back and punched Erin's arm.

"Ow!" Erin rubbed at what she could tell was the beginnings of a bruise.

"You idiot. Why did you run off like that? We're supposed to stick together." Liana's voice was shaky, and she cut herself off with a choked sob to rub at her eyes. "We always stick together."

Erin felt increasingly guilty at the rare sight of Liana crying. "I'm sorry." Liana scoffed and turned her head away. "Hey, I'm sorry, okay? I wasn't thinking."

"No, you weren't." Liana sighed and gave Erin a shaky smile. "Don't leave me like that again, okay?" Erin didn't respond, too concerned by Liana's tearstained face. Liana got back to her feet with a weary groan. "Time to find Jax." Erin looked down at the muddy ground, then back at the fires. "No." Liana stepped in front of Erin to block her view and held out her hands. "Enough of that. Let's go."

Erin grabbed hold of Liana and shakily climbed to her feet. "Wait," she said when Liana turned to go. She picked up the scroll she had left on the ground.

"What's that?" Liana shook her head. "Never mind, it can wait. Jax first. We'll have to walk, the horse is gone. I can only hope we'll reach the cave before Jax does, can you imagine how he'll react if he gets there to find us gone?" Erin tripped over the hem of her dress. The soggy fabric clung to her legs and slowed her progress. Liana held out a hand to steady her, then kept talking, as if to protect them from the sight of the bloody, churned up earth that surrounded them. "Bet it'll be worse than that time we ran off in the market during the harvest festival, remember that?" Liana cast a look at Erin, but Erin couldn't muster the strength to speak. Liana continued with a shaky laugh. "Thought his head might explode!" Erin tried to smile, but her cheeks shook with the effort, and she let out a gasping sob instead. Liana swiped her hand across her eyes with a grimace and fell silent.

It was a grim walk back to the cave, though the leaves were green and the birds still sang. By the time they reached their destination, Erin and Liana were leaning on each other for support and stumbling every few steps. Jax was waiting for them there, arms crossed, scowling.

"Where were you?" he asked.

Erin let go of Liana to sink to the ground at the base of a nearby tree, exhausted. She did not want to talk about where she had gone or why. She let the scroll of parchment roll out of her fingers and leaned against the tree trunk to close her eyes. She had found Marc's body, she had found Jax and Liana, but she had no idea where her parents were. A fleeting, irrational hope that she might find them alive and whole, somewhere far removed from the battlefield, seized her mind, but she then remembered that she had heard them leave for the festivities early that morning. They had been there.

"Where are Mom and Dad?" she asked Jax, dreading the answer.

Sorrow and regret passed over Jax's face. "Captured." Erin closed her eyes. Jax continued to speak. "Don't know where they're being taken. I'll have to assign some men to find out, back at the keep."

"Right," Erin said, and she made to pick herself up again.

"What's this?" Jax picked up the scroll and gave Erin a quizzical look.

"It's-" Erin waved a hand and busied herself with getting to her feet. "Well, read it and see."

Jax unrolled the parchment, and Liana looked over his shoulder to read along. His face grew darker as he read it through, and he rolled it back up with a snap, muttering under his breath. He stuffed the scroll into one of the saddlebags on his horse, fuming.

"Hayward gave it to me," Erin said.

"Hayward?" Jax narrowed his eyes. "That obsequious little weasel, I'm going to kill him."

"I'll help," Liana said. She turned to Erin. "We'll say no, of course. You're not going to marry that pile of dung."

Jax snorted. "Obviously not."

"No, of course not," Erin said. She felt a distant sense of relief that nobody expected her to sacrifice herself as a war bride. "Though he will make things difficult once I refuse him."

"Of that I have no doubt," Jax said. "Good thing I'm skilled at making things difficult myself, and so are you." He gave Erin a pat on the shoulder, and she smiled tremulously. "Come on, we've got to get home and make plans."

They made their weary way back to the keep, hiding whenever they heard the approach of another person. Hayward's betrayal loomed large in their minds. A golden haze fell over the farmlands and meadows they passed, and the sun set in a blaze of oranges and reds while they walked. The golden color reminded Erin of Marc, and it made her heart and stomach clench. She fixed her eyes on the dusty road in front of her and wondered if all beautiful sights would now hold an edge of sadness for her. They arrived at Norcliff under the purple velvet sky of dusk and took one of the secret back ways in to avoid the hubbub at the gate. News of the attack had reached town.

The three of them settled in the family living room, in an unspoken agreement to search for what comfort they could find. Liana fell into an overstuffed armchair, but Erin couldn't bring herself to sit and ruin the fabric of the furniture with her soiled dress. A little voice in the back of her mind told her to go and change into something better, but she was too tired to listen to it.

"I should go to the capital to report this heinous deed and ask for help," she said.

"You should," Liana replied.

Jax nodded. "We'll go with you." He stood just to the side of one of the windows, in the shadow of the blue velvet curtain, and peered down at the front gate. "But first, you'll have to make a speech. Reassure the people," he said.

Erin could think of nothing she'd like to do less at that moment than go in front of a crowd of strangers and tell them everything would be fine. "Must I speak to them right away?"

Jax kept looking out the window. "The more time passes, the more dangerous the rumors will become."

Liana gave Erin a once over. "Don't go giving a speech in that dress, though," she said. "And you should do something about your hair."

Erin giggled, then burst into laughter that forced its way out of her chest in great heaving bouts and stole her breath away. She grasped onto the back of a couch and gasped for air. "Yeah, that's the real problem with today. My hair's a mess." She whooped with laughter and covered her eyes with her hand.

"All right, Lady Erin," Liana said wryly. "Let's go get you ready." Liana ushered Erin into her room to wait while she helped the maids get a bath ready and shut the door behind her with the admonition to, "Get out of that disgusting thing. You'll feel better when you do."

Erin stood in the middle of her room and tried to take off her dress while holding it as far away from the rest of her surroundings as possible. Dried bits of reddish mud still flaked off onto the rug beneath her feet, and she winced, feeling as though her very presence contaminated her home with all that had happened that day. She rolled her dress and shift up into as small a ball as possible and left it on the floor, where it might do the least damage. By the time she had finished undressing, a warm bath was already drawn, and Liana and the maids had left. She sank into the lavender scented water with her tangled and messy hair hanging down her shoulders and back, and tried to soak in as much warmth as she could. It felt distantly good to clean away the grime that caked her skin, and the cleaner she got, the easier it became for her to think clearly.

The people of Hart Keep and Norcliff were hers, now, hers to guide and guard, to support and cherish. She had to talk to them, but she didn't have much to say to anyone, let alone thousands of people. What could she possibly say to soothe their fears? How could she comfort them, when she could barely comfort herself? She thought back to the speeches her father would make, optimistic talks with light, humorous asides to make the crowds laugh and cheer. "People want to laugh, and they want to feel good about their lives. Let them," he would say, when she asked him how he made speeches that people liked so much.

She didn't have much to laugh about, she thought as she began to undo her knotted braids and soap up her hair. The townspeople would want to know what happened. She wasn't sure she could talk about it without bursting into tears. They would want her to have a plan, some way to make them safe and keep them prosperous. The future looked dangerous and full of conflict to her, and she didn't want to pretend at optimism when she felt none. She ducked her head under the water to rinse out her hair and rose to wipe water out of her eyes and smooth her hair back. She couldn't pretend to be someone she wasn't, and she wasn't her father.

Erin stepped out of the bath and wrapped one of the thick towels around herself. She would tell them the truth of what had happened, and she would mince no words about the dangers they faced. They deserved a chance to prepare, the same as her. She wouldn't break the bonds of trust between her family and her people, wouldn't let catastrophe strike them unaware. She wasn't Hayward either.

She opened her wardrobe to choose a suitable dress, but they all seemed too pretty to suit the somber truths she would have to speak until she reached a gray silk gown, unadorned but well made, designed to let the skilled tailoring and quality of the material speak for themselves. She put it on and considered her reflection in the mirror. A knock sounded at her door. "Come in," Erin called, and Liana entered with a hairbrush and comb to begin the work of tidying her hair. Erin tugged at the long sleeves and bodice of her dress to make them lie straight and held out her arms for inspection. "How do I look?"

Liana hummed and finished pinning Erin's hair into a tidy, utilitarian bun. "There," she said and stepped back. "You look ready for war."

Erin looked at her reflection in the mirror and prayed it would not come to that, despite the little voice in the back of her mind that told her it would. She turned away and went back into the living room, where Jax remained, watching the crowd. He turned and nodded to her gravely. "You're ready."

"Am I?" Erin ran a hand over her hair and sighed out a breathy laugh. "I don't feel ready."

"You are." Liana followed Erin into the room holding a sapphire studded comb and gently fixed it to Erin's hair. "There," she said, and stepped back to smile. "The Hart colors suit you well."

Jax held his fist over his heart and bowed, rising to gesture out the front door to the main gates, where the crowd stood. "Lady Hart, your people await you."

Erin took a deep breath and walked outside, mind empty and eyes burning with repressed tears. The crowd didn't notice her at first, and the people continued to talk amongst themselves, but soon they saw her, in groups of two or three, then ten or twenty, and then everyone had turned their heads to face her. Erin would have preferred to have more time, but she suspected there was no such thing as enough time to prepare for the responsibility she was about to shoulder. Regardless, it was too late to change their expressions from worry and fear to something better, happier, too late for her to do anything but speak her mind.

"I expect you already know most of what I'm here to tell you," she began. "We were attacked by the Mortons. My fiancé is dead and my parents are captured. I must go to the capital and ask for assistance in righting this great wrong. I can make no promises that this will end well. All I can say is that I am still here, and so are you, and we will continue on as much as we are able. This may not be what you hoped to hear from me today, but it is true. True is how I mean to go on, true of heart and true of intention, true to my family and my people. This is how I mean to lead, for lead you I must. I am the last Hart left standing, and I mean to stand as long as there is a people and a place to stand for, as long as you still stand with me."

Erin looked out over the sea of strangers, their faces ranging from curious to unimpressed to shocked. None seemed particularly happy with what she had to say. Fair enough, she thought. She wasn't happy saying it, either. She gave one last wave to her people, who didn't cheer or applaud like they used to for her parents' speeches, and then she went back inside to plan the fortifications for town and the voyage to the capital.

3
Lady Hart

SILENCE WRAPPED ITS arms around misty rolling hills, punctuated only by the beating of hooves against dirt and the occasional snorts of the horses. The day was gray all around, Erin decided as roiling swaths of fog swirled past. She briefly imagined jumping out of the saddle and running into the trees to cut through the air as though flying through clouds. Anything to improve the destination of this journey. Erin, Jax, and Liana had traveled day and night to reach the capital, and this was the morning of their arrival. The ground sped beneath the feet of their horses, the road turned from dirt to gravel to cobblestone, and then they were trotting along the bustling capital roads and into the palace. The capital was vaguely familiar to Erin, who had visited many years ago with her parents to maintain trade and political alliances with various lords and ladies. She had spent very little time doing anything but sightseeing while her parents did the real work of politics in the palace.

When the cast iron gates with their spike-tipped bars opened to the inner palace courtyard, Erin felt sick with nerves. A pair of guards with large shields and javelins stood at attention by the towering front doors, and courtiers wandered the garden, hungry for fresh gossip to exchange amongst themselves like currency. Erin wanted to turn her horse around and leave for home, but the work she came to do was more important than her fear, so she rode with Jax and Liana through the gauntlet of onlookers to one of the smaller side entrances that led to the guest quarters.

The Hart name didn't rank high among the lofty guests the royal family received, so their rooms were simple and far from the central court, in a little-used wing of the palace. Once Erin, Jax, and Liana had set their bags down, they convened in the library near the main hall that connected their wing to the rest of the building.

"You'll need to arrange a meeting with King Ulrich," Jax said. "I can tell the steward that Lady Erin requests an audience."

"Really Jax, I don't think you've called me lady my whole life. Are you afraid my time in court will inspire me to put on airs?" Erin huffed, caught between a mix of tired amusement and irritation.

"Gonna have to start being formal. Never know who's listening," Jax cautioned.

"Like anyone will care what we do," Erin said.

Liana snorted. "They'll care because they'll be looking for ways to ridicule you, country bumpkin that you are."

Erin laughed. "Gee, thanks, Liana."

Liana sobered. "But we must give the impression that we are here to act as fancy and high-minded as the other nobles are pretending to be. We need to put on a show of stability. You must remember to play your part."

"Yes, fine, I know," Erin grumbled. She straightened up, crossing her ankles and folding her hands on her lap. "I'll keep up appearances."

Liana nodded, eyes twinkling. "Keep up the illusion even when you think you are alone, but -"

"But don't fool yourself into believing your lies and forget your true self, yes, I remember Jax's many lectures just as well as you do, Liana."

"Oh, I doubt that. You didn't get them at home as well as in training," Liana said.

Erin grinned. "True."

"What's this about my lessons? You wish there were more of them?" Jax teased. "I shall comply with Lady Erin's heartfelt plea for more tutelage."

Erin shook her head at the formal address one last time, and then resigned herself to the inevitable bowing and scraping that would be the bane of her existence for the days to come at court. It was short work to send a letter to the steward requesting a meeting with the king, and then Erin set about choosing her outfit. She picked a silken gray dress with a subtle blue sheen and a gleam of silver thread in the embroidery. The colors were based on the style of her ancestors, fierce warriors whose idea of formal attire had been a clean suit of armor. When she went back to the library, Liana and Jax had also changed into the simple gray uniforms of Hart family retainers.

"You look like a warrior," Liana said to Erin, who smiled ruefully.

"I'm going to feel ridiculous going in there, as if I'm preparing for battle," Erin said.

Liana shrugged. "Perhaps you should be. Court is much like a war of words, from what I hear."

Liana's prescient description stuck with Erin as she walked out to the gardens where court was being held that morning. Well-trimmed hedges lined the walkways, and a riot of flowers growing in intricate formations brightened the grounds. A lady in a robin's egg blue silk dress with delicate white lace accents walked up to Erin with a curious smile. "What is your name?"

"Erin Hart of Norcliff."

"I am Charity Green of the Southern Meadows. A pleasure to make your acquaintance." Lady Charity's blue eyes crinkled at the corners as she smiled, and her blond curls, swept up into a half bun, bounced as she turned. "Please allow me to introduce you to some of my friends."

"Thank you," Erin said, a hot coal of hope burning in her chest and warming her. She recognized the Green name. They sent fruit to the Harts in exchange for furs. She had not expected such an immediate welcome.

Lady Charity brought her to a circle of well-dressed lords and ladies. "Lady Erin, it is my pleasure to introduce you to Lord Ryan Tooley of Westhaven," a well-groomed man with black hair and a short goatee bowed courteously, "Lady May Merryweather of Eastvale," a thin lady in a deep red gown with luxurious, wavy brown hair took her red silk fan from her face, smiled, and nodded politely, "and Sir Jacques Steeltoe of the 43rd mounted regiment." A man with short-cropped blond hair and an amiable cast to his features grinned cheerfully.

"Well met, Lady Erin," said Sir Jacques. "And from where do you hail?"

"She's from Norcliff," said Lady Charity.

"Norcliff! My word, you've traveled far," said Lord Ryan. "I had thought the people of Norcliff preferred to stay close to home."

"We do," said Erin, and she took a breath, sensing an opening where she could share her story, but before she could begin, Lady May spoke.

"A rare find, Charity. What luck that we have met you, as everyone will want to know what brought you here!"

"And what is your reason for being here, if I may be so bold as to ask," Lord Ryan said.

"It's a long story, and not a very good one, I fear," said Erin.

"My, that does sound intriguing," Lady Charity said. "Go on, go on!" She fluttered her white lace fan, looking delighted.

"My fiancé has been murdered and my family imprisoned," Erin said. It pained her to speak the words, but she forced them out, determined to spread the news of the Mortons' wrongdoing.

"Goodness!" Lady Charity gasped.

"Ardent Morton's men attacked my wedding and slaughtered my guests. He then had one of his men, Hayward, who used to work for us, hand me a letter declaring his intent to wed me himself."

"How positively shocking," Lady May said, her fan frozen in the air as though she had forgotten she was holding it.

"Perfectly horrible!" Lady Charity said.

"If Ardent marries me, he shall inherit my family's keep and lands. I mean to make him face justice for the great wrong he has done to me and my loved ones."

Sir Jacques shook his head and tutted softly. "What a horrible thing for a young lady such as yourself to have gone through."

"Yes," said Erin, "it was horrible. Will you help me spread the news of the horror that has befallen my family and search for allies to help me fight against the Mortons?"

"Do not fear." Lady Charity grasped Erin's hands and patted them softly. "I will help to spread the word. There will be many people, I should think, who will want to express their sympathies."

"We had not heard of it at all," said Lord Ryan. "Norcliff is so far from the capital that it falls out of our notice."

"Tell me, Lady Erin, what was Lord Ardent's letter like? Was he very effusive?" Lady May asked. "Was it a truly terrible thing to read? Did he presume to order you about?"

"He stated his intentions and then said he expected a reply in a fortnight, so I have come here straight away to arrange a defense and to show him I cannot be so easily cowed." Erin spoke forcefully, the thought of the letter filling her once more with a sort of horrified anger, and there was a long silence after her words.

"Yes, quite," said Sir Jacques. "Very brave of you, I am sure. Shall we begin to spread the word now?"

"I think we had better," Lady Charity said. "It sounds as though there is not much time left!" She looped her arm through Erin's and proceeded to guide her from cluster to cluster of people. Erin had braced herself for the difficult task of telling her tale many times over, but she was relieved to find that her new friends quickly took over the task to regale group after group of the horrors Erin had faced. Erin only needed to nod or shake her head to confirm or deny speculations. The day passed quickly, and Erin did her best to remember names, but there were too many faces passing before her for her memory to keep. However, she left court feeling confident that at least her story would spread through the capital.

Liana was waiting for her when she went up to her rooms, and as soon as Erin entered she asked, "How did it go?"

Erin sat in front of her mirror and began undoing her braids. "I met some people who helped me to spread my tale. Many seemed sympathetic to my plight today. It bodes well." Erin picked up a comb to begin brushing her hair. "How did things go with you and Jax?"

"We reopened some long-closed channels of communication, and Jax is still out collecting information on the families at court." Liana stepped closer, so that her reflection could be seen in the mirror behind Erin. "Who were these people who helped you?"

Erin told Liana the names of her newfound friends, and Liana wrote them down in a list to look into their backgrounds tomorrow.

Erin went to bed feeling cautious optimism that this trip to the capital would bear fruit.

The next day was the time of the week that the king heard grievances and meted out solutions, aid, or punishment as he saw fit. King Ulrich held an audience for any lords and ladies who might seek his favor in the mornings, then held court for those cases from any commoners who had worked their way through the judicial system to his high office. Erin arrived early outside the throne room to wait for her chance to speak with King Ulrich. The people who left their audiences with the king before Erin all had grim, dissatisfied expressions, little changed from the looks they wore going into the room. Erin feared such a reaction to kingly justice did not bode well for her own chances at a fortuitous and speedy resolution to her troubles.

Soon enough, it was her turn to meet the king. The steward ushered her through the double doors, cleared his throat, tapped his staff on the floor, and announced her name. Erin curtsied deeply, and looked up and up the steps to the king's dais. King Ulrich wore a thick ermine cape over silk and velvet formal court clothes, and his boots were made of leather so highly polished that she could see the shadow of her reflection in them. He waved a negligent hand to gesture her closer, and she rose, took a few steps forward, and curtsied again as the steward closed the doors behind her. An array of nobles lined the sides of the throne room, drinking, eating dainty hors d'oeuvres, and whispering behind hands and fans, but the room was so large and the vaulted ceiling so high that the place barely seemed occupied. Erin focused her attention on the king. She needed this to go well.

"What brings the reclusive Hart family out from their beloved homeland to grace us with their presence?" King Ulrich said with a flat, deep voice that betrayed no inflection or emotion. He was a stern man with short salt and pepper hair beneath a silver circlet that sat lightly upon his brow. He had a dark gray beard grown out a few inches long. His face had the careful blankness that seasoned courtiers wore to prevent betraying feelings that might bring gossip down upon them. "If I recall correctly, we have not had a Hart seek an audience with the royal family since your father came to serve in the army as a boy. How is Finley these days?"

"Hard to say, your majesty, as he is currently missing. We think the Mortons took him hostage when they attacked during my wedding ceremony and killed many of my family and friends."

King Ulrich's face remained a carefully blank mask. "I am sorry to hear that. Please accept my condolences for your great loss."

"Thank you, your majesty." Erin rose from her curtsy. "I have come here on behalf of the Harts and Clairmauds to request aid from your majesty's army in righting the wrongs done to us by the Mortons and in freeing the captives the Mortons have taken."

King Ulrich held a hand up to his chin and rubbed a finger back and forth in a show of thought. "What misfortune, my dear. Of course, it is only right that you should seek to free your family from captivity, if that is indeed what has occurred. Have you any proof of these happenings?"

Erin stared. "My proof lies in the charred remains of the people who attended my wedding, who were burned in the meadow where I would have been married."

A collective gasp rose from the nobles watching in the audience, and Erin yearned for all the onlookers to go away. She didn't want her plea for help to become the day's entertainment.

King Ulrich sighed heavily. "Lady Hart, I am sure you feel that this situation is dire enough to require the aid of my soldiers, but the fact of the matter is, we simply cannot spare the manpower to help you. We are spread thin defending towns throughout the kingdom from bandits, and the northern border is beset upon by our bellicose northern neighbors, as you well know. The army is fully occupied securing our kingdom, especially with the increase in criminal activity lately. However, my sympathy for your plight is great, and I urge you to remain at court for as long as you must to gain support for your cause from your fellow countrymen."

"But my family has served you faithfully." Erin's voice rose in frustration. "We've watched the northern borders for generations. Surely that must count for something!"

King Ulrich looked past her to the steward and waved his hand.

"This way, Lady Erin," the steward said, stepping between her and the king.

"But-"

"The other visitors must have their turn," the steward said with iron-clad politeness as he ushered her out of the throne room.

"I wasn't finished," Erin said, but the steward had already turned his back on her to send in the next person to meet with the king and his court, leaving Erin frustrated and alone. "I had more to say." Erin watched, stunned, as the double doors closed once more and blocked her view of the court. Not wanting to return to Jax and Liana with news of her failure to secure royal assistance, Erin walked the halls of the palace in a daze, running over her brief audience with the king again and again, analyzing what she could have done differently, how she could have managed to get the help she needed for her home and her people. Everywhere she walked, there seemed to be people watching her and whispering about her, the ladies hiding behind their fans and the lords tut-tutting openly. She tried to make conversation, to continue to search for allies, but often trailed off in thought. Hours passed, and the sunlight filtering through the windows grew dim. Room after room was full of such spectators until Erin came upon a dimly lit chamber with a sole occupant reading a letter by the light of the fireplace. He stood out of his chair and folded up his piece of parchment at the sound of the door closing behind Erin. His face was pale, with a red mouth made redder by contrast to his skin, twinkling, cold blue eyes, and brown hair gathered into a ponytail at the nape of his neck by a thin, red velvet ribbon. He wore clothes of luxurious red velvet and silk, and a gold circlet rested atop his head. "Lady Hart, how unexpected," Prince Thomas said with a thin smile.

Erin dipped into a low curtsy. "Your highness."

"No luck getting help from my father, eh? News of your misfortunes has reached me. You've made quite an impression at court."

Erin remained silent, sure that to answer with a yes or no would be equally imprudent.

Her silence didn't seem to register for the prince, who continued speaking. "My father is always happy to take help, but try and get him to help you, and you'll be left hanging in the chill winds of solitude." The prince offered a jaded, sideways smile. "I'm sorry you didn't get the support you wanted, Lady Hart. If I was king, well." The prince tucked his letter into his pocket. "Things would have gone differently." The prince circled closer to Erin. "It is fortuitous that we should meet here, away from the prying eyes of court." He stopped before her. "You may tell me of your troubles, and I might be able to help you, for a certain cost."

Erin felt a chill run down her spine as the prince drew near, but she held her ground. "I need help defending my people from the incursions of our neighbors, the Mortons, who -"

The prince held up a hand. "Yes, yes, I, like everyone in court, have heard of the Mortons' dastardly deeds. There is no need for you to rehash the matter." He stepped closer. "All you must do is decide, how far are you willing to go, to get what you need?" In one fluid movement, the prince tangled his fingers in the hair on the back of Erin's head and pressed his mouth against hers in a bruising kiss. Erin's hands flew up and shoved at his shoulders out of pure reflex, but he would not move away. She tried to remember her training, but her movements were clumsy with shock.

A high pitched scream of protest rose in the back of Erin's throat, muffled by her lips, which were pressed shut against the assault. His mouth was harsh and closed off, and she could feel the wall of his teeth behind his lips and the bone of his chin pushed up against hers. She tried to back away, but he followed her until he had her pressed flat against the wall. He let go of her head to grab at her wrists and hold them against the wall. She threw herself from side to side, struggling to escape, and flinched in horror at the feel of his body against hers.

Someone gasped nearby. The prince stepped away at the sound and let go of Erin's wrists. Erin leaned further into the cold stones behind her, frozen in place, and tried to see who else was in the room. The prince wiped at his mouth and smirked at her before turning around to reveal a maid standing behind him, clutching a tray of food. Erin stared back with a mute plea for help, but the maid wasn't looking at her.

"I have brought dinner, your royal highness, as you requested," the maid said with a high-pitched, childish voice and a low curtsy.

"Yes. I'm afraid we got carried away." The prince looked back at Erin with a wink. Erin looked from him to the maid, who examined

Erin's features with unabashed interest. The prince pointed to a table by the fireplace. "Put it there."

"Yes, your highness."

The prince grinned at Erin. "You are dismissed."

Erin didn't wait to find out if he meant to dismiss her or the maid. She rushed past him, brushing her shoulder against his chest and shuddering at the feeling. The sensation of his touch crawled over her skin, and she walked stiffly along empty corridors, the courtiers now gone, gathered in the great hall for dinner.

The ornate decorations lining the halls of the palace were no longer graceful in their beauty, but cold and shadowed in the uneven light cast by the sconces on the walls. Everywhere she looked, she saw luxury that reminded her of the prince. She couldn't bring herself to stay in the palace for the night. Images of him sneaking into her room through some secret passage, aided by a loyal servant, ran through her mind with frightening power. She kept to the edges and corners of halls and rooms, jumping at sounds of servants passing and floorboards creaking on her way outside. Her mind imagined monsters within every shadow, and she went in search of the safety of her friends as if her life depended on it.

Erin found Jax and Liana in an empty stall at the back of the stables next to their horses and collapsed beside them on a wooden crate, heedless of the damage to her gown. "Nothing. It was all for nothing. We will have to return home empty handed," Erin said mournfully.

Liana raised an eyebrow at Jax, but he didn't react beyond moving a pawn forward on the portable chess board they had balanced between them on an overturned barrel. Erin struggled to catch her breath with great, heaving gasps, loud in the meditative quiet of the room. She stared into space as her heart slowed. When she was able to think about more than escape, she turned her attention to the chess board. Jax was likely to win in about three moves, but Liana was not one to give up a match until the bitter end.

Erin watched Jax make his moves to the rising frustration of Liana until he toppled her king. "Victory is mine," Jax said.

"One of these days, I'm going to wipe the board with you," Liana grumbled as she began to pack away the chess pieces.

"I have no doubt you will wipe many boards with many opponents." Jax leaned against the wall of the stable and looked at Erin. "Wouldn't you agree, Lady Erin?"

Erin gave a careless nod, staring at the empty space where the chess board had lain.

"My lady?"

"Hm?" Erin didn't look up.

Jax gave her arm a light touch, and Erin flinched. Jax's eyes flickered with concern. "It was always a possibility that the king would refuse to lend us aid, and yet something troubles you so much that you forget yourself. What is it?"

"The prince." Erin forced the words out in a grating voice. Liana halted in the middle of shutting the latches on the chess set to focus her attention on Erin.

Jax rose to his feet and searched the stable, checking behind doors and peeking through windows before returning to sit with artificial ease. He extended a hand to Erin. "Go on."

"I couldn't." Erin found it difficult to speak. "He wouldn't." She threw up her hands in disgust.

Jax frowned. "He also refused to help." Erin nodded in agreement. "Unfortunate but unsurprising. What else?"

"He..." Erin touched her lips, unable to say more.

Liana narrowed her eyes. "He trespassed upon you."

"Yes." Erin arranged her skirts around her in a desperate bid to maintain her composure.

"I see." Jax glared at the wall. "Did you make him pay for it?"

"No." Erin pressed her eyes and lips shut.

Jax bowed his head. "I will gladly collect your revenge for you, my lady."

"No!" Erin shouted. She took a deep breath and lowered her voice. "No. I was too surprised to act then, but I am better now. I will do it myself."

"Good," Liana growled.

Jax leaned forward to rest his elbows on his knees. "How can we help?"

Erin tapped at her lips in thought before catching herself and resting her hand in her lap. She turned to Jax with a determined glare. "I want revenge."

Jax nodded. "He's a prince. It will take time and money to get your revenge, and we already have a great task set before us. You'll have to be patient to see it done properly."

Erin nodded. "But it can be done?"

The dark shapes the dim lighting cast across Jax's face transformed him into a terrible stranger. "Oh, yes."

"Good." A need for justice filled Erin like a massive glacier that froze her from the inside out, protecting her from the snarling beast of shame that tore at her belly with wicked claws. She straightened her back and adopted the ruthlessly correct posture of a noblewoman. "As you so often remind me, every proper lady needs a hobby."

Liana giggled. "How else will we women fill the days and maintain our wits, such as they are?"

Jax's expression warmed with a fondness that chased away the hollows from his face. "I suppose I should be grateful you're not asking me to teach you needlepoint." He watched Liana and Erin laugh together, and when they quieted, he continued to speak. "I have a colleague here who is discreet and well-versed in the ways of court. She'll take well to you and your situation. I'll arrange a meeting for tomorrow." Jax paused. "If we're going to make life difficult for the king's heir, we may as well try to befriend the second in line. Do you remember who that is?"

"Duke Bavencian." Erin cast her mind back to memories of Jax's lessons on the nobility of the land. "He spends his days hunting and holding banquets at his castle to the west."

"Once we secure our alliances here, we could pay him a visit." Jax thought it over. "His favor would be doubly beneficial, for he maintains a large and well-rested army."

"But how do we manufacture an introduction?" Erin asked.

Liana tilted her head. "Would he take comfort in exchanging confidences with a pretty face?"

"No. The duke is a worldly man who will see through a seduction attempt. Besides, he has little lasting care for the women he beds." Jax tapped his fingers on the side of the barrel. "Hunting, though. He cares a great deal about hunting."

"Perhaps he'd enjoy having company on his trips, company that will bring him luck." Erin picked up a piece of straw from the floor and twirled it between her fingers. "Or a new huntsman, one who can bring out the best in his horses and dogs."

Jax nodded at Erin with approval. "I believe we can supply him with both."

4

An Invitation

IT WAS LATE afternoon by the time Jax reached the barracks, and the air was full of the lazy heat of a sunny summer day. Through the open windows came the sound of laughter and card games from soldiers enjoying their break before dinner.

"Hey, grandpa!" someone shouted. "I hear you used to be spymaster around here." Jax looked around and noticed a young soldier approaching from the barracks with a sadistic smirk on his face. When the soldier opened his mouth, Jax knew what was coming. He lowered his chin and firmed his footing.

"I also heard that you and Captain Raylance used to bunk together. Can you settle a bet that I have going? Who was the woman in the relationship?" The soldier's smirk morphed into a vicious grin. "My money's on you."

Jax waited for the mix of rage and shame that used to fill him at questions like these, when he was a young man in the barracks. It didn't come. A cool, calculating vindictiveness had taken its place. He looked at the young man in front of him and decided which weak spots to hit for most impact.

"I prefer men. If I wanted a woman in my bed, I would court you," Jax said, watching with interest as the soldier's face blanked in surprise before darkening with rage. Go on, throw the first punch, Jax thought. The soldier seemed speechless, which was a disappointment. Jax wanted to know if he was a screamer or a crier. He decided to throw oil on the fire. "You are quite handsome, after all. One might even say pretty. I'm surprised no man has laid claim to you yet. Is it because everyone finds your personality wanting?" He watched with delight as the soldier snarled. Jax tapped at his chin in thought, adopting a pitying expression. "Or is it because you're too poor?"

The soldier leapt forward with an angry shout, throwing his fist at Jax's face. A mistake. Jax ducked and drove his shoulder into the soldier's solar plexus. He heard a startled cough and bared his teeth in a grin, lifting the soldier into the air in a fireman's carry. Jax pivoted and slammed the soldier into the dirt where he lay spread eagled and groaning.

By this time the fight had gained a sizeable audience. Jax pretended to lose his footing and stumbled onto one of the soldier's outstretched hands, making sure to target the one most likely to be dominant. The sound of snapping bones reached his ears, and he listened with great satisfaction as the soldier screamed. He looked down and saw tears of pain drip down the sides of the soldier's face from eyes pressed shut. Jax smiled. Screaming and crying. Two for the price of one.

"So sorry," Jax stepped back and apologized with a courtly bow, noticing a sergeant elbowing his way through the onlookers. He raised his voice. "I lost my balance for a moment. It's difficult for a man of my advanced age to lift heavy things, you know. You shouldn't pick fights with your elders. We're delicate." He rubbed at his shoulder. "I think I pulled a muscle."

The sergeant stomped closer. "What happened here?!" He stared at the soldier on the ground. The glare dropped from his paling face as the sergeant caught sight of Jax. Good, Jax thought, that will make things easier.

Jax adopted a magnanimous tone. "Oh, you know these young-lings. They're so eager to prove themselves that they'll pick a fight with just about anyone."

"Of course. My apologies, sir, I didn't recognize you. Would you like to press charges?" The sergeant asked, his posture now ramrod straight.

"That's not necessary. Boys will be boys," Jax said, watching the soldier continue to cry in the dirt, now curled up on his side and cradling his broken hand. "I will only ask that he cover the cost of a physician for me." Jax rubbed at his shoulder again, wrinkling his brow in worry. "My shoulder hurts quite a lot."

"Yes, sir. I apologize for the inconvenience. Please send us the bill." The sergeant looked relieved to have gotten off so easily.

Not so fast, Jax thought. "Hmmm," Jax said, pretending an idea had just occurred to him. "As you may have heard, I take great pride in nurturing the next generation of warriors." He looked at the sergeant with an earnest expression. "I'm concerned that this soldier's breach of conduct will hold him back in his training. Do tell me, what is his name and where does he live? I'd like to visit once in a while to check on his progress."

Sweat beaded along the edges of the sergeant's forehead. "You are kind, sir, but surely someone of your stature is much too busy -"

Jax raised his hand with a gentle smile and looked down on the soldier on the ground, who stared upwards with horror. "Not at all. I assure you I take my duty to pass my wisdom on to the younger generations very seriously."

"I commend you for your dedication." The sergeant wiped at his brow. "His name is Marcus Goldsmith. He lives in the east barracks in room 20." Below them, Marcus whined and curled further inwards.

"Good man. You are clearly devoted to the advancement of the men in your charge. I'll be sure to notify your superior officer should the opportunity arise. Who are you?"

"Sergeant Williams, sir. Thank you, sir."

Jax nodded to Sergeant Williams in farewell. "I'll leave you to your noble work." He turned and strode away from the crowd, fixing the face, name, and location of Marcus Goldsmith in his memory.

He continued to walk with speed and purpose until he turned a corner and passed through the gates to the main palace. His back stopped prickling with the awareness of eyes watching him go, and he slowed to a more leisurely pace, breathing deeply to cleanse himself of the adrenaline from the fight. He looked up to the sky, thanking the heavens that he had stopped at breaking that soldier's hand. The inner calm he had learned to keep during his time at Norcliff began to trickle back to him, and he welcomed its return with relief. The capital is bad for my health, Jax thought with dark amusement. He would find Hadrian at a better time, not when he was so unsettled.

"Same old Jax."

Jax felt the full sting of the hidden insult in that comment and turned in the direction of the familiar voice. "Hadrian, old friend. How are you?"

"I'd be better if you didn't mess with the recruits," Hadrian Raylance, the captain of the royal guard, replied. He was as handsome to Jax's eyes as always, with his blond hair and striking green eyes. "I must say I'm surprised to see you back here. Are you taking up your old work once again?"

"No, I'm a changed man with a new family to serve and a new outlook on life."

"Is that so?" Hadrian gave Jax a considering look. "Which family would that be, or can't you tell me?"

"The Harts."

"A good family." Hadrian paused and frowned. "I was sorry to hear of Lady Hart's fall from grace in court today."

"I wouldn't call it a fall from grace so much as a personal tragedy," Jax said.

"Yes, I suppose that is another way to put it." Hadrian nodded. "A better way. The Hart family has served the realm well for generations. They deserve all due consideration."

"My thoughts exactly," Jax said.

"Would that I could help you, but we are currently engaged in battle with more and more brigands every day. It's gotten so bad that I've had to send out some of my guard to help."

"Are they truly brigands?"

"We can't be sure. They're awfully well-equipped and well-trained to be brigands, but they carry no marks or colors to identify them otherwise. It is as it is. We can only do our best with what information we have," Hadrian said. "The border is stable, and we have much to be thankful for in that."

"Indeed. May we meet again under better circumstances. I wish you well with your campaign."

"And I you, with your lady and your newfound purpose. If I have resources to spare in the future, I will send them your way."

Jax bowed his head. "I will do the same."

Hadrian held out a hand as Jax turned to go. "Jax, wait." Jax turned back around. "If you find yourself in dire need," Hadrian said, "send a message to me, and I will send you aid."

"Thank you, Hadrian," Jax said.

Hadrian nodded decisively. "Do not despair. Though your lady may never marry again, she can still live a full life. Norcliff is far enough away from the palace that she may start anew."

"I wouldn't say that she needs to start anew away from the palace," Jax said slowly.

Hadrian's eyes widened with surprise. "Haven't you heard?"

"Heard what?" Jax didn't like surprises, and this seemed like the harbinger of a bad one.

"Why, news of your lady's, er," Hadrian floundered. "Attempts to win the prince's favor?"

"What attempts?" Jax asked through gritted teeth.

"Why, that she meant to win his affections rather...brazenly." Hadrian coughed gruffly, visibly discomfited.

Jax's hands clenched. "Where did you hear this?"

"Well..." The captain shrugged helplessly. "Everywhere."

Jax blinked, the only show of surprise he allowed himself.

Hadrian looked confused. "Don't tell me you didn't know of this?"

"Excuse me," Jax said. "I must find Lady Hart and help her through this."

"Of course you must." Hadrian ran a hand through his hair. "I'm sorry, Jax. I thought you knew."

"You aren't the one at fault. There's no need to apologize. I must go." And with that, Jax walked as quickly as he could back to the guest wings to search out Erin and Liana, who were in the sitting room looking over a map of the kingdom to plan their visit with Duke Bavencian. Jax paused to take a breath, while Erin and Liana broke off their conversation to look over at him with surprise.

"What is it, Jax?" Erin asked.

"It must be positively awful, to have you short of breath," Liana said.

"There is news throughout the palace that you attempted to seduce the prince," Jax said.

Erin shot up out of her seat. "That I did what?!"

Jax held up a hand. "Don't rush to anger, now, we must think this through carefully."

"I will rush wherever I want to rush," Erin snapped. "I must go to court and defend myself!"

"Erin-!" Jax stepped forward to stop her, but Erin was already out the door.

Erin halted outside the gardens where court was being held in the flattering light of the setting sun and reminded herself to move with grace, catching her breath and patting down her hair. She stepped onto the garden path with the resolution that she would secure what aid she could from her newfound friends to fight not only the Mortons but also the rumors about her and the prince. She could not think about the prince without her skin feeling itchy and too small for her body. Her mind bubbled with hot, angry thoughts. She did her best not to linger on him, instead focusing on her duty to defend her home and herself from any and all threats.

It was difficult for Erin to find Lady Charity in the press of people, but eventually she found her with her back turned toward her to speak with the same circle of friends she had when they first met.

"Lady Charity, how do you fare on this fine day?" Erin asked as she reached the group. Lady Charity turned with a smile, which grew when she saw Erin.

"Lady Erin, what a surprise," Lady Charity said.

"Why should she not be this bold? Lady Erin has already proven her propensity to be shocking," said Sir Jacques.

"Lady is taking it a bit far, don't you think?" Lord Ryan asked. "I hesitate to call her one, after she has behaved in so ill mannered a way."

"Positively barbaric, but what can you expect from someone who lives so far north," said Lady May.

Shocked, Erin turned to Lady Charity in search of an explanation for her friends' attacks on her honor only to find Lady Charity laughing behind her frilly light pink fan. "Did you think we would not find out about your advances upon the prince last night?" Lady Charity asked.

"I don't know how you conduct yourself in Norcliff," said Lady May, "but here we do not fling ourselves at the prince like, like…" here Lady May seemed at a loss for words.

"Like a common whore?" Lord Ryan asked, and Lady Charity and Lady May's laughter turned ugly while Lord Ryan sneered and Sir Jacques shook his head in disapproval.

"That's not what happened," Erin said. "He came at me, not the other way around."

"It's no use trying to change the story now," Lady Charity said. "I have the events from the prince himself, as well as one other source I shall not name. Just think of what shocking behavior you must have displayed before Lord Ardent to have him react in such a manner. If he truly did. You have proven to not be the most truthful person, after all."

"It is ill-bred of you to try to shift blame to the prince," said Lord Ryan. "A more well-mannered royal you could not hope to find in any kingdom. His reputation is beyond reproach."

"I find that difficult to believe, given how he acted toward me," said Erin.

"I find it difficult to believe that you are still here," said Lady Charity. "You will find no sympathy from us for the mess you have made of yourself. Move along, now." She flapped her fan at Erin. "Move along." She turned away to talk again with her friends, and Erin found herself on the outside of the tight circle they formed. Tilting her chin up, she walked sedately through the crowd of chattering nobles, determined not to let their words affect her, but everywhere she went the other nobles turned their backs to her. She could hear their derisive laughter following in her wake. She remained there in the garden for another few minutes, not wanting to seem like she was running away, but it was hard for her to face the collective disdain of the crowd. Soon she walked away, seeking the shelter of her guest room with a stiff spine, back prickling at the sounds of whispers passing from noble to noble and servant to servant as she walked past. She would not give up, she resolved. She would talk with Liana and come up with a plan for how to deal with the forces rallied against her.

While Erin reunited with Liana in the guest rooms and told her the troubling story of her experience at court, Jax wandered the gardens of the palace, in the less populated sections. As he walked the paths, the memories of the meanings of the flowers around him slowly returned to him. Norcliff was too far north for the Harts to keep much variation in their gardens, so it had been years since Jax had seen the exotic blooms of the late Queen's gardens. For once, he found himself grateful for the royal family's strict adherence to tradition, as it meant the layout had remained unchanged.

He took out his sharpest dagger and began to collect his message. Yellow roses from the rose garden for friendship, optimism, and good health. Ivy off the stone walls for fidelity, petunias from the planters set at each gate for anger and a request for comfort. Viscaria, the gaily pink blossoms disguising dark implications behind an old assassin's invitation to dance.

He stared at the bouquet in his hands and considered. The yellow and pink were a cheerful combination loaded with irony, just the way Madame Neigely would like, while the ivy grounded the message in trust. There was still something missing to finish the bouquet. He wandered from yard to yard in the expansive gardens until he reached the cultivated meadow at the outskirts. He looked over the controlled chaos and smiled. A wild flower would do the trick, and he knew the perfect one. Black eyed susans, for justice.

He sheathed his knife and pulled out a length of black silk to tie the cuttings with a bow as he walked to the palace gates. One of the guardsman on duty smirked at the bouquet. "Going courting?"

Jax clutched the flowers to his chest and adopted a wistful air. "I seek a lady of the night to soothe my troubled soul."

The guards roared with laughter and waved him through before turning back to their game of dice. Jax took the long way to his destination and made sure to double backwards and sideways to check for a tail. Satisfied that he was alone after an hour of wandering in and out of pubs and through crowds, dodging the drunkards and bar brawls, he set out for Madame Neigely's tea house.

The tea house was situated in a quiet, leafy enclave set back from a city square lined with more sedate, orderly taverns and shops. The streets were wider, cleaner, and emptier here, with the occasional well-dressed stranger passing by on foot or horseback. Jax kept to the shadows, wary of being recognized in a place where there were no crowds to hide his face.

The gate to the tea house was cloaked in the shadows of cherry trees that drooped over the well-polished and intricately carved wooden fencing, with shrubs strategically placed to afford visitors privacy. Jax knocked once at the door and waited. Soon a window in the door slid open to reveal a cloaked face. The only visible features were a pair of striking blue eyes lined in kohl. Jax held up his bouquet for the gatekeeper to see. "A gift for the lady of the house."

A hand covered in intricate geometric tattoos extended out from the window to take the bouquet before withdrawing, and the window closed with the snap of a latch. Jax turned to sit on the cast iron bench next to the door and breathed in the heady scent of the roses growing up the trellises to either side of him. The carefully constructed atmosphere of luxurious ease made the wait pleasant. He was almost sorry for it when the gatekeeper returned to pass through the window a small bundle of rose leaves, a slip of paper, a bottle of ink, and a quill with the feather trimmed to a narrow point. Jax took the bouquet and smiled grimly. Rose leaves meant permission to hope.

Jax held the leaves up to a curtained window that glowed from interior light, miming a salute with the bouquet. He then turned away to write out a description of Erin's likeness, a time, a signal, and a place for the meeting. The gatekeeper took his message and disappeared, and Jax looked to the window, tucking the rose leaves into the folds of his cloak. A shadow appeared behind the diaphanous curtains and waved to him with slow grace. Jax swept his cloak behind him in a courtly bow and made his exit, retracing his wandering steps back to the palace. The meeting was arranged, and now there was little for Jax to do but wait and see how Madame Neigely and Erin got on with each other.

5

The Madame

MADAME NEIGELY TUCKED a black eyed susan into the brim of her hat and searched the square for someone matching Jax's description. A matching flower woven into the hairnet of a young woman caught her eye in the bustling crowd of merchants and shoppers. She stepped forward to make herself known and caught Erin's eye. "So you're the girl who won Jax's loyalty and made a royal mess of herself at the palace the other day," she said.

"You're well informed, Madame."

"I make a point of keeping track of the gossip that trips off the courtiers' tongues." The Madame went to a fruit stand and picked up a strawberry for inspection, looking at Erin out of the corner of her eye. "You should too, if you plan to survive your stay at the capital."

Erin glared at the baskets of freshly picked blueberries laid out before her. "I plan to do more than survive."

"Oh?" The Madame motioned to the shopkeeper. "Two pounds of strawberries, please."

"I seek…" Erin quieted as the shopkeeper came over to collect his payment and pack the produce into a small wicker basket.

"This way." The Madame walked past the stand and through a narrow doorway into a cool, dark apothecary. She swept past the man idling behind the shopkeeper's desk and held a curtain of deep green velvet to the side for Erin to follow. Erin went into the back room and stared up at the clusters of dried flowers and herbs hanging from the ceiling while the Madame set her basket of strawberries down on a black slate table. "You seek revenge."

Erin turned to stare at the Madame with burning eyes. "I seek justice."

The Madame's smile turned from polite to real. "Not such a girl after all." She pulled a key from a chain around her neck and unlocked one of the dark wooden drawers set into the wall to reveal tidy rows of glass vials. She picked up one vial after another, holding them to the light so that the rich hues of the liquids inside shone like gems. "The gossips say you seduced the prince, but anyone with an ounce of sense could see through that lie. He stole something from you, didn't he?"

"He stole a kiss."

The Madame set her vial back down and looked at Erin. "Yes, certain kinds of men do take those without asking. They do it because they want to possess all that we are as women, and they think that kisses will help them take our strength."

"You sound as if you speak from experience."

The Madame tapped her long, painted red nails against the cork stopper of a vial. "Extensive experience."

Erin stilled and looked at the Madame with complete attention. "How do you move past it?"

"You return the favor. Take what your thieves owe you for their crimes." The Madame reached to the back of the drawer and pulled out a vial of blood red liquid.

"What did they owe you?"

"What they stole." The Madame smiled and locked the drawer of vials shut. "A kiss for a kiss." She took Erin's hand and wrapped her fingers around the red vial. "Should you decide to collect your dues from the prince, you'll need to dress appropriately. He is royalty, after all. This is my favorite lip paint." She opened a small container made of lacquered red wood and took out a vial of clear liquid. "This is the antidote you must take before you use it." She handed the second vial to Erin. "Let me show you how to make more. You might need it, if you want to take back your home as well."

"You know about that?"

"I have heard that your neighbor threatens to steal your home. The rich and powerful say you have come to seduce the prince, and the court has agreed that you deserve whatever punishment you get for your audacity. There are few ways to survive as a woman when times are desperate, and your situation is desperate. You'll have to choose, just like the rest of us fallen women must." Madame Neigely sounded amused, despite the harshness of her words.

Erin frowned. "What can I do?"

"First, you must let go of any hope of a respectable man marrying you and giving you the comfort of children, hearth, and home. That door has closed to you. The men deemed good matches by the court will avoid you now, as any man concerned with his reputation must. You're going to have to consider your new best options. Your choices are limited. Your first option is to act like a soft and foolish girl and trick yourself into loving some brute who can protect you through marriage. There are many issues with this strategy. You must find such a man, marry him, and then keep him alive. And even after overcoming those challenges, the biggest problem with marrying a brute is that he won't protect you from himself." Madame Neigely gave Erin a hard look and plucked a dried flower with dusty red petals from the ceiling. She held out the flower to show Erin. "Heart's Blood. Five red petals to a flower, black center, leaves with jagged edges, must be dried. Dry it upside down, or the petals will lose their poison. You can find it at high altitudes in the late spring, and it grows near your home. It constitutes two fifths of the mixture. Steep it in boiling water. One flower will do the trick in a few hours. Use two to make it quick."

"Your second option," the corners of the Madame's mouth turned up into a poisonous smile, "is to forge yourself into steel and sharpen your edges, so that none may touch you without risking injury. I prefer the second option. As you know, life is uncertain, and husbands can die, just as easily as any other human."

Erin's face grew sad, and she nodded soberly. "I know it well."

The Madame began to sweep from one side of the room to the other, gathering supplies as she talked. "Mint, to disguise the taste. Must be dry. One fifth of the mixture. Beets, for color. Must be fresh. One fifth of the mixture." Madame Neigely plucked a knife out of thin air and began to chop the materials she had collected. "I am not, and never have been, a wife. I am every man's woman and therefore no man's woman. That's the price I chose to pay for the freedom to manage my own affairs. As a child, it was the only path to independence that I knew how to walk, so I walked it." Madame Neigely stopped chopping to examine Erin. "Do you have a path you know? I don't speak of the path to becoming the lady of a household, which is no longer an option. Do you know a path that you can still walk?"

Erin had already known her future had changed, but to hear it confirmed out loud struck at her so powerfully that she found it difficult to speak. "No," she forced herself to say, simple and unadorned, because it was the truth.

Madame Neigely nodded and resumed chopping. "Maybe it's better that way. It will force you to forge your own path. Regardless, I will educate you in some of what I know, should you need it." She rummaged through a drawer at her side, and rows of tiny glass vials clattered against each other.

"Desire," she said in a quiet voice while holding up a vial of red liquid to the light, "is a double edged sword that you must wield with care. You can make yourself attractive and compelling, and that will open doors for you. It will also catch the attention of powerful, hungry people who will want to control and destroy you." Madame Neigely began to crush and grind the chopped plants together using a black granite mortar and pestle. "That's the nature of hunger. It devours. Take care that nobody devours you. Only you can protect yourself from that." She gave Erin a wry smile. "Did you think someone else could?"

Erin thought of her fiance, torn and bloodied in the mud, and of the prince, betraying his duties as heir to the throne, assaulting her out of the blue. "Not anymore."

"Good." Madame Neigely smiled. "That means you've grown up. But do remember, you are not entirely alone. You have people who are here to help you." She showed Erin the vial of red liquid. "Add a mix of half rosewater, half red wine. One fifth of the mixture." She poured some liquid into the mortar and began to work all the ingredients together. "Are you sure you want to fight him?"

Erin frowned. "Yes."

"He's powerful."

"I know. I must have justice."

"Surely there are people better equipped to that task than you."

Erin thought of the guards and soldiers of the palace, all sworn and honor bound to protect the king and heir with their lives. "The people with the power to help me will not do it."

"How do you know that? Can you see into the future? Besides, doesn't the prince suffer enough by existing as such a horrible person, empty of all emotion besides malice? Imagine living that way, always seeing the worst, always trying to fill that inner emptiness and never succeeding. Isn't that enough punishment?"

"It's not about punishing him." Erin felt the truth of her words as she spoke them. "It's about protecting people. He won't stop himself, and nobody outranks him except the king, who doesn't seem interested in controlling his son's behavior. As long as the prince goes unchecked, he'll continue his malignant ways." Consumed by an urgent passion, she clenched her fists. "I know what he is. Others don't. It's my responsibility to act."

"Hmm." Madame Neigely plucked the stems of little star shaped white flowers from the ceiling. "The antidote is simple but vital. You must take it every time you use the lip paint." She held up the flowers. "Heart's Star. Five white petals, yellow center, three flowers to a bunch, fuzzy round leaves. You will find it at the same time and place as Heart's Blood. Dry it upside down, and match the number of flowers to the number used for the poison." She then took a green, leafy plant out of a bunch of dried plants on the table. "Elk Ear, five leaves for every flower of Heart's Blood used, must be fresh. Found along riverbeds in warm weather, spring and summer here, all year round further south." She ground them into a mush and unstoppered a bottle of clear liquid. "Two parts vinegar, three parts water, use one tablespoon for each flower added." Madame Neigely poured the mixture from her bowl into a thin glass vial and stoppered it. "Heat it until the mixture is smooth before taking it." She put the vials in a dainty pouch and tied the drawstrings into a neat bow before peering at Erin. "It may be your responsibility to act, but are you prepared to do what you must to see your task through to the end?"

Erin nodded. "I am determined."

"You'll have a difficult time of it, but in my experience, the struggle is worthwhile." She gave Erin the bag of vials. "This may help you some, when all other options are lost, and the knowledge I have shared will help you more. Should you find yourself lost or with nowhere left to turn, my tea house is open to you. I am always looking for apprentices."

"Thank you, Madame."

"None of that title nonsense. We're sisters, now, sisters in experience and sisters in knowledge."

There was little Erin could bring herself to do in response save nod sadly and say her goodbyes. She had lost a future but gained a friend. It was a small comfort to hold in her heart, on her long walk back to the palace.

6
Letters in the Night

Erin sought out Jax when she arrived at the palace and found him in the guest stables inspecting their tack. He smiled at her over his work repairing a small tear in a saddle blanket. "Did your meeting go well?"

"Yes." Erin sat on a bale of hay, glad to rest her weary feet and uncaring of the straw getting caught in her dress. "She was generous."

"I thought she might be."

Erin ran her fingers through her hair, tugging at her braids, and stared at Jax with a lost expression. "I cannot face another day of this torture. It is..." Erin sighed heavily. "Unbearable. I'm ready to leave."

Jax gripped at the hilt of one of his knives, wanting to draw it in her defense, but a blade could not defeat a memory. Erin went to stand by one of the stall doors to stroke the nose of the horse inside, and her gown dragged in the mud caked between the tiles of the stable floor. She was made for more than this, Jax thought, made to sit in a fine chair in a shining hall. He imagined laying the prince's head in the dirt at her feet and washing the floor red with the blood of her enemies. It was a pretty picture, but he knew it was wrong to want that sort of thing anymore. He tried to come up with words of comfort. "Do you remember what we did, the first time your life was in danger?"

"During riding lessons?"

"Yes."

Erin remembered her first horseback riding lesson and how she fell to the ground before the horse's hooves. Jax had chosen her first mount well, an old pony with a steady gait and gentle nature that had halted to avoid trampling her. Though her eyes had run with tears and her mouth had wobbled with fright, Jax hadn't allowed the lesson to end there. He had lifted her back onto the saddle and led her out to a lake beyond the town walls. The novelty of being in a place she hadn't visited before made her forget her fright. He had led her pony into the shallows of the lake where they could rest together in the cool water, a welcome relief from the hot, dusty air of the training paddock.

Erin ran her fingers over the well-oiled leather of her saddle. "We carried on until I wasn't afraid anymore."

"That's right. And now you adore horseback riding. Think of the joy you would have denied yourself, had you stopped then." Jax walked over and gripped her shoulder tightly. "You don't belong here, hiding from the world with no one but your old teacher for company."

Erin picked at the stitching on the saddle. "I always belong with friends and family."

Jax sighed. "Yes, and you are welcome to seek me out for comfort and counsel as often as you like. But then you must keep fighting. Let me tell you a secret I learned from an old soldier."

Erin looked up. "What is it?"

"A good fight will keep your fears from defeating you, no matter how the fight ends."

"There's nothing good about what has happened here." Erin's voice quivered, and her eyes overflowed with tears.

Jax hands clenched in fury, and he let go of Erin's shoulder to cross his arms. "Yes, there is."

Erin wiped at her face with clumsy hands and scoffed. "What?"

Jax began to pace, uneasy at the sight of Erin's tears. "You remembered your training-"

"No, I didn't. I let him grab at me! And the whole court knows - it cost us any potential allies we might have won!"

Jax help up a hand. "Let me finish. It's only natural for your emotions to get in the way in your first real battle. The important thing is that you escaped to fight again another day. Then you went out and measured the worth of your potential comrades in arms. You found them unreliable and have rightfully concluded that there is no more reason to stay here. You then made a successful trip to meet Madame Neigely and gained resources you may need to succeed at your goals." Jax stopped his restless feet to look at Erin. "You remembered my lessons. I'm proud of you."

Erin felt a pleasant warmth at Jax's rare declaration of pride, but it didn't wipe away her disappointment in herself. She impatiently brushed away more tears and tipped her face upward, willing her eyes to stop watering. "So you agree. We must move on."

Jax nodded. "The sooner the better."

Erin felt weak with relief. She had feared he would tell her they needed to remain in this untenable situation. "I'll gather my things."

"Wait," Jax said thoughtfully.

Erin paused. "What is it?"

"We've enjoyed the gift of our king's hospitality." With a flash of silver, Jax unsheathed a dagger to flip it in the air. "It would be rude to leave without a parting gift of value commensurate to the treatment we've received."

"What did you have in mind?"

"If you're earnest in your desire to bring justice to your..." Jax trailed off, and Erin knew it was out of caution against eavesdroppers. The reminder that the palace was full of spies set her nerves on edge. "Unwanted admirer." He settled on with a wry smile that Erin returned. "We might as well gather what information we can while we're here."

"Right," Erin said slowly. "A nighttime walk, I think, to take in the air."

"Perhaps by the royal wing, near the balconies," Jax suggested.

Erin nodded. "Let me get ready, and I'll go."

"And I will make our final preparations to leave tonight." Jax turned back to his work while Erin left for her rooms, walking quickly to avoid running into more courtiers.

Liana greeted Erin with a startled look from where she stood among the small pile of luggage she had packed for their departure when Erin burst into their shared sitting room. Erin locked the door behind her, relieved to escape the public eye and relax her expression from its mask of neutrality. Liana pressed a small pile of folded clothing into one of the saddlebags and asked, "Did you find what you were looking for?"

"Yes, and now I'm going to the royal wing to look for more." Erin pulled her favorite knives out of the hidden compartment in one of her bags and sat in an armchair to check them. "How go the preparations to leave? We'll leave tonight, once I'm done gathering information."

"This is the last of the packing," Liana said. Erin went to her bedroom and began to pull off the layers of her dress and under-things. Liana abandoned her packing to help Erin out of her intricately fastened clothing, and Erin sighed with gratitude as she put on her stealth outfit. The pants and shirt were loose, dyed in blacks and grays, with plenty of room in the shoulders and hips for movement.

Liana unpinned Erin's hairnet and held up a mirror while Erin tied a dark cloth over her head to hide her hair, which caught light like a beacon when left uncovered. Kneeling by the cold fireplace, Erin scooped up ash and patted it onto her face before rising to inspect her handiwork. "What do you think, Liana? Did I miss anything?" Erin turned in a circle and picked up her knives to slide them into place at her wrists, ankles, sides, and back.

Liana set the mirror down. "The prince won't know what hit him."

"Let's hope it doesn't come to that," Erin murmured and peeked through a gap in the curtains. The sun hovered over the roofs of the city, orange and heavy, and made the shingles and thatch seem gilded in gold and bronze. The sounds of people shouting farewells and doors clanging shut drifted up from the marketplace. Erin pulled back and rechecked that her knives were securely fastened in place. Her nerves fluttered at the thought of all the ways that her plan could fail, especially if people started leaving court for their rooms early. "Is dinner proceeding as expected?"

"Yes. The royal family has declared their intention to preside over the revelries long into the night. They've only just begun with the hors d'oeuvres." Liana stopped putting Erin's cosmetics in a travel bag to give her a concerned glance. "You don't have to be the one to do this, you know. You could stay here and pack, and Jax or I would be happy to take your place."

Erin rubbed the ash from her hands. "I know." She tugged on dark leather gloves. "I want to be the one to do it. Besides, what sort of lady would I be if I helped my own retainers to do their work?"

Liana nodded and went back to packing. "Imagine the prince doing servant's work."

"Cooking his own meals," Erin suggested with dry humor.

Liana snorted. "Burning his own meals, I'd say."

"Washing his own clothes."

"He'd be more likely to destroy his own clothes." Erin peered out the window again as Liana chuckled. The sun had set while they talked, and the sky was a deep purplish black with small pinpricks of light overhead from the stars. Erin picked up her climbing hook and rope and put on her soft climbing shoes with flexible leather soles.

"Jax and I will meet you at the stables, and we'll leave directly." Liana doused all the lights save for one dim, candlelit sconce. "Happy hunting."

Erin pulled the curtains open and sat on the window ledge. "May our journeys be fruitful and our reunion swift."

Liana held her fist to her heart. "Let nothing stand in our way."

Comforted by the ritual of her family's customary farewell, Erin swung her legs out the window, secured her climbing hook between a gap in the stones of the tower, and pulled herself out into the air.

While the tower had been built so that the outer walls were as smooth as possible, time and weather had roughened the surface and widened the cracks between the great square blocks. Erin tested each foothold before shifting her weight upward, gripping onto edges and gaps with her climbing hook, hands, and feet. A shifting breeze tugged her clothes this way and that, but long hours of practice scaling the cliffs of her home under Jax's critical eye kept her mind focused and her ascent steady.

Soon she fell into a rhythm of hook, hand, and foot, one after the other, pulling herself up and up into the gloom of the night. Fate smiled down upon her with the gift of an overcast sky that obscured the moon and helped her gray and black outfit blend into the air, stone, and shadow around her. Sometimes she climbed near a window and had to make sure to give a wide berth if there were lights on inside, but most windows were darkened, the occupants all intent upon remaining at the dinner where the king and prince could better notice them. Finally she neared the top. The prince lived in the second highest suite in the palace, above a wing of rooms that were his to do with as he pleased. Only the king's rooms were higher. Erin began to slow down and proceed with extra caution, unwilling to be caught outside the prince's domain.

She reached the balcony connected to the prince's rooms and settled in just below the balustrade to listen for signs of life. The marble floor was silent, with no click of boots or rustle of cloth, and no voices sounded from within. Erin pulled herself over the railing and onto the balcony, where she crouched to the ground to hide. She half-hunched, half-crawled to the archway leading into the prince's rooms, minimizing her silhouette by moving swiftly between pieces of furniture until she could step out of view of anyone who might think to look up from the ground or a window.

Erin prowled through the opulent rooms inside, checking to make sure they were empty while also getting her bearings. The bedroom was draped in reds and oranges, and Erin hated the look of the slashes of bold colors against the bone white marble walls and floors. Everything about the room screamed violence from the colors to the weapons to the stuffed game hanging off walls to the furs lining the floor with heads still attached.

Erin found a narrow gap in the wall, set off to the side in what looked like the prince's sitting room, and walked through to find a small den. Shelves lined the narrow space and left just enough room amid the books and papers for a desk and armchair. Another archway led out to a parlor with gaming tables. Erin stood in the curtained archway and checked again that nobody lurked in the long, grotesquely shaped shadows cast by statues and furniture.

Reassured that she was alone, Erin began to look through the papers lying on the desk, making an effort not to move anything out of place. She scanned the first letter. The cover page was innocuous.

Brimley,

On your way to your lands, could you pass this along to our mutual friend? You know how he is about propriety, so be sure to hand it off in the right way. Don't die of boredom out there in the sticks – we'll go on a hunt soon enough to give you some diversion.

In Friendship,

HRH

Erin shook her head at the disdain the prince held for his country and turned to the next page, which she read with increasing horror.

Morton,

I'm holding up my end of the deal with getting you Norcliff. If you want to continue to benefit from my support, you'd better give me results with Varnall. Don't your bandits want to get rich? Tell them they can keep some of what they manage to steal, or come up with a reward system for raiding a village, or something. Don't you know how to lead? I don't care how you do it. Get me more gems and favor with the north, or suffer the consequences. Varnall doesn't accept empty promises, and neither will I.

Impatiently,

HRH

Erin stared at the words on the page and tried to think through what they meant. She couldn't fathom why a prince would want gems when he could go to the royal treasury any time and would soon inherit the entire kingdom. She flipped back to the first letter, but it gave no hints about his motives.

The click of a door opening interrupted her reverie, and she hurriedly set the letters back down to jump behind a curtain as she heard two pairs of footsteps draw near. She pressed herself against the wall and rose up on her toes to reduce the amount her feet could be seen between the bottom of the curtain and the floor. A man began to talk, and she recognized the prince's nasal tone of voice instantly. She stiffened in fear of discovery as the two people walked so close that the fabric of the curtain swayed when they passed her hiding place.

"We'll depart directly," said the second man, whose voice she didn't recognize.

"The night's festivities should provide adequate cover." Erin heard the rustle of papers. "Here are my letters for you and Morton. Be sure to deliver Morton's directly to him, would you? We can't afford to let this fall into the wrong hands, and I know how fond you are of delegating, Brimley. This is one task you must do yourself."

"I would never do less than see personally to any task you gave me."

"Just the same." The prince sounded amused.

"I'll leave immediately, your royal highness."

"As you should. Now, I must get back to the party before anyone misses me, and you have an appointment to keep."

The curtain rippled again as the prince and Lord Brimley walked back out. Erin stayed where she was until their voices faded behind the slam of a door. She ran to the balcony on tiptoes and climbed as quickly as she could down to the ground. Sneaking along the alleyways in the service area outside the palace's inner walls, she reached a clearing behind the stables where Jax and Liana waited with the horses.

"We have to follow Lord Brimley!" Erin said as she accepted a cloak from Jax and leapt into her saddle.

Jax cocked his head. "Why?"

"He has letters – proof of the prince's wrongdoing! The prince is working with the Mortons! We need to get that proof!"

"Quiet," Jax hissed. "Do you know where Lord Brimley is going?"

Erin kept her voice to a furious whisper. "To see the Mortons!"

Liana grinned. "We can take the shortcut and intercept him at the border to the Morton estate."

"No." Jax scratched at his chin. "No, we must keep our eyes on this Brimley. He could surprise us, and we'll need every scrap of evidence we can get if we want to discredit the prince."

"He just left," Erin said. "We can catch up to him at the outer gate." With their plan set, they urged their horses forward into the night.

7

A Fork in the Road

LORD BRIMLEY CHOSE a strange, weaving path out from the palace, sticking to back roads well sheltered by the old growth trees that made up the royal hunting forest.

"I don't like the look of this," Jax said as they followed Lord Brimley through the forest at a safe distance. "These are the actions of a man hiding a dark secret."

"I'd say the letter he carries is quite a dark secret," Erin replied, and they fell silent, urging their horses onward, out of the capital city and into the wilds after Lord Brimley.

All was quiet save for the occasional hoot of an owl and the quiet thump of hooves against dirt, the sound obscured by the much louder rattle and creak of Lord Brimley's carriage in the velvety silence of the forest at night. They rode through the night, and around them, so slowly that they scarcely noticed it, it grew quieter and quieter until the sound of the carriage was unnaturally loud in the stillness. Erin loosened her knives in their sheaths, and out of the corner of her eyes, she saw Jax and Liana do the same. Erin felt a prickling at the back of her neck, as if something lurked in the wood, and she strained her ears for some indication of what might be out there. A branch snapped in the distance, and Erin drew a knife as Jax signaled them to slow. Then everything exploded into motion as men burst from the brush to either side of Lord Brimley's carriage, yelling and brandishing their weapons. Jax brought his horse to a halt, and Erin and Liana followed suit. They hid themselves among the trees while bandits tied up Lord Brimley and his men and ransacked his carriage.

"The letters -" Erin whispered but fell silent as Jax pointed to a chest of papers that the bandits had seized and tied to one of their packhorses. The ransacking of Lord Brimley's belongings was over quickly, and soon the bandits began to disappear back under the cover of the brush.

"They're getting away with the papers," Erin said and took a step forward to follow them.

"Wait!" Liana grabbed Erin's arm. "We can't leave Lord Brimley, what if there's more the prince asked him to do?"

Jax rubbed a hand over his mouth and grimaced. "We'll have to split up."

"Lord Brimley will probably go to the Mortons and tell them the prince's message in person," Liana said.

Jax turned to Erin. "I was going to wait to bring this up until we reached Morton's lands, but Erin, you're too recognizable to sneak into Morton Manor unnoticed, and it's too much of a risk to have you there besides. We need you to lead our people and make our alliances with the other nobles. Will you follow the bandits?"

"Only if you take Liana with you," Erin said. "The Mortons are a dangerous family to go visiting, and I would not have you caught there alone."

"It's equally dangerous to follow the bandits -" Jax began, but stopped as Erin raised a hand.

"No. You've trained me for this practically since infancy. I can follow a bunch of bandits."

Jax shook his head. "Erin, it's dangerous for you to travel alone -"

"I order you and Liana to follow Lord Brimley, and I'll follow the bandits and do the best I can to recover the prince's letter."

Jax nodded slowly. "Very well, milady. Shall we rendezvous at Hart Keep in three days' time?"

"Three days," Erin agreed.

Jax held his fist to his heart, and Liana followed suit. "May our journeys be fruitful and our reunion swift."

Erin did the same, smiling fondly at the familiar words. "Let nothing stand in our way."

With nothing more to say, the three split up. Liana and Jax remained near the bound and gagged group of Lord Brimley and his men, and Erin rode in pursuit of the quickly departing bandits. She had expected them to stop soon and break camp to run an inventory of their loot and celebrate their good fortune. They did stop to rest, but they didn't celebrate. Erin hid behind a tall oak with a wide trunk and watched the bandits set up a tidy, well run camp with a regular changing of the guard along a well defended perimeter. They acted too well-disciplined and organized in Erin's opinion, like professional soldiers instead of the way Jax had taught her a band of criminals might behave.

By the next day of following the bandits through the forest, Erin's back ached from her continual hunching behind trees and rocks to avoid detection. She had set her horse free to return to the stables in order to stay hidden. When they weren't attacking targets with furious speed, the bandits were orderly and swift, though their clothing was ragged and their stature unimposing, with a general look of malnourishment. The man who barked orders at the rest was cut from a different cloth, observant, tall, and wide as a boulder on his formidable battle horse. He had set a tight watch over the stolen goods overnight, and Erin's eyes were blurry from staying up and trying to see a way past the guards.

The bandits wound their way along the side of a mountain and into a river valley, and Erin had to focus on her feet, made clumsy from exhaustion. She was so tired that it took her a few moments to recognize the sound of hooves beating into the ground at a furious gallop. She looked up to notice that the bandits had formed a tight ring around their carts of stolen goods and faced outward with weapons drawn and eyes roving from side to side. As the sound of horses grew louder, she began to hear metal clashing with metal and men shouting battle cries. She looked but could see nothing until she whirled around to find a cloud of dust rising from under the feet and hooves of a group of soldiers coming into sight over the top of the hill behind her.

A man in a full suit of armor on a black horse raced ahead of the rest with his sword drawn. Erin leaped to the side of the trail to hide herself behind a thicket just before the man galloped past with a roar of challenge at the bandits. Erin leaned to the side to keep an eye on his progress and watched the gap between him and the rest of the soldiers grow. Dread rose within her, and she murmured, "He's too far ahead." She could not bear to watch such a lionhearted man die at the hands of a band of criminals.

She drew her knives and sprinted out from her cover, calling out to the charging man, "Slow down! Slow down, wait for everyone else!" He showed no signs of hearing her words and continued his charge. She cursed to herself as he threw himself to meet the closest bandit in battle with a clash of sword against sword. The bandits broke from their formation with vicious grins and ran to surround the man on his horse and block his path to escape.

Erin gasped for breath and willed her legs to run faster as she held her knives before her in a defensive position. The man was almost completely surrounded, and he wheeled his horse about to swing his sword from side to side while the men below him grabbed at his legs and saddle. He struck down man after man, but it was not enough. There were too many, and soon enough a rail thin man succeeded in cutting the man's saddle from his horse.

The soldier fell out of sight, and Erin's stomach dropped at the sight. "Idiot!" she shouted in lieu of a battle cry as she reached the bandits and raised her knives. She slit throats and stabbed at hamstrings in a wild bid to clear a path to the unhorsed soldier. All she could see was the confusion of metal around her and the acrid smell of blood as she did her best to move forward. She stabbed her knife between the ribs of the large man in front of her and weaved between two others to find the soldier, snarling and holding his ground against the men surrounding him.

"Behind you! A way out, behind you!" She shouted and leapt at the bandit trying to stab the soldier in the back. He killed the two in front of him and turned to take in the sight of her, with the bandit falling away from her knives with blood spraying from his neck onto her already stained clothes. The sound of the rest of the soldiers reaching the bandits and joining the fight brought Erin a rush of relief, and the arrival pulled the bandits' attention away from the two of them for a moment.

The soldier nodded to her with a startled expression just visible through the gaps in his helmet, and then there was no more time to talk. They turned their backs to one another as more attackers climbed over the bodies all around. Erin hacked and cut and snarled at whoever approached with furious determination. She could not tell how long the fight lasted, only that it seemed to take forever and no time at all until there were no more bandits to fight.

She blinked sweat out of her eyes and wiped her blades on the tunic of a corpse beside her before sheathing them. All around her, soldiers dealt death blows to men writhing on the ground and rifled through the stolen goods piled at the center of the battleground. Erin bent forward to rest her hands on her knees and tried to recover her breath.

"What's your name, my good man?" A deep voice asked as a hand clapped her on the shoulder.

She straightened her sore back with a hiss and turned to the soldier who had brought her out of hiding. "Erin." She let the hood she had worn to hide her red hair from the bandits fall and sketched a curtsy in spite of her lack of skirts. The gesture was a habit ingrained in her by her mother, who had stressed the importance of using politeness and diplomacy whenever possible.

The man took a step back and pulled off his helmet to reveal gently curling black hair plastered to his head and a severe but handsome face barely softened with surprise. He stared at her, opening and closing his mouth in silence as she rose out of her curtsy and looked up at him.

An older man with light gray hair rode up on a graceful bay stallion. "My Lord!" He dismounted and swept his cape behind him to rest a hand on his sword. "How many times have I asked you not to go rushing ahead without us?!"

The lord's mouth snapped shut and his eyes narrowed with irritation, though he did not take his eyes off of Erin. "Yes, yes, there's no need to shout, Arnau. I'll be more careful next time."

Erin watched with surprise as the lord bent into a courtly bow, took her hand, and kissed the air above it. Off to the side, Arnau muttered under his breath and lifted his gaze to the sky. "Forgive me, milady. I did not realize," the lord said.

"You are forgiven." Erin pulled her hand back as soon as he finished bowing, wiping her dirty hands on her shirt self-consciously. She knew he had called her a lady out of kindness, for she did not look the part in her travel-worn clothes. His eyes followed the motion of her hands before snapping up to meet her gaze. Erin looked to the side and tried to come up with an explanation for herself and her actions. She had not expected to meet a lord in a fight against bandits. She had not expected to meet anyone.

"I'm relieved. I'm also in your debt. How may I repay you for saving my life?" The lord observed her with a curious intensity while Arnau crossed his arms and scowled at her.

Erin cast her eyes about, uncomfortable under the lord's scrutiny. As she looked around, she noticed a soldier opening the trunk with its precious letters to rifle through its contents. She looked back at the lord. He could claim everything here, if he wanted, as spoils of victory. She needed to find out what he planned to do with that trunk of letters.

"You could give me your name," she said.

The lord peered at her face again, more closely this time, before replying. "Of course. I am Hugo Castelli of Xycabria. You travel on my lands."

"Forgive me, my lord, I did not know." Erin sketched another curtsy, taking care to do it with the clumsiness of someone with no rank. She looked up to see if she had convinced him that she was beneath his notice, but he remained attentive and focused on her. "If it's not too much to ask, could you give me a place to rest for a few days? I have traveled many miles and am weary from the road."

"Certainly, you may stay at my manor and dine at my table. I would like to know more about my savior." Hugo walked away to collect his horse while Arnau continued to watch her suspiciously. Erin kept her eyes on the ground but watched Arnau in her peripheral vision. Hugo rode back on his horse to stop at her side and extend a hand down to her. "Ride with me and rest your weary feet."

Erin stared up at Hugo in alarm. She wouldn't be able to keep an eye on the trunk if she was next to a lord at the center of everyone's attention. "I couldn't, my lord." Erin searched her mind for an excuse. "I don't know how to ride," she blurted out and smiled in relief. No lord would suffer the awkward bumblings of a peasant girl on his war horse.

"No matter, I won't let you fall. Come." He stretched out his hand to her again, and she took it, unable to think of a way out. "Put your foot in the stirrup and step up. I will do the rest." She followed his directions, and he lifted her behind him with a grunt. "There. No trouble."

Erin stared at the broad metal shoulder plates of Hugo's armor. Her hands fluttered from his shoulders to his waist and back, hovering over the polished metal now scuffed with grime from the fight. Thrown by his patience for her, she couldn't decide how to hold onto him.

He reached back to grab at her hands and place them on his stomach before clicking his tongue at the horse. "Hold around my waist. There is no room for propriety when you may fall off otherwise." He waved at Arnau, who had resumed scowling at his lord, and shouted to his men, "Pack up and return to the manor. Tonight, we feast!" The soldiers raised a ragged cheer before falling into line behind him.

"My lord, please allow me to accompany you," Arnau called out, hastily mounting his horse and falling into a trot beside them. He gave Erin a suspicious look. "Tell me, lady, what is your name?"

"Erin." She didn't give her surname, though Arnau paused like he was waiting to hear more.

"A beautiful name for a beautiful lady," Hugo said, and Erin could feel the vibrations of his voice in her fingertips through the metal of his armor. Hugo pointed out a cluster of buildings against the horizon. "There is my home. I hope you enjoy your stay, for I am grateful beyond words for your assistance today."

Erin had no response, equal measures flattered and horrified by the attention Hugo was giving her. She felt a blush rise in her cheeks and cast her eyes downward, holding a hand to the side of her face in an attempt to hide it.

"You say you have no skill in riding, yet your seat on the horse is quite well-balanced, Lady Erin," Arnau said, and Erin quickly put both arms around Hugo's waist again.

"Beginner's luck, perhaps," she said, and fixed her eyes on Hugo's home as it drew near. It looked like a cross between a castle and a fort, situated as it was at the top of a hill, surrounded by a small city, and guarded by tall and sheer walls. Erin felt awe at the sun-baked, golden stone walls rising up from the ground before them as they rode over a drawbridge to the main gate. The moat beneath them sparkled in the setting sun. Light caught on the dust from the road and the insects that skimmed the water's surface, which picked up the last bit of sun in its ripples and shone waving rays of light on the people passing over the water. Men and women took off hats and set aside their burdens to bow and curtsy to Hugo and his soldiers as they rode past. Erin marveled at the absence of beggars lining the road, so different from the chaotic mess of the capital.

Inside the gates, tidy houses and shops lined the cobblestone streets, and a scattering of merchants bustled to and fro, closing up the windows and doors to their shops and packing up for the day. Dogs yipped and horses nickered, and a hum of conversation filled the streets. There were no loud shouts or large crowds. Erin enjoyed the tranquil sense of efficiency in the way people cleared a path for the soldiers and returned to their business without the pomp and circumstance that accompanied the progress of lords and ladies on the streets around the palace. Hugo and Erin galloped ahead of the rest of the group up a steady incline to the towers at the top of a hill, which were built from a sand colored stone that gave off a warm glow in the evening light.

Hugo led the horse through another gate and into a circular courtyard with a cheerful fountain bubbling in the center and well pruned trees lining the edges. He stopped his horse before a flight of steps leading up to thick oak doors propped open by a pair of servants who bowed in welcome. Hugo handed his reins to a groom and swung his leg over the horse's lowered neck to leap out of the saddle. He then held a hand out to Erin, who took it and slid to the ground with as much grace as she could muster. He steadied her with a polite hand on her waist as she stared down and gained her footing, uncomfortable with their closeness.

"Join us for dinner tonight, milady, for you played a part in our victory, same as any man in my company, and I would like to get to know you better," Hugo said. "Maria will help you."

A maid came forward from the group greeting the returning soldiers and curtsied. "Please follow me, milady," Maria said and began to walk indoors before Erin could get a word in edgewise. Erin was loathe to spend too much time with the lord and his bewildering kindness, and with the sharp eyed Arnau, who seemed to see past her disguise with ease. She had to stay to recover the papers despite her fear of discovery, though, so she followed the maid to her rooms and prepared for supper.

8

An Unfamiliar Dance

ERIN WORE A borrowed gown made of deep blue velvet with white lace that flowed along the hems of her sleeves to add a graceful eloquence to her movements. The maid who helped her prepare wove small white flowers into her hair, and Erin took a moment to admire the neatness of her appearance after the wear and tear of travel and battle. Erin thanked Maria for her help, and Maria nodded silently before leaving Erin to her thoughts with the same brisk efficiency she had applied to helping Erin get ready.

Erin ran a hand gently over the delicate blossoms in her hair and marveled at how put together she could look when inside, she was full of unease. She had hoped to keep a low profile, but she doubted she could escape attention as a guest of a lord. She stepped out of her rooms and looked around in search of the way to dinner only to find Maria waiting outside her door with a lantern that lit up the warm stone corridor.

"Follow me if you please, milady," Maria said, and she showed Erin the way down a flight of stairs to a great hall where a large dinner table stretched from one end of the room to the other, with a space at the far end for a dance floor. Lord Hugo sat at the head of the table, and when Erin followed Maria into the room he stood from his chair and waved her over. Maria curtsied and stepped back, and Erin thanked her once again before joining Hugo.

"Please, sit, milady," Hugo said and held out the chair to his right. "I have reserved this place of honor for you."

"Thank you, milord." Erin sat and attempted to hide her nerves as well as she could by eating a spoonful of the tomato soup the servants had ladled into the white porcelain bowls.

"I should be the one thanking you, milady. Without your help, I might have met my end on the battlefield today," Hugo said.

"Yes, you might have done, and then where would we be?" Arnau spoke up from his seat to Hugo's left. He nodded to Erin. "Milady. Thank you for gracing the table with your presence."

"Yes, thank you," Hugo said. "If you weren't here, Arnau would likely be yelling at me. So you see, you have saved me again, and I am doubly grateful."

There was a pause in conversation as the servants set down platters of lightly grilled chicken and vegetables all along the table. The dinner was an unusual mix of formal and informal. Gilded porcelain and crystal tumblers were on the table and people dressed in fine clothes, but the conversation was loud and carefree. The festive air was infectious, and Erin could almost forget about her mission to recover the prince's letters in such amiable company.

"You seem surprised, milady. Is my home so unusual to you?" Hugo asked as Erin looked down the table at the other dinner guests.

"I must confess, I had not expected to meet a lord during my travels." Erin felt herself relax a little into the friendly ambiance. "I did not know you were a lord at all, when I first saw you, but rather thought you to be a soldier."

"An overzealous soldier," Arnau muttered. Hugo threw back his head and laughed, and Erin giggled, hard pressed not to join in on the overall atmosphere of celebration.

"You must have traveled far to not recognize me as lord of these lands," Hugo said, and Erin was back on her guard, fearful of slipping in her disguise. "Where did you say you were from, again?"

"A farm at the capital, near the palace."

"How odd to meet a woman traveling such a distance alone," Arnau said.

"My family had nobody to spare to accompany me."

Hugo tilted his head and gave her a searching look. "Did you not have a brother or other relative who could make the journey?" Hugo asked, and Erin's stomach dropped. She had done just what she had hoped not to do and captured Lord Hugo's curiosity.

"He needed to stay behind to work the farm."

"I see," Arnau said. "How did a farmer's daughter come to learn to fight?"

"My uncle was a soldier." Erin's mind raced to find acceptable answers to Hugo and Arnau's questions. "He didn't mind me tagging along when he taught my brother and cousins."

"How tolerant of him," Arnau said. "Sounds like he knew better than to trust other people's opinions on right and wrong. Smart man. Truths are much more difficult to find than opinions, and more precious because of it." Arnau leaned forward over the table and said, "Where exactly are you from, Lady Erin? Could you describe your home to me?"

Erin took a breath to speak when a great swell of music sounded to loud cheers from the other dinner guests. People began pushing back their chairs and migrating to the dance floor, and the room filled with the sound of a lively tune and the footsteps of the people dancing.

Hugo pushed his chair back and stood. "I'd like to dance."

"You wish to dance?" Arnau raised his eyebrows. "That's unusual."

"Not so unusual with such a lovely dance partner as I hope to have." Hugo turned to Erin. "Would you do me the honor of accompanying me?"

"My lord?" Erin froze, not needing to fake her unease.

"What is it?" He looked down at her with an amused expression.

She reached for an excuse that he would accept. "I don't know the steps."

"It's a simple dance, and I'll lead." He held out a hand, and she took it for the sake of appearing courteous. He helped her to her feet and led her to the dance floor. As they walked, he frowned. "Strange, how smooth your hand feels."

Erin concealed the twitch in her shoulders by lifting them in a shrug. "My family dotes upon me and keeps me from work that would give me calluses."

"How fortunate." He grasped her other hand and pulled her toward him, and she stared at his shoulder, covered in fine silk and inches from her nose. He towered above her, and she did not like being this close to another man anymore.

"Yes," she said in a distant voice, as though she spoke from miles away. "Fortunate."

"I don't recall you telling me the final destination of your journey."

"I don't recall you asking me before now." Erin deliberately trod on Hugo's foot, and he winced in pain. "Oh no! I'm so sorry, milord, I'm really not good enough at dancing to keep up with you."

"Nonsense, it was a mistake anyone could have made."

"Nevertheless, I do believe I must cease dancing with you, to protect your feet from further injury."

Hugo smiled wryly and said, "Very well, Lady Erin. Let me escort you off the floor, at the very least." He tucked her hand through his elbow in one smooth movement and walked her out of the area set aside for dancing. He seemed about to speak when a lady with a flirtatious smile walked up.

"Lord Hugo, are you looking for another dance partner?" The lady asked.

"As a matter of fact," Erin said, "he is. Please, don't let me keep you," she said to Hugo and walked away, making a beeline for the closest exit into a sparsely occupied hall. She took a deep breath and let it out slowly. "That was close," she whispered as she made her way back to her guest room. "Too close." She resolved to find the letter that night and leave first thing in the morning, before Lord Hugo or his inquisitive second in command, Arnau, asked any further questions to which she might not have a good enough answer.

Back in her room, Erin changed into her travel clothes, covered her hair with a hood, and walked back out into the corridor to follow the first servant she saw carrying what looked like goods taken from the bandits. She kept to corners and shadows cast by the flickering torch lights and made sure to keep a leisurely pace. She did her best to act like she belonged there to avoid suspicion, until the servant came to a door flanked by two guards.

Erin quickly walked into another room off the hall, and found herself confronted by the sight of Hugo.

"A-ha!" Hugo took a step forward, and Erin backed out of the room and into the guards who had moved from the vault door to waylay her. Left without an avenue for escape, Erin straightened her shoulders and marched back into the room to face Hugo. "So you are here for more than you appear to be." Hugo's face became dark and foreboding, and he walked closer until he loomed over Erin. "Out with it. What were you sniffing around the vault for?"

Erin crossed and uncrossed her arms and shifted back a few steps. She could see no way to talk herself out of this mess. "The bandits stole something, something I need to prove a man's guilt. A letter."

"A letter." Hugo huffed out a laugh. "You risked your safety for a letter? It must be quite a crime this man of yours is guilty of committing."

Erin tilted up her chin. "It is quite a crime. Almost treason, as a matter of fact."

Hugo frowned. "Treason, eh? That is serious indeed. I'd like to read this letter myself."

Erin hesitated. She wasn't sure that she trusted this strange man with his disconcerting kindness and fierce intensity, but she needed allies, and he had treated her well so far. "If I show you the letter, will you let me keep it?"

"That would depend on what the letter says. I make no promise save that I will be more inclined to lenience if you act in good faith and show me what you wanted to steal so badly."

"Steal?" Erin asked, incredulous. "How can I steal what has already been stolen?"

"We did not steal these goods. We recaptured them."

"They were stolen first, just the same."

"I see your point," Hugo said, "but the fact remains that I want to know the nature of this treason, in case it's an issue that will affect my people."

Erin couldn't argue with that, knowing the weight of concern that she felt for the safety of her own people. "I see no harm in that," she said and walked back to the vault with Hugo following. "It's in the chest of papers you took from the bandits. There should be two letters from the prince. One is addressed to Lord Brimley, the other to Ardent Morton." She waited at the door of the vault for the guards to unlock it, which they did at a nod from Hugo. She walked into the vault, bypassing the gold and silver to go to the wooden chest and open it to reveal the letters. Hugo stepped forward and took the letters out to read them with a frown.

"This is serious indeed. The prince has been behind the increased criminal activity lately?" Hugo scowled. "Many good men have fallen in battle with these bandits who act with the prince's support. I have stretched my coffers to the limits to defend my people from these incursions." He threw the papers back into the chest and crossed his arms, frowning deeply. "He must be stopped."

"Yes, he must," Erin said, and a small spark of hope kindled within her. "Will you help me stop him?"

Hugo gave her an appraising look. "You? Stop a prince?" He smiled. "Do you plan to step on his feet until he begs for mercy?" He held up a hand to stop Erin from responding. "No, no, I know it's no laughing matter. Yes, I will help you. You'll need all the friends you can get, and I must protect my people." There was no uncertainty to his voice, and Erin marveled at his confident air.

"Thank you," Erin said. "I confess I had not expected to find an ally on this journey. I had merely hoped to recapture the letters."

"Well, you can consider me caught as well," Hugo said with a wry smile. "Indeed, I am thoroughly captivated, my lady."

Erin felt a blush rise to her cheeks and she turned away to hide it from sight. "Will you travel with me to my home, to make a plan to stop the prince and the Mortons from carrying out their plans?"

"I will, but there's one problem," Hugo said from behind her.

She turned around to look at him, worried. "What is it?"

"I don't know where you live," Hugo said.

"Oh." Erin's face burned with embarrassment. "Norcliff. I'm Erin Hart, of the Norcliff Harts."

Hugo's eyebrows rose. "Lady Hart, a pleasure to make your acquaintance." He swept a deep bow that left Erin feeling tongue-tied.

"Likewise." Erin pretended to curtsy, holding out the hem of her tunic in the place of skirts. Hugo looked amused at the sight but did not comment. Erin straightened and adopted a businesslike tone of voice to hide her embarrassment. "We should leave as soon as possible. Friends of mine have followed Lord Brimley, a compatriot of the prince, and we plan to rendezvous at Hart Keep."

"We shall leave at first light, my lady." Hugo bowed again before striding out the door, leaving Erin alone with the letters and a bewildering mix of bashful happiness and anticipation where before there was only grief, shame, and solemn duty.

9
Hart Keep

ERIN AND HUGO arrived a day later at Hart Keep to find the halls cleared of servants and the decor from Erin's ill-fated wedding still on display. The majority of the townspeople were working on fortifications along the rings of the walls meant to keep out intruders, and Erin was met with grim faces and bows or curtsies at every gateway on the path to the keep. The townspeople watched in silence as Erin and Hugo rode by, a sharp contrast to the cheers that would greet Erin and her parents on their return from excursions in the past.

"Your people are a quiet lot," Hugo said as they dismounted at the keep entrance and left their horses with the groom.

"They're worried, and I don't think they know what to make of me yet. Which makes a pair of us," Erin said with wry humor.

"What do you mean by that?" Hugo offered Erin his arm to guide her up the steps, and she accepted with bemused tolerance.

"I came to power through unexpected means, with a fiancé lost and the Hart leadership scattered by the massacre that was my wedding." Erin's voice cracked on the word massacre, but she kept going. "They've had little time to acclimate to me or my ways, as I have had little time to adapt to my change in circumstances."

"You sell yourself short if you think you're adapting badly," Hugo said.

"Thank you," Erin said as they walked through an inner courtyard with a small pond built out of stone where brightly colored red and orange goldfish swam to and fro. Erin paused by the little waterfall that fed into the pond and trailed her fingers over the water's surface. Just a few days ago, she had sat by this pond and daydreamed of how she might live as a wife and, someday, mother. "How quickly life can change," she murmured.

"That is the nature of life, to be changeable," Hugo said. "But we can hold that which is dear to us and keep it well, so that it may last through the trials of each day."

Erin smiled sadly and thought of her wedding ring, lost in the chaos of the attack. She would have liked to have kept it, to have a less ephemeral memento than the wedding decorations that still lined the halls of the keep which would be cleared away soon enough. She watched the fish swim with their scales glittering as they caught the light. She still had her family home. She still had this moment, by the pond, in the courtyard with Hugo watching her, arms crossed, with a heavy brow and sympathetic expression, while fish swam with graceful flicks of their fins, and light danced along ripples in the water's surface.

Erin let out a heavy sigh and turned to face Hugo. "You're right. We must hold that which is dear to us close, as well as we can, for as long as we can."

"And when all seems lost, I've found that life has a way of surprising me with just what I need to get through another day."

Erin looked at Hugo, standing tall and resolute in her family's courtyard, and she felt a lightening of her spirit. Here was a friend, a brave companion, who she had met by chance and who was willing to travel out of his way to help her and protect their nation. She was not so alone after all, and hope was not lost to her. She smiled at Hugo, who gave her a slight smile, no more than a subtle twitch of the lips, in return. "I would like to show you my home, Lord Hugo, if you're interested in seeing it."

Hugo bowed his head. "I would be honored to see it, Lady Erin."

Erin gestured around them. "We can start where we are. This is the central courtyard," she said, and they walked along the interior garden, which was lined with archways leading off into other rooms. Ivy twined its way up the walls and along the columns between the arched balustrades of the second floor balconies. A stairway in the back led to the basement and second floor. "Above us are the family bedrooms and the guest room, where you're welcome to stay." They passed an archway to the dining room. "We take our meals..." Erin trailed off. With her parents missing, she would be the only one left to eat in the dining room. The sight of the rows of empty chairs made her sad. "We took our meals in there." They stopped in the archway, with Hugo following Erin's lead. There were wedding bouquets still adorning the table, slightly wilted now, with the blooms drooping. "The living area is this way." Erin led Hugo to the opposite side of the courtyard. It, too, seemed forlorn and empty, and Erin missed Liana and Jax with a sudden pang. "The study is this way." She led Hugo farther into the central courtyard to the study where her father did his work. She paused in the archway, struck by the sight of the papers still lying on her father's desk where he had left them. She had to clear her throat before she could speak. "The library is over here." She steered Hugo to the opposite side of the courtyard. Here, at last, was a place where she could find comfort, with the shelves of books set into the walls and the reading armchairs with their high armrests, well suited to supporting books. It was with relief that Erin led Hugo into the library. "I've spent many hours here, both as a student with my tutors and while reading for pleasure." She led Hugo back into the courtyard. "Let me show you the way to your guest room," she said.

They walked up the stairs, the pair of them, and it occurred to Erin that her parents had walked up these stairs in a similar way, arm in arm, on quiet evenings when there were no festivities to attend or company to entertain. She unwound her hand from Hugo's arm and climbed the stairs faster. She wasn't here to find a new beau. She didn't think she could, couldn't see a way to fill the gaping void that the death of Marc had left in her heart, and she didn't like how Hugo reminded her that the emptiness was there.

Erin showed Hugo to the guest room. "Here you are," she said briskly. "I'll leave you to rest now." She walked quickly away, through the hall, down the stairs, and back to the library.

A book lay open on one of the tables in the library, and Erin leafed through the pages. It had been a gift from Marc, a book of maps that they had pored over, considering the places they could travel before their time came to run the Clairmaud estate. Erin's eyes welled up with tears that she brushed away angrily. She had been looking at this book in the days leading up to the wedding and dreaming of what might be. She had traveled to the capital since then. It had not been what she had dreamed of, and Marc hadn't been there to lighten her days and share her joys and sorrows. She closed the book and put it back onto the nearest bookshelf. She would have to let these old dreams go.

Erin walked back out into the courtyard to sit by the pond, but a restless itch at the back of her mind grew so troubling that she got to her feet and began pacing in an attempt to shake off her unease. She wandered into the living area in search of she hardly knew what to find Hugo standing with hands clasped behind his back, looking at the portrait of her family that hung over the fireplace. Hugo turned to face her as she marched into the room to regard her with a raised eyebrow.

"I find myself at loose ends, and I don't like it," she said.

"I too find waiting most distasteful," Hugo agreed.

"Shall we go and see what we can do to help with the fortifications while we wait for Jax and Liana to get here?"

Hugo nodded. "I like that idea much better than sitting here and twiddling my thumbs." He offered her his arm, which she took with a discomfited smile, still thrown by his courtly gestures toward her.

They walked to the first inner wall which had some parts carved out of the rock of the cliff behind the keep. A man with close cropped brown hair and a matter of fact bearing walked up to Erin and Hugo and said, "Hello, are you here to help with the fortifications?"

"Yes. I'm Erin, and this is Hugo," Erin said. "How can we help?"

"Eliot Cooper's the name, and that gate there needs more supports." Eliot pointed out the gate he meant, a small wooden doorway with wooden struts holding it shut. "You can get more poles from the pile there." He pointed out the pile and then went back to the business of directing the placement of wooden poles against a large gate to hold it shut against the possibility of a battering ram.

Erin and Hugo went to the pile of poles and carried one together to set against the door. A woman stopped by them on her way to get more supports to say, "Thank you for your help. I'm Anna." She extended her hand for Erin to shake.

"I'm Erin, and this here's Hugo," Erin said.

"Well met," Anna said before walking away.

"Why do you not tell them your rank? Why do you let them tell you what to do?" Hugo asked as they took a pole from another volunteer to stack against the door.

"Because I don't wish to make a fuss, and the people here know what they're doing better than I could. They know what to do and the best way I can help get it done. There's no need for a Lady Erin here. Erin the volunteer, on the other hand, can be of use."

"Rank is important among my people," Hugo said. "We may be relaxed in times of peace, but we make a point of being aware of it so that we may act in an emergency or during a conflict where decisions must be made and followed quickly. Isn't this an emergency?"

"Yes, and everyone is listening to the person who knows best what to do, which isn't me. Each person has their strengths to contribute. I'm here to help, and that's all. I know how best to maintain my keep, and the people who live here know best what needs to be done to protect their homes. They know the weak spots of their portion of the wall. This is how we work together, here in Norcliff."

"I see," said Hugo, "but I still think the chain of command is vital to survival in a crisis. My people have survived many battles by following it, through the ages."

"Perhaps for you, your way is best suited to your way of life, as our way is best suited to our way of life.

Hugo bowed his head courteously. "As you say, Lady Erin."

"Please, we may dispense with the titles."

"I respect your ways, but I must hold true to my own, and they dictate that I honor you as a lady," Hugo said.

"Very well, Lord Hugo." Erin felt a small loosening in the tightness in her chest that she had felt since meeting Hugo, a relief that Hugo still wanted to keep the distance of titles between them, despite her talk of dispensing with them. She felt such a bewildering mix of attraction and caution toward Hugo that she didn't know how much closeness she would be able to bear.

10
Picking Flowers

WHEN ERIN AND Hugo returned to the castle, sweaty and dusty from their work, they found Jax and Liana's horses tied to a post near the entrance. Erin rushed into the keep with Hugo following behind at a slower pace to find Jax and Liana resting in the living area. Erin greeted them enthusiastically while Hugo waited in the door frame for an introduction. "This is Hugo Castelli of Xycabria," Erin said, when Jax gave Hugo a questioning look. "He's shown interest in helping us with our mission."

"You took a risk by giving him that information," Jax said evenly.

"He had the letters in his possession, and to get them back, I had to tell him why I needed them," Erin said.

"A dire problem," Hugo said. "And one that needs addressing."

"Well then," Jax said, "I am Jax, the weaponsmaster."

"And I'm Liana, assistant weaponsmaster and lady's maid."

"Well met, both of you." Hugo bowed politely, and even disheveled from a day's labor, he cut a dashing figure to Erin's eyes, with his sweat-soaked shirt showing his broad shoulders and strong arms.

"And now to business, for the news we have for you is grave indeed," Jax said. "Lord Brimley visited the Mortons even without the letters. They're keeping your parents in their dungeons, and bandits have begun to gather outside the manor's walls."

"Word among the townspeople is that Lord Morton aspires to take other families' lands by force, starting with ours and the Clairmauds'.

The Mortons mean to take advantage of the chaos the bandits sow," said Liana.

"Attacks on homesteads along the northern border are on the rise, and they already occupy the attention of the king's army," Jax said. "Frederick Clairmaud is traveling home from university to fill the gap left by the death of Marc and the capture of Lord and Lady Clairmaud, who the Mortons also keep locked away."

"Those are not the only people the Mortons keep under lock and key," Liana said. "Townspeople who disagree with the Mortons' actions have also been imprisoned. A rumor has spread on the streets that an army from Varnall is being smuggled in to strengthen the Mortons' and the prince's position."

"I worry at this news, and at the possibility that this army may turn into an invading force," Jax said. "Their loyalty to the prince is likely to be extremely conditional and easily swayed."

"This is grave news," Hugo said. "The Varnallans value property and land gained through conquest as trophies. My many years of fighting against their bandits can attest to that. The prince may believe they are his allies, but I have difficulty believing they could be allies to anyone besides themselves."

"We must spread this news far and wide," Erin said. "The prince risks the safety of us all with his ill-thought out actions, and we must free the people the Mortons have unjustly imprisoned."

"We should travel to Duke Bavencian's castle by first light tomorrow," Liana said. "We must act quickly before the prince puts any more of our people in danger."

Jax rolled out a map on the table, and they began to plan out their journey to the duke's castle to plead their case before the king's brother.

The next day dawned crisp and bright, and the group of four got an early start to their day long trek across the rolling meadows and gentle hills that lay between Norcliff and the duke's castle. They rode through a lightly wooded glen, and sunlight filtered through the pale green leaves of silver-white birch trees to either side of the path, dappling the ground in shifting layers of light and shadow. Erin drew her horse up beside Hugo's to say, "I must thank you again for helping us, Lord Hugo."

"There's no need to thank me," said Hugo. "I would do more besides, to repay my rescuer. Your quick thinking may have saved my life, and a life debt is no trifling matter."

"You owe me nothing, for I acted as anyone might."

"Perhaps," said Hugo, "but it pleases me to help you, so help I shall."

Erin nodded. "Thank you," she said before riding forward to travel next to Liana.

"I see you've found an admirer," Liana said in an undertone. "And what a handsome admirer to have. I commend you." She giggled, and Erin reached over to push lightly at Liana's arm.

"Stop that. He's here to help us secure the nation against a threat to its safety, not to admire me," Erin whispered.

"Then why does he stare at you so?"

"He does?" Feeling self conscious, Erin ran her fingers over her braided hair and straightened her tunic, sneaking a glance behind her to find Hugo talking with Jax about their favored weaponry. She turned back and glared at Liana.

"Ah, yes," Liana said. "I can see how you are impartial to him." With one last amused look, she rode ahead to scout out the trail, leaving Erin behind, face burning with a deep blush. She felt confused at how swiftly her feelings had turned, from loving Marc to mourning him, and now to her newfound interest in Hugo, which didn't cease no matter how improper she felt it to be. She didn't understand herself, and part of her felt ashamed of her reaction to Hugo.

Later that day, they stopped atop a gently rolling hill to have lunch in the shadow of a large oak tree, with a meadow of wildflowers spreading at the base of the hill. While Jax, Erin, and Liana sat and ate traveler's bread, Hugo walked to the bottom of the hill to pace the meadow and keep watch.

"How did you manage to meet Hugo Castelli?" Jax asked Erin.

"He attacked the bandits who stole Lord Brimley's papers," Erin said. "I helped him fight them off. Then, he had the letters we needed, so I went with him to his home. Why do you seem surprised?"

"The Castellis are notoriously reclusive. They stay within their borders maintaining their army or go on long campaigns to protect the kingdom but spend little time socializing outside their homeland. Hugo Castelli is known for his fighting prowess and his solitary nature. I was surprised to find him with you."

"He did tell me that he owed me a life debt," Erin said. "He insists on helping me even though I told him he doesn't owe me anything."

"He would. Life debts are a serious matter in Xycabria. No wonder he's here," Jax said. "That explains it. You should take care not to demand too much of him, for he will most likely feel honor bound to do it."

Erin nodded seriously and went back to her traveler's bread. Jax's words confirmed what she had feared, that he regarded her as someone he was duty bound to help and not as someone to admire. She felt disappointed relief at the settling of the matter of how Hugo viewed her, and she resolved not to think on it further.

Her resolution did not last, however, because Hugo came back from the meadow with a bouquet that he presented to her with a gallant bow. "For your consideration, Lady Erin," he said.

Stunned into silence, she took the bouquet and looked at the flowers it contained. There was purple aster, for love and daintiness, white clover as a request to think of him, lavender for devotion as well as silence and caution, and chamomile for patience. Erin stared at the strange mix of flowers until Jax plucked the bouquet from her hands.

"What is this? Aster for daintiness? Lavender for silence and caution? This doesn't suit Erin at all."

Hugo frowned and spoke slowly, "Forgive me, Lady Erin, for any offense I may have caused. I did the best I could with the blooms I could find in the meadow. I will try again." He turned and walked away before Erin could speak.

"What are you doing accepting flowers from the likes of him?" Jax asked Erin. "We barely know the man."

Liana snatched the bouquet out of Jax's hands. "Then we should get to know him before judging him, shouldn't we?" She handed the bouquet back to Erin. "He has done Erin no wrongs yet, has he?"

"He has not wronged me," Erin said and smelled her bouquet thoughtfully.

The journey was tenser after that, with Jax shooting Hugo

disapproving looks and Erin's heart fluttering with a mixture of happiness and guilt every so often as she caught sight of her bouquet peeking out of the saddlebag where she put it.

That night, Erin and Liana slept in a separate room from Jax and Hugo at the inn they found in a town close to the duke's castle. In the morning, Erin came downstairs to the breakfast table to find Hugo waiting for her with another bouquet, this time of white roses and violets.

"Oh, my," Liana said from behind her as Erin viewed the flowers. Erin admired the blooms, the violets for thoughts of love and the white roses for honorable intentions.

"I hope these meet with your approval, Lady Erin?" Hugo asked.

Erin paused. Should she accept these flowers at all, so close to Marc's death? She considered Hugo, his earnest expression and warm, dark eyes. "Yes." Erin took the flowers and blushed while Liana giggled and Jax grumbled into his porridge. It was with some excitement that Erin sat down and had breakfast, but it faded away to nerves as they mounted their horses and rode to Duke Bavencian's castle, now visible on the horizon.

11

The Hunt

DUKE BAVENCIAN'S CASTLE was made of a light gray stone the same color as the boulders bordering the moat that surrounded it. Ivy and roses grew up trellises and along the rough hewn stone walls to create a general appearance of unforced beauty. Erin, Jax, Liana, and Hugo rode over a cobblestone bridge to the front door where Jax announced that Lady Erin and Lord Hugo had arrived to the two guards who stood watch. Soon, a well-dressed butler with a refined manner led them to an ornate main hall where Duke and Duchess Bavencian sat on a slight dais. Some visiting nobles milled about the room, all wearing hunting clothes, checking their weapons and talking amongst themselves. The duke wore well tailored hunting clothing of fine cotton and leather while the duchess wore a silk dress of gold and burgundy.

"Welcome, travelers, please do come in," the duke said happily, and the four walked up to the dais, Jax and Liana trailing behind a little bit. "What brings you to our home?"

"Your upcoming hunt," said Erin. "Lord Hugo and I would like to join you on one of your renowned outings."

"How wonderful," the duke said and rose from his chair. "It is fortuitous that you arrived when you did, for we are about to go hunting now. You are welcome to join us, should you not be too tired from travel."

Duchess Bavencian then spoke from her chair, "I will remain here, and would welcome your company if today's hunt is too strenuous after your travels."

"No, I welcome the chance to join you on your hunt," said Erin.

"I, too, accept your invitation, for we did not travel for long this morning, and our horses are well-rested," said Hugo.

Duke Bavencian clapped his hands together. "Excellent. Shall we?" He gestured toward the front doors, and the crowd of nobles began to drift outside to pick up spears from a pile by the doors. It was a sunny day, and the hunters congregated beneath a cloudless blue sky with birds chirping while hunting dogs bayed. Erin liked the cheerful ruckus raised by the hunting party, and it was with high spirits that the group set out into the Duke's forest.

"We hunt wild boar," Duke Bavencian told the four of them as they followed the pack of hunting dogs. He hefted his spear into the air with a rakish grin. "May the best man catch the best boar," he said and urged his horse onward.

Erin exchanged a meaningful look with Jax and Liana, who separated from the main hunting party to loop around whatever boars they might chance upon while Erin and Hugo stuck with the main group. It was a merry party, and few of the nobles seemed overly concerned about catching anything, with the notable exception of Duke Bavencian, who rode with the huntmasters and their hounds. Erin rode to the front of the group to keep a lookout, and Hugo followed.

"Are you an avid huntress, Lady Erin?" Hugo asked.

"No, but I am an avid protector of my people, and the winning of Duke Bavencian's favor would be a great help toward securing their safety in the days to come. What about you, Lord Hugo? Do you find sport in hunting?"

"No. I find little pleasure in the leisurely pursuit of an activity meant for survival for many. In Xycabria it's dishonorable to waste food and resources for sport. We only hold hunts so that the people may eat. That being said, I understand how it can be viewed as beneficial to practice at an activity to hone a skill, and hunting is a valuable skill."

Just then, a great baying went up from the hounds, and the dogs surged forward into a sprawling thicket of low lying brush. Out from the thicket bounded a large boar with the whites of its eyes showing and its nostrils flared. The duke charged at the head of the hunting party toward the boar, and the boar charged, too. Neither faltered, drawing closer and closer with swift fury, and the huntmasters and nobles gave cries of consternation as the boar tossed its head, with its thick, sharp tusks gleaming ivory-white and pointed toward the duke's horse. The duke tried to rein his horse in, but he was going too fast to stop or change course, and the hunting party watched with increasing worry the collision course the duke and boar ran until an arrow flew out of the woods and into the boar's side. The boar broke off from its charge with an enraged squeal, and the duke struck the killing blow with a well-aimed spear throw.

The other nobles clapped and cheered, and Duke Bavencian bowed and waved with a flourish of his hand. "Thank you," he said to the onlookers, and then he squinted in the direction of the spot where the arrow came from and said, "Whose arrow saved me from potential calamity? I would like to thank you properly for your timely aide."

Jax and Liana rode out from the forest. "I shot the arrow, your grace, and Liana here brought my attention to the boar in the first place," Jax said.

"A team effort," the duke said. "I'm grateful for your collaboration, for you may have saved me and my horse from a horrific goring. If I'm not mistaken, those are the Hart colors you wear, are they not?"

"They are, your grace," Jax said.

"Lady Hart," Duke Bavencian said to Erin, "with your blessing, I would like to hold a ceremony to honor your prescient servants."

"I would be pleased to attend it," Erin said.

"Good! Then it's settled. A feast, upon our return!" The hunting party cheered, and the duke sent runners ahead to tell the kitchens to prepare. The group set off back to the castle at a leisurely, rambling pace while the huntmasters corralled their hounds and gathered the boar and assorted other game felled by the hunters.

The main hall of Duke Bavencian's castle was ornately decorated, with rows of paintings lining the walls in the salon style and a long main table with ornately carved and gilded gold armchairs at one end of the table where the duke and duchess sat. In an alcove of the room past the other end of the table, a quartet of string musicians sat, including a cellist, two violinists, and one person playing the viola. A well-polished parquet floor of reddish brown wood gave the room a warm and welcoming feel, and there was ample space for dancing and conversing by the musician's alcove. A large contingent of servants bustled through the room, bringing out platters of food and refilling drinks as the hunting party sat to eat. Jax and Liana occupied seats of honor to the duke and duchess' right while Erin and Hugo sat to the left.

"How long have you served the Hart family?" Duke Bavencian asked.

"About two decades," said Jax.

"Since before I was old enough to remember," said Liana. "Lord and Lady Hart raised me with Jax's help alongside Lady Erin as a companion."

"I don't suppose I could convince either of you to leave Lady Erin to serve me, could I?"

"I'm afraid not," said Jax.

"We're happy where we are," said Liana. "It's our home, and Lady Erin is as dear as family to us."

"You're lucky to have loyal servants," Duchess Bavecian said to Erin. "There is always a demand for skilled people, and I work tirelessly to find such exemplary servants as yours."

"I am lucky," said Erin, "and glad to have them in my life." She smiled at Jax and Liana, who smiled back.

"Don't sell yourself short, my love," the duke said to his wife and gestured at the servants in the room. "We have quite a large number of exemplary servants, ourselves."

"Yet these servants saved your life," the duchess said. "I do so worry about you on your hunts, husband, and the added peace of mind that would be brought by the knowledge that you have such skilled protectors as Lady Erin does would be priceless. What if they had not been there today? What might have happened?"

"Ah, my love." The duke took the duchess' hand and patted it soothingly. "Do not dwell on might haves and could have beens. I am here before you, healthy and whole, there is a delicious feast before us, and now we have made new friends in Lady Erin, Lord Castelli, and

Lady Erin's wonderful servants." The duke turned to Jax and Liana. "Pray tell, what are your names?"

"Jax, at your service," said Jax.

"Liana, your grace," said Liana.

The duke turned back to his wife. "We have met the noble-hearted Jax and Liana, who did us a great service today, and who we would be honored to have as friends."

"It is I who am honored, your grace, by your friendship," said Jax.

"I am honored as well," said Liana.

"Excellent." The duke turned to Erin and Hugo. "I hope you will stay a few days, so that I might repay you and your servants for your kindness. I would like to bestow some favor upon Jax and Liana, though I am not decided yet as to what."

"We would be delighted," said Erin.

"Good. Then it's settled," said the duke, and he called a servant forward to say, "Prepare rooms for our four guests here and treat them well."

"Yes, your grace," said the servant, and he exited the room.

"And now, let the festivities begin!" The duke clapped his hands to cheers and raised glasses from the hunting party, and the quartet began to play a lively dancing tune. People rose from their chairs to dance, and Erin's heart grew light at the jubilant atmosphere. She waited for Hugo to ask her to dance, but it was to no avail. Hugo continued to eat and make conversation with the noble sitting next to him on his other side.

Erin waited for a break in conversation and said to Hugo, "Why have you not asked to dance with me?"

"I learned my lesson at our last dance. My foot still twinges from the memory of your stepping on it. Nay, Lady Erin, I am not given to dance and invited you to do so before as a way to converse with you and gain a measure of the character of the woman who had protected my life with such admirable ferocity."

Erin's stomach sank. She was surprised to find that she wanted to dance with Hugo and was disappointed to be denied the chance to do so.

"If you would like to dance, there are a number of suitable partners I could introduce you to," said the duchess.

"No, thank you," Erin said. "That's not necessary. I only thought to ask Hugo as he has been my companion during my travels, and we had danced before. I am not much for dancing either, as it happens."

"Very well." The duchess flipped her ornately decorated fan open and fluttered it. "Do let me know if you change your mind."

"There is one thing I would like to ask of you, your grace," said Erin.

"Yes?" The duke focused his attention on Erin. "What is it?"

"May we be granted a private audience with you tomorrow, to discuss some matters I believe will be of great importance to you?"

The duke raised his eyebrow and turned to Jax and Liana. "Is this the favor you wish me to bestow upon you?"

"Yes, your grace," said Jax. Liana nodded.

"Very well. I'll see you in the audience chamber after breakfast," said the duke before rising from his chair. "And now, no more serious talk." He offered his hand to the duchess. "Wife, would you grant me a dance?"

"Yes, husband," said the duchess, and the pair walked to the dance floor.

"That went well." Hugo finished his drink. "I'm off to rest and prepare for tomorrow," he said, and he rose and walked out of the room.

"We should retire too, milady," Jax said.

"In a moment, Jax," said Erin. She lingered to watch the duke and duchess dance with grace and precision, the kind that only comes from knowing your dance partner well enough to coordinate steps. She imagined dancing with Hugo in such a familiar way, and the heat rose in her cheeks. Then she thought of dancing with Marc, and the heat dissipated, and all she felt was sad. She turned away and rose from her seat. "You're right. We have an important task tomorrow and must be well-rested," she said, and they retired for the night.

The next day, breakfast was a quiet affair, with most of the hunting party resting late into the day after the celebrations of the night before. Erin brought down the prince's letters in her travel satchel, and it was not long at all before a manservant came up to the four of them where they sat and ate to say, "His grace awaits your presence in the audience room." They rose from their seats and followed the manservant to a room with intricately painted flowers adorning the paneled walls and a geometric design laid out by the wooden floorboards. The duke and duchess sat on a dais at the far end of the room and gestured them inside when the manservant opened the door to announce their presence.

The duke did not speak until the manservant had left and shut the doors behind him. He then gave the four of them a critical look. "You're imagining things if you think I don't know you came here to request my aid for something. A Hart and a Castelli, outside of their beloved homelands? Most unusual." The duke pointed at Jax. The lace under his cuff swayed at the motion, and he stopped pointing to rearrange the folds with unaffected nonchalance. "You're Sir Jax, of course. The world at large may not remember you, but I'm not so arrogant as to think the past cannot harm me." With the lace settled to his satisfaction, the Duke gave Jax a piercing stare. "I must confess I'm a trifle offended that you thought I wouldn't remember you, sir. As I recall, I sat in on the last few of your reports before your retirement."

Jax swept a courtly bow. "My most humble apologies, your grace."

The duchess flipped open her fan and used it to cover the bottom half of her face. "Your modesty does you credit."

"Now that we all know who we are, I would like to hear the real reason for your coming here." Duke Bavencian rested his elbows on the arms of his chair and steepled his fingers.

Erin stepped to the front and dipped into a low curtsy in a show of respect. "We bring ill tidings from the palace, your grace."

"Do you indeed?" The duke began to look bored. "You should know that I pride myself on my ability to keep up to date with the goings on at court."

Erin bowed her head. "I have no doubt you are well-informed, your grace, but this is information of a particularly delicate nature."

"How irregular." The duke exchanged a glance with his wife. "Do go on."

"I have intercepted correspondence of an incriminating nature between the prince and a friend of his." Erin pulled the papers out of her satchel and unfolded them to show the duke. "He intimates a scheme that could damage the sovereignty of the throne."

The duke laughed. "I seriously doubt that my nephew would act in a way that would put his inheritance in jeopardy."

"Be that as it may," Erin offered the papers to the duke. "I implore you to read these letters and consider the consequences of his plans."

The duke looked at the papers held out to him and then back to Erin. "Oh, very well," he said, gesturing impatiently at the papers. Erin stepped forward to deliver them to the duke with a curtsy. Duke Bavencian took them, sighed, and began to read. His expression grew more thunderous as the silence stretched. He glared at Erin and shook the letters in the air. "He cannot be serious."

"He is," Erin said. "I heard him plotting with another lord, the Lord Brimley mentioned in the first letter."

"That fool," the Duke murmured, exchanging a glance with his wife. "That grasping idiot. He puts the stability of our entire kingdom at risk for the paltry favors of our hostile northern neighbor."

Erin could taste victory. "We hoped you would join us in our effort to protect the kingdom from such folly."

Duke Bavencian considered Erin, tilting his chin up and narrowing his eyes. "Lady Erin. Have you ever wondered why I remain in the country, so far from the culture and diversions of the palace?"

Looking up at his haughty demeanor, Erin worried that she had miscalculated. "No, your grace."

Grim amusement flickered across his features. "There is a crown in my family. It rests very close to my head. It has haunted the edges of my life since I was old enough to understand what it meant to be king. My brother, and now my nephew, are all that stand between myself and the nightmare of the throne. I had hoped they would remain there for the rest of my days." He sighed and rubbed at his brow. "Now you bring me news that leaves me with little choice. I can begin a battle to take up that dreadful power, or I can witness the potential collapse of my beloved homeland, knowing that I could have prevented it. I wish to do neither. Forgive me if I do not welcome you as a friend today."

"Do you mean to say you would rather not ally yourself with us, your grace?" Erin ventured, afraid that they would not gain the duke's assistance after all.

The duke looked tired. "No, I don't mean to say that. I merely mean to say that this is a dificult decision, and I will need some time to think about it."

"Is there anything we can do to make the decision easier?" Erin asked.

"You can leave me to my thoughts," the duke said, and with a wave of his hand, he dismissed them from the room.

12
A Tea and A Treaty

"That didn't go badly," Jax said once they were back in the hall outside the audience room.

"It didn't go well, either," Erin said with a wry smile.

"There's hope yet," Jax insisted, and upon returning to the guest wing, they retired to their guest rooms to wait on the duke's decision.

Around mid-day, while Erin sat in silent vigil with Jax, Hugo, and Liana, a lady's maid in a white linen gown came into their sitting room and curtsied deeply. Jax looked up from where they were going over a map of the Morton estate and asked, "What's this?"

"Her grace requests the company of Lady Erin in the garden," said the maid. "I am here to show you the way, milady."

Erin shared a glance with Jax and rose from her seat. "I would be delighted to join her. Please direct me to her."

Duchess Bavencian sat in a rose garden with a silver and porcelain tea set arrayed on an ornate table with cast-iron rose vines twining up the legs. A cluster of nobles milled about while a small band of musicians played, and a few danced to the music. "Lady Erin," the duchess said. "Please join me for tea."

Erin sat across from the duchess and accepted a teacup full of a flower-scented white tea that a lady's maid poured for her before retiring behind a screen delicately painted with roses in bloom.

"You're an odd creature, to travel with Lord Hugo virtually unchaperoned over such a distance," the duchess said. "I confess I am curious to learn more about you." The duchess flipped open her fan and lightly fluttered it in the air. "I fancy myself something of a matchmaker, you see. Why do you concern yourself with matters of state, when your personal situation is so dire? I would think you'd spend all your energy on finding a new husband, and you have quite the eligible bachelor traveling with you."

"I attempted a marriage, once. It did not take."

"Yes, we heard news of your misfortune, both at what would have been your wedding and at the capital."

"Then you know something of why I might hesitate."

"I do." The duchess raised her cup of tea to Erin. "To the fallen."

"The fallen." They drank together with a solemnity that clashed with the airy music playing in the background.

The duchess set down her drink with a satisfied sigh. "Still. There's no earthly reason why you should let that impede your search for a new husband."

"There is no such search."

"No?" The duchess nodded at the men and women dancing nearby. "Love may strike at any moment, Lady Erin."

"Love has run its course with me." Erin felt curiously out of breath as she recalled her fiance's smile and gentle strength. "There's no room in my heart for more."

"Love can be cruel. I know that aspect well." The duchess nodded her head slowly, and fatigue stole across her face, making the lines around her mouth and eyes seem careworn instead of cheerful. "Love can also be inevitable. When you care about someone, you act the fool because you must, not because it's in your best interest. Love leaves little room for self-preservation." She clapped her hands and became the merry lady of the house again. "But that is no reason not to enjoy yourself! Husband hunting is most diverting."

Erin frowned at the thought of courtship with a stranger, of all the uncertainties and small awkwardnesses that might occur. A small voice in the back of her mind offered that things weren't going so badly with Hugo, but she ignored it. She didn't want to encourage the duchess' matchmaking. "I have no interest in the endeavor."

"You're a woman, Lady Erin. Your interests don't matter to society at large." The duchess seemed amused by Erin's stubborn refusal. "The nature of your womanhood won't go away merely because you wish it gone. You were born with the ability to bear children and raised under the expectation that you would one day run a household. Should you rebel against the role society has placed upon you, you risk your security and your happiness. You will always be in danger, and you will always pay a price for independence."

The undeniable truth of the duchess' words weighed Erin down into deep exhaustion. She bowed her head and thought of Ardent Morton. The threat of a future as his captive wife followed her like a pack of hounds baying for the kill, as if she was a fugitive with a bounty for her hand in marriage. "I would pay a far steeper price for obedience." Her voice cracked with rage.

"I see." The duchess sank back and refilled her teacup. "I will still offer you my help, should you one day change your mind. You must use all the resources at your disposal to strike the best bargain for your future that you can, my dear." She began to pick at the foods laid out around her. "If you need help negotiating the price you pay, I would be glad to help you. I'm well versed in balancing my household's budget, and it's important to keep a careful eye on the accounting. You don't want to come away after a great deal of effort and expense only to find yourself worse off than you were before."

Erin smiled. "I'll keep that in mind."

"See that you do." The song ended, and they watched the dancers part with bows and curtsies, to be replaced with new couples, who leaped and twirled into a faster dance. Erin picked out Hugo prowling through the crowd at the far end of the garden, mingling in search of allies and information. The duchess lightly tapped at Erin's elbow with her fan to catch Erin's attention. "Do you have much planned for tomorrow?" the duchess inquired while her eyes tracked the dancers.

Erin examined the duchess' gently smiling face for hints at the reason behind the question, but the cheery expression was like a blank wall. "Not yet."

"I like to take my breakfast in my personal gardens from time to time. Do join me, should you find yourself in need of a friendly ear."

"I would be happy to."

The duchess nodded as if something important had been settled and rose from her chair. "Please excuse me, Lady Erin." She accepted the hand of a well-dressed nobleman. "I believe I shall dance while the music is good. You should consider doing the same." And with that, the duchess joined the nobles' intricate, delicate dance to the lively, light tune the musicians played. Erin remained in her chair and watched the revelers for a time, thoughts resting on Hugo and his refusal to dance with her the night before. She had wanted to dance, then, and she had thought he might want the same. She couldn't tell what part of his courtly behavior toward her was because he felt obligated to treat her well due to the life debt he believed he owed, and what part of his behavior was because he genuinely liked her. She took a red rose from the bouquet on the table and twirled it in her hand, carefully avoiding the spiny thorns along the stem. He had given her roses. She smiled slightly. Roses were not something a man would use to repay a life debt. Of that, at least, she was certain. However, she was also certain that she was still mourning Marc. How could she open the door to this opportunity when her life was in such disarray? How could she move on so quickly from a man she had known all her life?

Erin got to her feet and began to walk the garden, smelling her rose thoughtfully from time to time until she came upon a small chapel set a little way back from the main path. She walked up to the door, and, finding it open, stepped into a room lit up in jewel tones from the sunlight filtering through brightly colored stained glass windows. Erin walked into the long, narrow main part of the chapel and was surprised to find Duke Bavencian standing in the aisle between the rows of pews and staring up at the royal blue ceiling dotted with stars painted in gold leaf that shone in the filtered sunlight. Without turning to look at Erin, he began to speak, and his voice echoed against the stone walls. "Are you religious, Lady Erin?"

"Sometimes." Erin thought of her feeling of serendipity, before her wedding, and the devastating feeling of loss afterward, how nothing had eased her sorrow. Then she remembered her gratitude at discovering that she wasn't alone after all, once she had met up again with Liana and Jax. "My faith comes and goes."

The duke turned to look her over, as if he hadn't truly noticed her until just then. "Faith can do that, can't it." He ran a gloved hand over the back of an elaborately carved wooden pew. "I don't hold much faith in all…this." He waved a hand at the splendor around him. "In my travels, I have mostly seen it as another tool used to control the proletariat. Occasionally, however." He walked over to a stained glass window and opened one of the panes to look out on his gardens. "Occasionally, I feel the urge to come here, just in case it might make a difference. You can never be too careful, when dealing with fate." He cast a glance back at her. "You're sure of your information on the prince?"

"I have shown you the letters and told you what I overheard."

"Yes. You have." The duke smiled wryly. "I suppose that's all the certainty one can get, in life."

"Does this mean you'll help us?"

The duke sighed and shut the window, dusting off his hands. "I suppose. Provided you don't make it too inconvenient for me."

"Thank you."

"Don't thank me yet. This could end with us in our graves," the duke said. "Call upon me when you have need of my aid, and I will help you. As for me, I must see if I can talk my nephew round to some sense."

Just then, a messenger burst into the chapel, panting for breath. "Your grace, bandits are attacking the village!"

"What?!" The duke straightened to his full height. "How dare they attack my people! This insult is not to be borne. Ready my horse and notify the guard. We ride to the village as soon as possible."

"Yes, your grace." The messenger bowed and ran off while the duke turned to Erin.

"This is most unusual, to have such an attack so far into the center of the kingdom," the duke said. "It seems I'll be helping you sooner than expected, now that my nephew's scheming has brought trouble to my door."

"We'll support you in the defense of your people, for no person should have to face this fight alone," said Erin.

"Thank you, Lady Erin," said the duke. He turned toward the door. "Let us depart to make our preparations." Erin and the duke parted ways once they had left the chapel, and Erin rushed through the sunlit garden, catching Hugo's eye, and made it to the guest quarters to find Jax and Liana in the sitting room going over plans to infiltrate the Mortons' estate. Hugo entered behind her.

"Hurry," Erin said, "Bandits have attacked Duke Bavencian's people in the nearby village. We must prepare for battle and help him."

"Indeed we must," said Jax. "The prince's allies grow bold."

The four of them went to their rooms to get their weapons. Erin got her blades to arm herself and changed out of her dress into her travel tunic and trousers to allow for better movement. When she was done, she went to get her horse and join the guards arrayed before Duke Bavencian in the courtyard.

"We ride!" the duke said, and the group of them rode toward the village, where they could hear screaming and the clash of metal against metal. As the duke's army of guards crested the hill that lay between the duke's castle and the village, Erin could see the bandits look up in fear and anger. They wore unmarked clothing and fought with weapons in good repair with an unusual skill that the villagers couldn't match. As Duke Bavencian's guards engaged in battle, Erin saw the bandits begin to retreat.

"Capture them alive," the duke roared as he swiped with his sword at attackers to the left and right. "We need them for questioning!"

The battle was soon over, and the duke stood in the rubble and debris from the fight as the bandits ran from the guardsmen. The guardsmen gave chase, and one caught up with a bandit, holding onto him by the back of his shirt and yelling "Who do you work for? Tell me!" The bandit broke away from the guardsman's grasp without answering, and that was the closest the guards came to capturing a prisoner.

The duke sheathed his sword with a sigh, wiped the sweat from his brow, and turned to Erin at his side. "Strange, isn't it, that they were so quick to run? It's as if they feared discovery."

"Yes, very strange," said Erin.

"If I find that my nephew gave his blessing for this attack, I will be very displeased." The duke watched over his guardsmen, who were helping the villagers get back to their feet and straightening out the damaged market stalls that lined the street.

Hugo walked up to the two of them, looking furious, and Jax and

Liana followed close behind. "How dare they run from a fight they started," said Hugo. "How dishonorable, to abandon battle like that."

Jax shrugged. "Sometimes, it's better to run and live to fight another day."

"Still, I find it suspicious that they abandoned their looting so easily," said the duke. He nodded to Erin. "I'll have to start preparing my army after all, if only to protect my home and people. You were right to bring my nephew's treacherous actions to my attention. I'll help you as much as I can."

"Thank you, your grace, for your friendship," Erin said, and she felt an easing of the tension in her chest from finding that she had a friend in Duke Bavencian. The future seemed brighter and safer standing there with friends old and new.

"We must form plans, but not here," said the duke. "We'll discuss this further tomorrow, at my home. There's no telling who may be listening."

13
Morton Manor

ERIN HAD SLEPT little, and she was the first down to breakfast the next day, followed soon after by Jax. He stopped in the doorway upon seeing her and tilted his head slightly.

"You're up early," he said.

"So are you," she pointed out.

"Fair enough," Jax said. He walked into the room and served himself from the buffet style breakfast spread, then sat at the long dining table across from Erin. "What occupies your thoughts so much that there's no room for rest? You know we have a great deal to decide today. Decisions go better with a well-rested mind."

Erin broke apart a roll of bread into smaller and smaller pieces with a nervous energy that wouldn't let her fingers rest. "I worry about my parents."

"Ah." Jax nodded. "You're right to worry. Ardent Morton clearly intends to use them as leverage to pressure you into marrying him."

"I also worry that he'll do the same with Lord and Lady Clairmaud."

"Your worry is valid," said Jax.

"We have to do something," Erin said. Jax hummed his agreement and buttered his scone. "I think we should free them before we go any further in our plans to stop Prince Thomas, so that they can't be used as leverage against us."

"I think you're right." Jax bit into his scone.

"Good." Erin poked at her boiled egg with a fork. "I thought you might disagree."

"Your concerns are well-founded, and I confess the idea of Lord and Lady Hart imprisoned weighs upon my mind. We should plan a jail break."

"Yes, we should." Erin nodded and began to eat with a newfound appetite and purpose.

Just then, Hugo came into the room to join them and piled food onto his plate. "All this travel has made me very hungry," he said and began to eat. Shortly thereafter, Liana also made her appearance, yawning and sleepy-eyed still.

"What are all of you doing, awake so early?" Duke Bavencian swept into the room a few steps behind Liana, soon followed by Duchess Bavencian. "And what have I missed? I had hoped to be here before all of you, the better for me to avoid missing anything."

"We mean to ride to Morton Manor to free Lord and Lady Hart and Clairmaud," said Jax.

"A jailbreak!" The duke rubbed his hands together. "How diverting."

"I'd like to travel with you, with your permission, Lady Erin," said Hugo. "These happenings concern me greatly, and I hope we might prevent further bloodshed by acting to weaken the strategic position of the Mortons and Prince Thomas. A jailbreak may be just the thing to take the wind out of their sails."

"Excellent idea," said the duke. "Meanwhile, I'll attempt to track my nephew down and see if I can talk some sense into him."

"Then our paths align," said Jax, "for my information network tells me that the prince has gone on a hunt in the wilds that border the western edge of the Morton estate and might be staying with them."

"We should travel together," said Liana, "to pool our resources and better guard ourselves against attack from any bands of brigands we may encounter."

"I'll bring some of my guard with me. That should scare them off." The duke turned to his wife. "My dear, do you mind me leaving you to run the estate alone for some time?"

"Not at all," said Duchess Bavencian. "We'll manage, though I will of course miss you, my love."

"It would serve as a useful distraction if you make a procession out of your trip," said Erin. "It would take attention away from our efforts to free the Mortons' prisoners."

"All this talk of cloak and dagger activities is exciting, I must say." The duke smiled. "But why stop there? Why don't you disguise yourselves as members of my retinue and sneak off to free the prisoners while I meet with my nephew?"

"A good idea," said Jax.

"It's settled, then," said the duke, and he sent a servant off to get him paper and a quill, which he used to write two letters, one to the prince and one to the Mortons to announce his intentions to visit. "I'll tell them I'm looking for a diversion," said the duke, and he signed his name with a flourish before sending off a messenger to ride to the Mortons ahead of them.

Erin, Hugo, Jax, and Liana donned servants' garb and blended as well as they could with the retinue that the duke assembled to travel with him. It was a more comfortable ride to travel with the duke, who stopped often for breaks and meals. The duke's guard consisted of seasoned men who could be identified by their battle-ready stance, yet they were merry in their own way, quick to joke or share a tale to pass the time.

The land between the Bavencian and Morton estates was green and fertile, with plots of farmland stretching out to the horizon on either side of the road. Cows, sheep, and horses grazed in their pastures, and wildflowers dotted the side of the road. The surroundings were so peaceful and beautiful, with bees bobbing among the wildflowers and the faint buzz of insects interrupted only by the sound of a gentle breeze, that it was easy to forget the seriousness of their mission and their destination at the end of the road.

On their second day of travel, as they stopped for lunch, Erin sat on a log across from Hugo and marveled that he was still with them. "Why do you still travel with us?" she asked. "Don't you have responsibilities to think of at home?"

"I bear a far greater responsibility to keep my home and my people safe, and if the prince persists in his dangerous dealings withe Varnall, he might bring ruin upon us all. He must be stopped," Hugo said.

"You speak as if you feel strongly on this," said Erin.

"That's because I do feel that way," said Hugo. "My father died in battle with Varnall during the war these many years past."

"That was a long time ago, and we're at peace now," said Erin.

"If you can call their constant raiding peace."

"Be that as it may, all the proof of the prince's dealings that you have to go on is a letter shown to you by me, a person you just met. Why do you believe me?"

"I have battled against Varnallan brigands a long time and am intimately familiar with their avarice and thirst for destruction. Furthermore, you may have saved my life, and such a deed is not one I shall soon forget."

Erin's stomach sank. "Oh," she said, "I've told you before, you don't owe me for my aid."

"I will stand by your side regardless," said Hugo.

"I see. You're a good man to do so," said Erin, and she went back to her travel bread, her spirits dampened. She wanted more from Hugo. She wanted, she realized, a declaration that his interest in her was what kept him there. She shook her head at herself and finished her meal, feeling foolish and off balance.

As they traveled, Hugo collected flowers and once more gifted her with a bouquet of daisies, dandelions, and white clover. Erin accepted the gift, with Jax snorting disdainfully, but the bouquet only made her more confused. She wanted to tell Hugo that he didn't owe her his heart in payment for her help. Part of her wanted the flowers to be just flowers, given for fun, with no deep meaning behind them, and part of her wanted them to be gifts of intent. She wanted to be enough of a reason for flowers all by herself, and she didn't know how to tell Hugo that. She didn't know if that was what she should want, so soon after Marc's death, so soon after what the prince had done. She didn't know if she should tell Hugo to only give her flowers if he really meant them, or if saying as much might push him to grander gestures to please her. Instead, she accepted the gift with a smile and focused on the path ahead.

Soon enough, the Morton estate loomed large and grim on the horizon with its gray stone walls and long, narrow windows. Flags hoisted up from the highest point of the roof signified the presence of Prince Thomas and Lord Morton. By the time Duke Bavencian's party rode up to the front door, a butler with a neat as a pin suit, tidy mustache, and close cropped hair had appeared out of the depths of the manor to greet them. "Good day, your grace," he said, and he bowed deeply before holding open the door for them. "We have prepared rooms for you in the east wing. Please follow me."

The foyer had a large, winding staircase that led up to the second floor and split to come down on either side of the room, and they passed between the two flights of stairs to go into a long, dimly lit hall with dark, paneled walls. Portraits of Morton ancestors painted in earth tones with severe expressions lined the walls, and flickering sconces cast long, moving shadows along the walls and ornately patterned red and brown carpet. The butler left them to their rooms with a pair of servants waiting upon the duke out in the hall, and when all their travel bags had been set down and the duke had changed from his leathers into formal clothing of luxurious velvet and lace, the servants guided the party into the parlor, where Prince Thomas, Lord Repent and Lady Purity, and Ardent and his sister Prudence sat and played cards. Erin lingered at the back of the group, worried that Ardent or Prince Thomas might recognize her, but their eyes skated over her to focus on the duke.

"Lord and Lady Morton," the butler said, "may I present Duke Bavencian and his retainers."

"Good day, your grace," Lord Morton said. "Be welcome in our home."

"Hello, Uncle," said Prince Thomas. "We shall make a merry hunting party tomorrow."

Duke Bavencian gave a shallow bow and swept his arm out to include his small group of servants. "I have brought help with me, as you see, to ease the burden my visit may lay upon you and to smooth the way for us at the hunt." He turned to the group of servants that included Erin, Jax, Liana, and Hugo. "Leave us now, and see what assistance you can offer the servants of the manor."

The butler bowed. "Thank you, your grace, for your thoughtfulness.

I will see to it that they have tasks to complete." He turned to the group of servants. "Follow me."

The group followed the butler down the stairs to the servants' quarters and arrayed themselves before him to await their orders. "We have a lot to do with your master and the prince visiting at the same time, so don't shirk your duties," the butler said. He then divided them up into two groups. "You'll help with serving," he told one group, "and you'll help with cleaning," he told the group that included the four of them. They followed the butler to the dishwashing area. "Handle the dishes with care, they're from Lady Morton's finest set," he said before leaving them to their own devices, as there were no dishes to clean yet besides the kitchenware used to prepare the food, which was already set out to dry.

"Go," whispered one of the servants to Erin, "quickly, before others come who might keep track of our number."

Erin nodded to Jax, Liana, and Hugo, and one by one they peeled off from the group into the general chaos of the kitchen staff putting together a meal. They met up in the dimly lit hall outside the kitchen.

"Quickly now," said Jax once they were all together. "The dungeons should be on this level, if my information is correct." They walked quietly down the hall, opening door after door in search of the prison cells. Each door opened to storage rooms and pantries until they reached a cast iron door at the shadowy end of the hall. It was locked when they tested it, so Jax took a few pins out of his pocket and swiftly picked the lock.

Footsteps sounded behind them, and they hastily opened the door and hid behind it. Erin peered out through the small grate that served as a peephole to see two servants walk into the back hall to get food from one of the pantries.

"That was close," Liana whispered.

"Shh," Jax shushed her, and they stepped back from the door. "We must move quietly and with all possible speed, for every moment we're apart from the group is another moment when our absence might be noted." He led them down the darkened hall. Sparse torches barely lit the area with flickering light, and Hugo picked one up out of its holder and held it aloft to make it easier for them to see the way ahead. This hall was dimmer than the last and had a bare appearance, with no doors leading into storage rooms or paintings decorating the empty walls. There was a slight dampness to the air, and a far-off dripping sound was the only noise to be heard besides the sound of their footsteps. At the end of the hall was another locked door, this one made out of bars of iron. Jax took longer picking the large, intricate lock, and the door opened with a squeal of the hinges. They walked into a cool, dark room, to find Ardent Morton, Hayward, and an armed group of soldiers.

"A-ha!" Ardent pointed at them. "I knew I recognized you!" He waved to the soldiers. "Capture them!" The four of them struggled against the soldiers who grabbed at their arms and closed cuffs around their wrists.

"Keep the lady here, and take the rest away," said Hayward.

"No!" Erin shouted, but she couldn't stop the soldiers from wresting her friends away from her.

"Erin?" Came a voice out of the depths of the dungeon. "Is that you?" The dirt-streaked face of her father appeared out of the darkness of one of the cells. "It is you! Erin!"

"Erin?" Came another voice, and Erin's mother appeared in the opposite cell.

"Mom! Dad!" Erin renewed her struggle against the soldiers who held her.

"Don't let her get away!" shouted Ardent. "She owes me an answer to my proposal, and I will have it now."

"I'll marry you," Erin shouted, "just let them go!"

"No!" Hugo yelled and swung out at his captors.

Ardent turned to Erin and held her by the chin with a thumb and forefinger. "Ah, good, you've decided, then." He looked sideways at Hugo, then turned to Hayward. "Lock them up to make doubly sure Lady Erin will keep her word by reminding her of what she stands to lose if she doesn't."

"Don't let him use us against you," Jax shouted just before he, Liana, and Hugo were dragged out of sight.

"We must bring her to Prince Thomas and Lord Morton," Hayward said. At Hayward's order, the soldiers dragged her away from the dungeons, through the dank hallway back to the servants' quarters and up the stairs to the dining room where the prince, the duke, and the Mortons sat at a long table made of deep brown, well-polished wood.

"What's this?" Lord Morton asked from his seat at the head of the table. He looked to Ardent. "Why are you late to our meal, boy, and why have you brought such an unsightly guest with you?"

"This unsightly guest is to be my wife, father," said Ardent, "for she is Lady Erin of Norcliff."

"Sit down, boy," said Lord Morton, and Ardent seated himself. "Now, what is the meaning of this?"

"Father, we found her and a group of her friends attempting to free our prisoners from the dungeon. They came with Duke Bavencian as part of his retinue of servants."

"Uncle?" Prince Thomas gave Duke Bavencian a narrow-eyed look. "Did you know of this?"

"Certainly not." The Duke straightened in his seat. "I'm as surprised by this as the rest of you."

"I find that difficult to believe," said the prince. "Throw him in prison, too," he told Hayward, "for we can't risk our activities becoming known to the world at large, and my uncle is quite the raconteur. I'm sure you would spread news of our work far and wide, given half a chance."

"Imprison a duke?" Lord Morton looked scandalized. "That's taking it a bit far, isn't it?"

"Do you want the duke's army at our doorstep?" asked Prince Thomas.

"That's what will happen, if we imprison him," said Lord Morton.

"But we shall have him as a hostage," said Prince Thomas. "Which we wouldn't, if we set him free and then had to deal with him returning at the head of his army. I can't let him foil my plans. My treaty with Varnall is at a delicate stage at the moment." The prince turned to Hayward. "Imprison him."

"Now, wait just a minute," said the duke, "Your father would disapprove of you speaking with the north -"

"My father is content with his past glory. He won't budge, even when there is an opportunity to be grasped."

"The cost -"

"Is one I'm willing to pay."

"You may, but have you asked the people most likely to be affected by your grand plan? The ones who will pay that price for you? You shouldn't ally yourself or our nation with such unsavory companions, who act in such terrible ways to our people. You bring unnecessary strife to our lands."

"The people will see that I'm in the right. More importantly, my father will see I'm in the right, and he'll respect me as an equal. I'll inherit the kingdom then, and I'll have earned my place -"

"You can't earn leadership by acting in such a nefarious way! Don't ally yourself with those who wish our people harm, who steal and commit acts of violence against us. You must stop. You must not sacrifice our people to your need for success."

"They're a price I am willing, nay, must pay, as a leader of men." The prince waved a hand imperiously. "You'll see. You'll all see. I'll show you. I've gone too far to change course now."

"There is always hope. There is always a chance to change."

"No. I must see this through. I'm so close to glory, I must go the rest of the way. You'll be grateful for it, in time."

"Then you're lost to me. Your goals come at a cost I'm not willing to pay. Furthermore, the citizenry may surprise you with their unwillingness to pay the price you've set for them. Stop this, Nephew. Stop now, before it's too late."

"No! I will not stop - I will not wait for my time to be great any longer. This is my time to get what I want. This is my time to shine bright as a leader, to bring power, glory, and riches to my family's name, and if you aren't with me, then I don't need you here."

Erin listened to the prince with increasing horror. There was a hole in him where things like acceptance and peace should be, and he had filled it with greed, lust, and power. She almost felt sorry for him. Almost.

"Nephew -" the duke began.

"You'll thank me for this, in time."

No, Nephew -"

"You're dismissed."

"Don't do this -"

"Guards! See this man to the dungeon."

Hayward looked to Lord Morton, who sighed and gave a slight nod. Hayward bowed. "Yes, your highness," he said to the prince. "Take him away," he ordered the guards who weren't restraining Erin, and they grabbed hold of Duke Bavencian.

"I say! Unhand me," cried the duke, but the guards didn't let go and began to march the duke out of the dining room. "You'll live to regret this!" He yelled to the prince, who smirked at the duke as he passed.

"I'll certainly outlive you, at the very least," the prince sneered.

With the duke gone, Erin had no more allies in the room, and it was with some fear that she watched Prince Thomas turn his attention to her.

"Lady Erin," Prince Thomas said, "I believe you have an engagement to keep." He motioned to Ardent Morton, who stood up and gave Erin a proper bow.

"I'm glad to see you in good health, my lady," said Ardent, "and I'll endeavor to keep you in such."

"I would be in better health," Erin said through clenched teeth, "if you would free me and my friends and family."

"All in due time," said Ardent, "all in due time."

"Really, Ardent," said Lord Morton. "I fail to understand what you see in the girl, especially now that she's interrupted our meal in such a bothersome fashion." He looked Erin up and down in her travel-stained clothes and frowned. "She's certainly not much to look at." He waved a hand. "But her lands are worth the effort it will take to polish her. Take her away, and keep her away until she is fit to be seen."

"Yes, my lord," said Hayward, and he began to lead Erin away from the dinner, to her despair.

14

An Undesirable Engagement

"Come along now, mistress," Hayward said to Erin, who struggled against her captors as they frogmarched her out of the dining room and to a guest room where a young maid awaited her. The soldiers released her into the room, and Erin turned her face away as Hayward stepped closer. "Things would go better," he said, "if you cooperated." He stepped in front of her. "I worked hard to arrange this match for you, my lady, and it's much more suitable than your engagement to that Clairmaud boy. The Mortons know what's what, and they live in the proper way, unlike your parents or your departed fiancé's family. I would think you'd be grateful for the opportunity to better your situation."

Erin crossed her arms and glared at the wall. "I have nothing to say to you, Hayward."

"We shall see about that, my lady," said Hayward. "In time, I believe you'll learn to value my help."

Erin listened to the receding sound of Hayward's footsteps as he walked away and waited until she heard him close the door with a soft thunk before she turned to the maid. "I don't want to be made beautiful," she said.

The maid cast her eyes to the floor and curtsied. "Begging your ladyship's pardon, but it's an honor to look your best for Lord Ardent. You're lucky to have captured his attention. And," the maid added, hands trembling, "Lord Morton will be angry with me, should I fail in my duty to prepare you to be seen."

Erin sighed. "Very well," she said, "Do what you must." She watched in the mirror as the maid brushed and braided her hair into an intricate bun held up by pins adorned with rubies. The maid then helped her into a black silk dress with red accents, in the Morton colors. The maid stepped back, work done, and curtsied before leaving Erin alone with her reflection, which looked like that of a stranger, pale and bleak like she was attending a funeral. The rubies clashed with her hair, and she scowled at them.

A knock sounded at her door. Erin turned to face it and said, "Enter," expecting Hayward, but the door swung open to reveal Ardent on the other side.

"I'm here to escort you downstairs," Ardent said. Erin took the measure of him for a moment in an effort to understand why he wanted to marry her so badly. His narrow face, sharp chin, and high cheekbones, along with his short, straight black hair and dark brown eyes, gave him an austere, serious look.

"I'm not good company at present," said Erin.

"That may be. However, my parents and the prince await your presence, and they'll be less disposed toward benevolence the longer you make them wait." He offered his arm, and Erin rested her hand gingerly in the crook of his elbow. They walked down the hall and stairs, and it was like when she would walk with her mother or father to greet a guest except that the details were all wrong, the hall narrower, her mood lower, and the company more grim.

"Why have you not imprisoned me?" she asked.

Ardent looked surprised. "You are to be my wife. That's hardly the way to begin a lifelong relationship."

"Neither is holding my family and friends hostage."

Ardent cocked his head slightly to one side. "But it is preferable to a more final, violent end, is it not?"

"Oh, all right," she said with ill grace and privately thought that at least this way she had more of a chance to break herself and her friends free. "You have a point."

"I rather thought I did," said Ardent. "It's my duty as your future husband to see to your comfort, and I thought you might feel more comfortable like this."

"I would feel more comfortable if you weren't threatening my friends and family," she said.

"Perhaps," said Ardent, "but then you might not be here at all, and you would likely not have agreed to take my hand in marriage."

"You are correct, I would not," said Erin angrily.

Ardent's face was blank and his eyes seemed empty and dark in the shadowy corridor. "Yes, I thought that might be the case. But do not fear, I shall honor you as my wife, and Prince Thomas has a plan that will address the incessant looting along our northern border. His plan will make our future much safer and more prosperous."

"His plan will put us all at risk," said Erin.

"That's where we differ in opinion." Ardent's mouth turned up at the corners into a slight smile. "We're having our first fight as a couple. I am told that it's healthy to argue a little with your spouse. It means we are honest with each other."

"And what better way to ensure my honesty than to hold the safety of my loved ones over my head," said Erin.

"It may not be the best way, but it does seem to be working, as you have agreed to marry me and seem to be speaking very honestly with me." They reached a door made of dark wood, and Ardent stopped them before going in to turn to Erin with a serious expression made more grave by the severity of his features. "You may speak freely with me when we are alone, but take care in this company. My parents and the prince will not suffer your impudence as I do." Then he opened the door, and they walked into the drawing room.

Erin felt painfully alone as Prince Thomas and Lord and Lady Morton turned to look at her and Ardent standing in the doorway. She did not want to be around any of them, especially not the prince, who smirked at her from where he stood holding a glass of red wine. Lord and Lady Morton were more austere looking than their son, and Prudence sat straight-backed and proud in a black and red gown much like Erin's. The room was dimly lit and paneled with dark brown wood, and there was deep red upholstery on the heavy looking furniture.

"I have brought Lady Erin, with an improved appearance," said Ardent.

Lord Morton looked Erin up and down and sniffed. "She looks suitable enough."

Lady Morton nodded to Erin's red and black gown. "Her colors are better now." Erin stood straight backed and stoic, though she yearned to leave the room and the judgmental stares aimed at her.

"She looks almost unchanged to me," said Prudence. "Ardent, why must she wear the same colors as me? That makes me look unimaginative. Besides, I have more of a right to the colors than she does."

"I was not the one who chose the gown, sister," said Ardent, "and besides, as future sisters, doesn't it suit you to be of the same mind when it comes to fashion?"

"All I know is our family colors suit me better than they could ever suit her," said Prudence.

"That was never in doubt, dear," said Lady Morton. "Don't you agree, your highness?"

Prince Thomas chuckled. "Women's fashions interest me little, but yes." He looked down his nose at Erin. "You wear the colors better, Prudence."

Lady Morton sat back in her chair, looking satisfied. "There, you see, dear?"

Prudence arranged her skirts around her to the best effect. "I suppose I'm satisfied." She bowed her head to Prince Thomas. "Thank you, your highness."

Ardent led Erin to the armchair opposite his mother and sister and said, "Please take your ease, my lady, and get to know my family."

"That's not necessary, brother, as we all know she's not marrying you for your family," said Prudence.

"Even so," said Ardent, and he helped Erin to a chair, where she reluctantly sat.

"Greetings, Lady Erin," said Lady Morton, and apparently done with introducing the ladies of his family to Erin, Ardent joined his father and the prince on the other side of the room.

"Lady Morton, Lady Prudence," Erin said. Finished with the formalities, she strained to hear what the prince was saying.

She could make out a faint, "We'll start seeing more raids as they collect their price, and you can expect some disorder at the northern border, as is to be expected of a large army on the move," and then Prudence interrupted Erin's listening.

"My brother puts his whole heart into any venture he sets out to do, but I'm not so sure you're worthy of him or our family," Prudence said.

"Is that so," Erin said, and she tried to hear more of what the prince was saying.

The prince continued with, "And that's the price we must pay for consolidation of power. It will all be worth it when we command two armies and have twice the amount of land and resources. Lunland will bow at our feet. With more power and a firm alliance, we can stop the Varnallans from harassing our border, as you so desire. I have it all planned out."

"Do you have any hobbies, Lady Erin?" Lady Morton asked.

"A few," said Erin, still trying to hear what was being said across the room.

"I enjoy embroidery, myself," said Lady Morton. "A well-embroidered message of perseverance is among my chief objectives when I sit down with a needle and thread. I find the old sayings inspire temperance and fortitude in those who read them, even just in passing."

"Have you studied the old Morton sayings?" Prudence asked. "I've read and ruminated on them all."

"I confess I'm not as well-acquainted with them as I perhaps ought to be," said Erin.

"We shall continue to point the Varnallan brigands in the directions you give us, though the price of their destruction is rising, and I find it increasingly difficult to countenance the cost of our alliance," Erin caught Lord Morton saying.

"Peace, friend," she heard the prince say. "You'll be well-rewarded for your loyalty."

"That is a gap in your knowledge we can work to close," said Lady Morton.

"Hm? Ah, yes, indeed," Erin said.

"She doesn't converse very well, does she," Prudence said to her mother.

"We'll have to work on that, too," said Lady Morton.

"I may not converse prettily, but you will find that I hear and think well enough," Erin said, feeling stung.

"That remains to be seen," said Prudence.

"Prudence! Mind your tongue," said Lady Morton. "It's impolite to point out such faults, no matter how true they may be."

Erin clenched her teeth together and forced a smile. She needed to stay in the room to hear what she could of the prince's plans, no matter how much she wanted to leave.

"How are you ladies faring?" Prince Thomas abandoned his conversation to join them, to Erin's frustration. He was not likely to continue talking about his plans right in front of her.

"We are becoming fast friends, as future sisters should," said Prudence.

"You will find, your highness, that my daughter is capable of befriending all manner of folk, no matter how undesirable," said Lady Morton. "It's one of her many virtues."

"A rare and valuable trait for a woman to have," said Prince Thomas. He smiled at Prudence, who demurely cast down her eyes.

"Thank you, your highness," said Prudence.

"You set an example many a young lady ought to follow." The prince cast a glance at Erin. "No matter how stubbornly they may resist."

Erin felt sick to her stomach and shifted her weight in her chair. The prince grinned menacingly, and a chill crept up Erin's spine.

"What were you discussing so secretively over there?" Prudence asked.

"Oh, formalities and business matters," Prince Thomas said airily. "Nothing worth boring a young lady over."

Ardent walked over to stand by Erin. "We were discussing our treaty with the north -"

"Silence, boy," said Lord Morton. "You may have fallen to the questionable charms of the Hart girl, but the rest of us can still see reason and know to keep private business private."

"Yes, father," said Ardent, and he went to sit across from Erin, who felt awkward and uncomfortably like an interloper, though she wanted to stay to hear more. There was nothing more to hear, however, as Lady Morton turned the conversation to pleasantries and flirtations. She continued to point out her daughter's good qualities to the prince, and soon they began a game of cards. Erin could not bear to play cards with the captors of her family and friends, so she rose from her chair.

"Please excuse me," she said to Ardent, who half-rose out of his chair to follow her. "No, please don't let me take you away from your game. It's only that I am tired and wish to retire to my room for the night."

"Very well," said Ardent, and he motioned Hayward forward from his post by the door. "Hayward, please escort Lady Erin to her room."

"Yes, my lord." Hayward ushered Erin out of the drawing room and into the hall. "You see, my lady," Hayward said as they walked down the hall. "Lord Ardent is a good match for you. He has been quite solicitous tonight, has he not?"

"He would be truly solicitous if he didn't hold the safety of all the people I know and love over my head the way he does."

"They will only be imprisoned until your wedding and will be freed once the transfer of your titles and lands to the Mortons is complete."

"Oh, because that makes all of this okay," Erin said angrily as they reached her room. "Just leave me be, Hayward."

Hayward held her door open for her to pass through, and he bowed gracefully. "Yes, my lady," he said and closed the door. Erin could hear the click of the lock sliding into place, and she paced furiously into the depths of her room. She caught sight of her reflection in the mirror and snarled silently before pulling a ruby encrusted pin from her hair. She stopped just before throwing it onto the small table in front of the mirror and tapped her finger against the pin in thought before baring her teeth in a vicious grin. She walked back over to the door leading into the hall and settled down in a nearby chair to count the steps of the guards who walked the hall, pin clutched tightly in her hand.

15

Twice Imprisoned

LATER THAT NIGHT, as the shadows cast by the candles that lit her room flickered along the walls, Erin picked the lock on her door slowly and quietly with the pin from her hair, pausing each time a guard walked past the door. Finally, after much effort, the lock snicked open, and Erin waited with bated breath for the passing guard to reach the end of the hall and turn the corner. Then, she opened the door, just a crack first to peek through and make sure the hall was clear, before fully opening it. Stepping out of her shoes to walk barefoot in silence, she picked up one of the candles by the brass handle of its holder and snuck out into the cold and forbidding hall. Sticking to the shadows, she slipped down the hall and crept down the stairs to the basement, where she ran into a guard who looked as surprised to see her as she felt. She quickly leapt into action as he fumbled for his sword, hit him over the head with her candlestick, and struck him unconscious.

Taking his keys from where they hung on a hook in the wall, Erin unlocked the main door into the dungeons and walked straight into a second guard who gave a startled shout before she managed to strike him unconscious, too. Worried that someone might have heard the guard, she waited in silence but didn't hear anyone approaching.

"Erin? Is that you?" Erin heard someone whisper in the darkness, and she held her candle high to reveal the faces of her friends in the flickering, uncertain light. "Erin!" Hugo grabbed hold of the bars of his cell to get closer to her, and after she unlocked the door to his cell, he piled out to hug her to him. Erin could feel the tension in her shoulders ease at his reassuring touch. She sank into his embrace until Jax coughed from his place in the neighboring cell. They broke apart, Erin blushing and looking away from Hugo to glare at Jax.

"About time you got here," Jax said as she unlocked his door and then Liana's.

"We've been working on an escape plan," Liana said and showed Erin the knife hidden in her sleeve. "I managed to sneak this blade past them. I was going to pick the lock the moment their backs were turned long enough."

"I suppose I wasn't needed to break you out, then, but I'm still glad to see you." Erin hugged Jax and Liana tightly.

Jax was the first to disengage from the hug, and he stepped back to say, "Your parents are here." He motioned to two cells farther into the gloom.

Erin ran to her parents' cells and cried softly, "Mom! Dad!"

"Erin?" Came a voice from a pile of rags in the corner of one of the cells, and Erin's father stood to reveal a face smudged with dirt and surrounded by matted hair.

"Erin, is that you?" Erin's mother came into the light from the shadowy corner of the cell across from Erin's father. She had tangled hair and wore a ragged and stained dress that was once beautiful. She reached out through the bars of her cell to cup Erin's face. "It is you!" Her mother gasped and held her hands to her mouth as Erin unlocked the doors to her parents' cells, and Erin's father wrapped them both into a warm hug. Erin stepped back from the hug with the largest smile she had worn in a long time.

"It's good to see you," said Finley.

"The sight of you makes my heart glad," added Evelyn, and they stood there, leaning upon each other for a long moment while Jax took the keys from Erin's hand and freed Lord and Lady Clairmaud from the neighboring cells.

"Lady Erin," said Lord Clairmaud as he wrapped an arm around his wife's shoulders. "It's good to see you alive and well."

"We weren't sure, you see," said Evelyn. "I was so worried that you had been caught in the fighting and that something had happened to you." Evelyn wiped the tears from her eyes and held Erin closer. "Thank goodness you're here, safe."

"Not safe yet," said Finley. "We've still got to get out of here. And who, pray tell, are you?" he asked Hugo.

"Hugo Castelli, at your service," said Hugo.

"Castelli, eh?" Finley crossed his arms. "I've heard of you before. Didn't you once lead a band of mercenaries?"

"For the right client," said Hugo. "We were selective about whose offer we accepted."

"Hm. No doubt you'll be helpful in a pinch, should we run into trouble on our way out," said Finley.

"And how did you come to be one of our rescuers, Lord Castelli?" Evelyn asked.

"Hugo, please," said Hugo. "Your daughter saved my life."

"Did she?" Finley patted Erin on the back. "Well done of you," he said to her. "I, too, am grateful to find you safe."

"Enough talk," said Jax as he returned to the group. "I can't find Duke Bavencian."

"He's not in one of the cells?" Liana asked.

"No, I checked," said Jax.

Finley looked stunned. "You came here with a duke?"

"Perhaps they're keeping him in one of the rooms upstairs," said Erin.

"We don't have the time to search," said Jax.

"We can't leave without him," said Erin. "He's only here because of us."

"We have to get moving," said Jax. "We can come back for him once we have your parents and the Clairmauds safely out of the grasp of the Mortons and the prince."

"You go," said Erin. "I must stay and find him. It's our fault he's here."

"If you stay, I stay," said Hugo.

"Why's that?" Finley asked, and Erin winced. Finley narrowed his eyes at her. "Erin?"

"We don't have time for this," said Jax. "If we're going, we have to go now." He took a torch from its holder on the wall and led the way back to the dungeon entrance. "Come on! We can plan our rescue of the duke once our own rescue is complete." They began to climb up the stairs in silence until they reached the landing, where Jax motioned to them to be quiet before pointing to a guard with his back to them. He crept forward and quickly knocked the guard unconscious before dragging him out of sight and into a storage closet. They snuck out through the empty dining hall and into the foyer, where they ran into another guard, this one facing them.

"The prisoners have escaped!" The guard shouted before Jax managed to hit him over the head.

"Run!" Jax said, and he held out an arm to steady Evelyn as they broke into an uneven run, Erin's parents and the Clairmauds moving more slowly than the rest. It was a shock to Erin to see how difficult it seemed for her parents to move quickly, and she hung back to run with them, worried they might trip or otherwise hurt themselves. Hugo looked around until he found her and fell into step at her side while Liana led the way.

"Don't wait for us," Erin said to Hugo. "Go as quickly as you can!"

"I won't leave you behind," said Hugo, and he remained by her side. The group reached the front door and ran out into the courtyard, where two more guards awaited them. Jax and Liana quickly dispatched them, and the group rushed down the cobblestone path.

"Stop there!" Erin heard a shout come from the house, and she looked behind her to find Ardent running outside in his breeches with a robe hastily thrown on. Behind him, the prince followed in his evening wear. "Stop, I say!" Ardent shouted, and Lord Morton appeared close behind him and the prince with a fresh contingent of guards. Erin slowed, turned, and raised her fists.

"Go on ahead! I'll take care of this," she shouted to the group.

"No, you go on ahead," said Hugo, who stopped and turned to stand with her.

"Both of you, hurry up and come with us!" Jax said as he continued on with Erin's parents, the Clairmauds, and Liana, who was helping Lady Clairmaud to run.

There was no more time to talk as the contingent of guards reached Erin and Hugo, who fought them as well as they could without weapons, though the guards managed to restrain them as Ardent and the prince caught up with them.

"You have run from us for the last time," said the prince. "We'll marry you off to Ardent first thing tomorrow morning, and all this ridiculous running about will come to an end."

"No!" Hugo shouted, and he redoubled his struggle to free himself, growling angrily.

"Put the mercenary back where he was," said Prince Thomas, and a pair of guards began to drag him back to the dungeon.

Ardent stood a little off to the side, talking to one of the guards. His chest heaved from exertion from his run. He caught Erin's gaze, wrapped his robe around himself and tied it shut, and walked closer to Erin.

"Your friends may run free for now, but there will be no more places for them to hide once we marry and your inheritance becomes mine," said Ardent.

"My parents will never allow it," said Erin, tilting her chin up defiantly.

"Your parents with have no choice," said Ardent. "Not if they want to see you again." He turned to the guards holding her. "Take her to the dungeons this time," he ordered, and the guards marched her back through the manor, with Ardent walking alongside them. When they reached the empty cell across from Hugo's, Ardent turned to the guards. "How did she escape?" he asked.

"Picked the lock," said one guard. He pointed to the guard still lying unconscious on the floor. "Knocked out whoever she came across, crept downstairs, got the keys and freed everyone, my lord."

"Ah, but picked the lock with what?" Ardent stepped closer to Erin to curl a lock of her hair around his finger. "Your hair has escaped from its bounds, milady," he said. He then plucked out the remaining ruby-encrusted hairpins, and Erin's hair fell free in waves down her back. She shuddered in revulsion.

"Unhand her," Hugo shouted from the cell across from Erin's, and one of the guards who wasn't holding Erin rattled his sheathed sword against the bars of Hugo's cell in warning.

Ardent stepped back to hold up the hairpins. "Clever of you," he said to Erin. "You will not escape so easily this time." He turned to the guards. "Double the number of guards posted in the dungeons." He smiled slightly at Erin. "Your new hairstyle only enhances your beauty, Lady Erin. I look forward to our wedding day."

Hugo snarled from his cell while Erin clawed and kicked at the air, but the guards merely shoved her into the cell and shut the door. Erin pounded her fists against the bars of her cell as the lock clicked into place. "You can't keep us here!" she yelled, but the only sound that met her was that of Ardent walking away and his men returning to their posts.

Erin sighed and peered through the bars at Hugo, who scowled darkly in the direction that the guards had left. "Are you all right?"

Hugo stepped closer and looped his arms through the bars of his cell to lean toward her. "I'm fine, for I am near you."

Erin frowned impatiently. "Why do you say such things to me? You don't owe me your heart for my help."

Hugo tilted his head to the side, and some of his curly black hair, loosened from its tie by his struggle, fell across his face. He tucked it behind an ear and said, "I don't speak out of a sense of indebtedness. I say such things because I truly feel them."

"Oh." Erin nodded slowly, not sure what to say.

"Did you want me to stop?" He shrugged self-deprecatingly. "It is a bit much, isn't it, after fending off Ardent's advances all night."

"No," Erin said. "No, I don't mind." Her face was hot with embarrassment, and she was grateful for the dim lighting in the dungeon which she hoped hid any redness in her cheeks.

Hugo smiled slowly. "Then I shall continue to give voice to my feelings for you."

Erin nodded and looked at the ground, feeling too bashful to meet Hugo's eyes. "All right."

"Do you share my feelings?" Asked Hugo.

"I…" Erin didn't know what to say. Some part of her was still afraid of saying the wrong thing. Another part of her wasn't ready to say anything to a man she'd only known for a few days. She flicked her eyes up to briefly meet his. "I'm sorry that you're captured here with me."

"Is that all?" Hugo asked with a slight smile.

Erin looked at her feet. "We should make a plan for our escape, and for what to do about Ardent marrying me."

"Yes, that is a predicament," said Hugo, and Erin looked up to find him frowning darkly. "I don't want you to marry him."

"Then you're in good company, for I don't want to either," said Erin.

"I had not doubted I was in fine company," said Hugo. "You are among the finest company I have ever had. I should like to remain in your company for all my days, even if I must weather imprisonment to do so."

Erin could feel her face heating up again. "Be that as it may, I would rather see you freed."

"Only if you are free along with me," said Hugo. "And I don't want you marrying him out of concern for my well-being. I would suffer more knowing that I was the reason you married that man than I would suffer from the trials of imprisonment."

Erin shook her head. "You're a good man to say so, but I would suffer at the thought of you locked up down here because of my refusal to do what Ardent and the prince want of me."

"I'll be imprisoned regardless, for I have the feeling they don't mean to free me no matter what you or I do," said Hugo. "So there's no need for you to fret on that score."

"I can't refuse them when it might mean you stay down here all your life," said Erin. "I must see if I can bargain for your liberty, for you mean too much to me to see you caged when you are meant to be happy and well and most of all, free."

Hugo smiled crookedly. "I mean that much to you?"

Erin looked down at her feet. "I won't be the reason you remain down here."

"And I won't be the reason you marry Ardent," said Hugo. "So we had better make a plan that ends with both of us free. Not to mention, we still must find Duke Bavencian."

"Agreed," said Erin, and she sat on the floor and rested her back against the wall. She had no more ideas for escape, with no hairpins left to pick the lock and no way to avoid the guards by the dungeon entrance even if she did manage to escape her cell.

Hugo sat facing her and stretched his long legs out in front of him to cross them at the ankle. "We'll find a way out together, don't worry."

"I confess I'm out of ideas," said Erin.

"An opportunity will arise," said Hugo. "Everybody makes mistakes, and our guards are no less human than the rest of us."

On that hopeful note, they sat quietly facing each other, waiting for their keepers to slip up and present them with an opportunity.

Erin thought back over finding her parents and was struck by her father's odd reaction to Hugo and the way Prince Thomas had called Hugo a mercenary. She looked to Hugo, who sat in his cell with his eyes closed.

"Why did my father and the prince call you a mercenary?" Erin asked.

Hugo opened his eyes. "Your father did to see if he remembered the history of my family correctly, and I imagine the prince wanted to shame me for the way my people have had to earn money to make ends meet."

"So you have been a mercenary?"

"Yes," said Hugo. "My men and I had to live by the blade when I was younger. The crops failed, famine struck, and we needed to support our families somehow. So I and the men who served me became a band of mercenaries. The work came easily for us because we had been well-trained, and we soon had more work than we could do and were able to pick and choose our assignments. I did all I could to ensure our fighting remained honorable, though I did face difficult decisions when we started out. We never fell to serving thieves, though. We went hungry when those were the only jobs on offer."

"Were you mercenaries for long?"

"A few years. Eventually, the farms recovered and we could go back to only fighting the brigands who threatened our borders. The experience changed the way I viewed the world. I became more lenient with those who broke the law out of desperation and more supportive of those who worked undesirable jobs to put food on the table. Other nobles look down on me because of it, but the experience made me a better man and a better leader, I think."

"I think you're a good man," said Erin.

"Thank you, Lady Erin." Hugo smiled. "I think you are a good woman."

Feeling shy, Erin fell silent again, her view of Hugo slowly evolving into something difficult for her to define.

16

An Unwanted Wedding

IT WAS DIFFICULT for Erin to gauge the passing of time down in the dungeon. The scant lighting afforded by the widely spaced torches didn't give a hint at what time of day it might be, and the knowledge of her place in time became another comfort taken from her. The only hint at the passing of the day became the guards who walked by the cells every so often. Erin and Hugo kept silent company with each other, and Hugo took to sitting by the entrance to his cell, next to the bars, eyes hooded with sleep. Erin sat across from him, with both of them occupying spots that gave them a view of the hall.

Some interminable stretch of time later, the entrance to the dungeon clanked open, and in walked a pair of guards with Duke Bavencian held between them and the prince walking behind them. Erin and Hugo stood as the group drew near.

"If you aren't going to support me, then I don't want to hear your complaints, and I certainly can't let you leave free to share your complaints with anyone else." Prince Thomas pointed to the darkest cell, farthest from the entrance. "Put him there."

"This is most unconscionable of you, nephew," the duke said in a strained voice as he fought against his captors.

"Is it?" Prince Thomas laughed. "I hadn't noticed. I was too busy protecting myself from the possibility of you turning against me and telling the world of my plans."

The soldiers shoved Duke Bavencian into his cell. The duke

stumbled in, then straightened and began brushing off his clothing. He turned and, having regained his bearing, walked up to his cell door where the prince stood. "It's not too late," said the duke. "Stop this foolish behavior before the consequences of your actions become irreversible."

"I had rather thought that to be the point of my plans," said Prince Thomas. "Nobody will have the power to undo all I have done and am about to achieve. Besides, should there be any negative consequences to my actions, I'll simply order someone else to bear them."

"You're making a mistake," said the duke.

"Am I? From what I can tell, I'm the free man and you're the one in the prison cell," said Prince Thomas. "Enough of this. You've said your piece, I've rejected your advice, and now we're done with each other. I'm a busy man and don't have time to waste."

The duke took a step back, away from the prince. "So be it."

"Indeed," said the prince, and he walked back to the entrance, taking a moment to smirk at Erin and say, "Lady Erin, prison life suits you."

"It suits me better than allying myself with you, that's for sure," Erin said defiantly.

The prince's smirk turned into an ugly scowl. "Then may you have all the time in the dungeons that you like." He glared and then grinned nastily. "And you may find yourself working with me sooner than you think upon your alliance with Ardent."

"There is no alliance, only a forced agreement to marry," said Erin.

"Regardless of how you came to it, the fact is that soon you'll marry Ardent, and all your land and people will become his, which means they also become mine." The prince's grin grew to show his sharp eyeteeth. "Rest well, Lady Erin. There are many changes that await you tomorrow." He gave her one last vicious smile and continued on his way out of the dungeon.

Duke Bavencian sighed and rested his hands on his hips. "That went worse, much worse, than I had hoped." He sighed again and shook his head. "The prince is lost to me. I couldn't reach him." He looked at Erin and Hugo. "I tried all the arguments I could, to no avail. He won't turn away from his path."

"I could have told you that," Erin said.

"I had to try," said the duke. "He's family, after all. But if there's one thing the royal family learns, it's the importance of putting the kingdom before blood. This land is our closest and most important life source, and I can't forsake it." The duke fell silent and withdrew into the depths of his cell with a deep frown, and Erin and Hugo went back to their seats facing the hall and each other, on the lookout for guards. Erin watched the light flicker and listened to the far off dripping noise that was the only sound besides the faint noise of Hugo and Duke Bavencian breathing.

Erin felt herself lulled into a kind of resting state by the quiet of the dungeon, so it was startling for her to hear the loud grating of the doorway to the dungeons opening. She picked herself up onto her feet and peered into the gloom to find Ardent walking toward her. Hugo swiftly got to his feet, too, scowling darkly.

Ardent ignored Hugo, his gaze fixed upon Erin, and he stopped to stand just outside her cell. "This all could have been avoided," he said.

"I don't see how," said Erin, anger making her voice come out forceful and brittle.

Ardent looked Erin up and down thoughtfully and said, "You're in such dire straits, Lady Erin. I would save you from them if I could. Would it really be that bad to marry me?"

"You're holding me against my will. What's more, we don't love each other."

"How do you know? What if love is something you learn over time? We could grow to love each other. I would honor you as my wife."

Erin spoke sharp and fast, her temper rising. "If imprisonment is how you honor your future wife, I don't want any more honoring. Why don't you honor me by giving me a choice?"

"Because then you wouldn't choose me," Ardent said.

Erin paused, struck by Ardent's grim acceptance of the way things were. "You don't know that."

"I do know. And the question is moot now, since you've said yourself that you wouldn't choose a man who treats you like this. It's too late to change the way things are."

"It's never too late to change," said Erin.

"Yes, it is." Ardent turned to go. "Goodnight, Lady Erin."

Erin leapt at him through the bars of the cell and hit the back of his head. Ardent stumbled and slumped to the ground. "Goodnight, Lord Ardent," she said.

Hugo grinned. "I couldn't have said it better myself."

Erin reached out and grabbed hold of the fabric around Ardent's shoulders to pull him close enough for her to get the keys clipped to his waist. She tested the keys with shaking fingers until she found the one that worked and stepped free from her cell with the click of the lock. She went to Hugo's cell and tried all the keys in his lock but couldn't find one that worked.

"Don't worry about us," said Hugo. "Go and free yourself."

"I would not truly be free without you by my side. My worry for you would be like a new prison," said Erin. "I can't leave you here."

"Good, for I would rather not be left," said the duke. "Please free me, at least, before you go."

Erin tried to open the door to the duke's prison, but again, no key worked. She crept to the dungeon entrance and listened for sounds of life on the other side of the door. She heard the sound of footsteps coming closer, and her heartbeat quickened before a guard said, "Don't go in there."

Erin breathed a quiet sigh of relief.

"Why not?" asked the guard closest to her hiding place.

"Lord Ardent is in there. He requested privacy."

"All this activity is bad for my nerves," said the closer guard. "And I have a splitting headache from where that prisoner hit me."

"You should have stayed on your guard better."

"You don't know how vicious that girl's blows are." The nearer guard fell silent for a moment. "Shall we check on them, just to show that we're doing our jobs?"

"Are you afraid that girl will come back and hit you again?" The other guard laughed.

"Not just the girl," said the closer guard. "The man with her moved like a soldier. And I want Lord Ardent to see that I do my job well."

"You can posture all you like, it doesn't change the fact that you let a girl get the drop on you."

"You wouldn't have done any better, in my place. Don't under-estimate her." The closer guard sounded sulky. "I am going to check on them," he said, and Erin stepped swiftly back as the door to the dungeons swung open. "You-" the guard shouted, but Erin silenced him with a punch to the head, and he slumped to the ground. She ran into the guardroom, where the other guard was rising from his seat.

"Halt -"

But Erin did not halt, instead twirling into a high kick that knocked the other guard unconscious. "You shouldn't discount women," she said to the slouched over guard before taking the key ring off the hook on the wall beside him. She hurried back into the dungeon and quickly unlocked Hugo's cell. Hugo stepped out and swept Erin into a hug so tight that he picked her slightly up off the ground. Erin held onto his broad shoulders and smiled widely as Hugo set her back on the ground.

"My rescuer, at it again," said Hugo.

The duke cleared his throat. "I'd like nothing more than to be rescued as well," he said.

Erin felt the heat of a blush rise in her cheeks as Hugo stepped back, grinning. She hurried to the duke's cell and unlocked his door, fumbling a little with the key.

"Thank you, Lady Erin," said the duke as he stepped out of his cell. He walked over to the dungeon entrance to arm himself with a sword from one of the fallen guards. Hugo took the sword from the other guard, and Erin took a knife out of one of the guards' boots. The duke put his borrowed sword and scabbard through his belt and sighed heartily. "I feel like myself again." He gestured to Erin. "Lead on, Lady Erin, our fair heroine."

They crept up the stairs to the ground floor, came out behind the bookshelves of the library, and began to sneak through the empty dining hall. Shadows lingered in the gloom of the unlit room. The ceiling was high and dark, and Erin had to reach her hands out to make sure she didn't run into anything as her eyes adjusted to the lack of light. She could hear faint, far-off voices as they crept closer to the main entryway until suddenly the voices grew rapidly louder, and Hugo, the duke, and Erin rushed to hide behind the table and chairs.

"I dislike the idea of imprisoning a duke, your highness," Erin could hear Lord Morton saying.

"It's fortunate, then, that I'm the one who imprisoned him and not you," said the prince. "Besides, my uncle is weak-willed, and values luxury above all else. There's no need to fear him. We can buy him over to our side, once he's spent an adequate amount of time learning what life in the dungeons is like as his other option."

The sound of footsteps and voices faded away again, and the duke rose out of his crouch with his fists clenched. "That impudent little worm thinks he can intimidate me into allying with him? Well, he can think again. I am tougher than that, and am capable of as much of a show of force as any other man, though I find such shows to be distasteful to the extreme," he whispered furiously. "It takes a real man to appreciate the finer things in life!"

"I do not doubt that you could best the prince in many arenas, should you put your mind to it," said Erin soothingly. "But please, contain your anger until we have escaped, your grace."

The duke subsided and said, "My apologies, Lady Erin. Let's depart from this dreadful place."

They crept into the entrance hall and out through the heavy, dark doors into the warm air of a summer night. The frogs and crickets made a chorus of nighttime sounds, and the three of them ran into the forest with quiet footfalls and bated breath.

17
An Old Alliance

It was a long run through the forest before Duke Bavencian held up a hand, panting a little bit. "I'm not as young as I once was, and these old bones need rest," he said before sitting on a nearby boulder. He wiped the sweat from his brow, the lace gathered at his wrists accentuating the movement. "What's our plan?"

Erin rested her hands on her hips and tried to catch her breath. "Jax will take my parents back to Hart Keep, and he'll stay there to arrange for our rescue. We can rendezvous with everyone there."

The duke nodded, his breath coming more slowly. "Very good," he said. "And how will we be getting back to Hart Keep? Not by foot, I hope?"

Hugo opened his doublet to show coins sewn into the side. "We can hire horses at the nearest tavern."

"Good," said the duke. "All this running is most unnatural for a man of my station."

"We must get there quickly, then, before news of our escape begins to travel, so that nobody is on the lookout for us," said Erin, and with that, they were off again. The nearest tavern was kept by a dour man of few words. He took their payment and rented out horses for them to take to the waystation in Norcliff, and the travel went faster after that. There didn't seem to be a search out for them yet, and they were galloping swiftly down the main road from the Morton's flat, sectioned off farmlands into the rockier terrain of Norcliff by the time the sun rose. It was with little trouble that they made their way from there to Hart Keep, and soon they had walked up to the town walls, where the guards stood to attention at the sight of Erin, though she wore travelstained clothes, and her hair was a windblown mess. Word of her arrival traveled quickly, and soon her flag was hoisted up to join her parents' flags flying from the tallest tower of the keep. Erin stopped to look at the three flags waving in the breeze and felt her throat grow tight and her eyes begin to water. She cleared her throat, wiped at her eyes, and quickly rejoined Hugo and Duke Bavencian, who had gone on a little ahead of her. She was glad to return home, after all this time, and find her parents waiting there for her.

By the time they reached the front door, Finley and Evelyn stood within the doorway waiting for her, and they gathered each other close in a hug before parting.

"We thought you were still imprisoned!" Evelyn said, stroking her daughter's wild hair. "What a relief to find you returned to us so soon after our parting." She tugged Erin into one more hug, tighter than the last.

"Thank you," Finley said to Hugo and the duke, who shook his head.

"Don't thank us, for we did very little," Hugo said with a crooked smile. "Lady Erin freed us, as well as herself."

"Your daughter is quite the fearsome warrior," said the duke.

Finley laughed, and the laughter seemed to take the years off him so that he was once again the same as before his imprisonment. "I know it well," he said. Then he grew serious once more, and his face was gaunt from hunger, and a patchy beard hid his slight smile. "We'll need warriors like her, in the battle that's coming."

"Enough of that for now," said Evelyn, and she shepherded them into the keep. "First we must rest and recuperate from the trials we have overcome."

Jax and Liana came up to them, and Liana hugged Erin with a laugh, saying, "I knew they couldn't keep you for long!"

"You've done well." Jax gave Erin a nod of approval.

"She's our savior," agreed Hugo.

Jax grunted and said, "So you're still here, then, and still spouting that nonsense."

"Nonsense?" Finley asked with a raised eyebrow. "What nonsense would that be?"

"The man's courting your daughter," said Jax.

"Really?" Finley looked to Erin for confirmation, but she couldn't speak from embarrassment. "The mercenary?"

Hugo looked suddenly grave. "I hope to one day earn your approval, Lord and Lady Hart, as I hope to earn your daughter's heart. Please allow me to continue courting your daughter. Though it was begun in an unconventional way, it was begun in earnest, and I haven't broken any rules."

"No, he hasn't," said Jax. "I can give him that much."

"I don't know about this," said Finley. "Jax, we'll speak more on what has been going on, later. As for you, Lord Hugo, I trust you'll be patient enough to wait for approval from me and Evelyn before proceeding?"

Hugo, bowed his head. "I'll be patient."

"Dad," said Erin with a scolding tone, "really? He doesn't deserve to be treated in this way. He's been nothing but solicitous with me."

Finley sighed and looked to Evelyn for help. "Erin, dear," began Evelyn, "we don't doubt you kept to the codes of courtship as well as you could, but you're new to this. That's why your father and I must speak with Jax about what has been going on. You haven't had to judge a man's character before this. You and Marc knew each other inside and out from growing up together. This mercenary is a stranger, to all of us, and we must learn if he is worthy of courting you."

"While you're judging Lord Hugo's character, is there some food and wine to be had?" The duke asked. "I find myself in want of a meal after our travels, and I'm sure my compatriots would like one as well."

"Yes, of course," said Evelyn. "Follow me."

They soon came to the dining hall, where Lord and Lady Clairmaud sat. "Erin, how good to see you," said Lady Clairmaud, and she rose to give Erin a hug. "We were glad to hear of your arrival."

"Yes, we were," said Lord Clairmaud. "Here, sit down," he rose and pulled out a chair for Erin. "You must be tired from your journey."

Hugo and the duke sat as well, and servants came out with platters of food for the group to share.

"We were just speaking of our plans to return home," said Lady Clairmaud. "I find myself eager to see Frederick once again, safe home from school."

"I, too, am eager to return home," said Lord Clairmaud. "We must gather our forces to meet this threat from the prince and the Mortons."

"It would go better," said Lady Clairmaud, "if one of the Harts came with us, to rally our soldiers and show them the old bonds are still strong, with or without a wedding to join us together."

"I'll go," said Erin, looking to her parents. "You just got back and are in no shape to be traveling all over the country."

"I'll go, too, then," said Hugo. "I'll watch over her."

"And Lord and Lady Clairmaud will watch over you," said Jax.

"I don't know if that's such a good idea," said Evelyn.

"Jax, go with them," said Finley. "Someone will need to chaperone them on the way back, and we can keep in touch with you by carrier pigeon if need be."

"Mom," Erin said in a pleading voice.

"We'll need Jax here, to clear the way for our plans with his information network, though, dear," said Evelyn to her husband. "Liana can chaperone them."

"Liana is just a girl herself," said Finley.

"Liana will have to suffice," said Jax. "Lady Hart is correct, I have much work to do."

"I'll keep them safe," said Liana, "and ensure that there's no impropriety." She smiled a little. "Finally, a chance to show that I know better than Erin."

Erin laughed. "In your dreams, Liana."

Liana grinned. "Yes, this shall be a dream come true for me."

Erin sobered. "We'll return with the old alliance between the Harts and Clairmauds as strong as ever."

"Hear, hear," said Lord Clairmaud, and after that the conversation turned to small talk and niceties as the group took their rest and ate to regain their strength.

The next day dawned bright and clear, and Erin packed her bags and went out to the front courtyard to find Hugo already there, mounted on his horse and holding the reins to hers. "Lady Erin," he said, bowing from the saddle.

Erin stared, and behind her, Liana giggled. Erin curtsied belatedly. "Lord Hugo, thank you for getting my horse." She tied her saddlebags to her horse and mounted up while the stableboys came out with horses for Liana and Lord and Lady Clairmaud.

"My, such punctuality is to be admired," said Liana, and Lord and Lady Clairmaud exchanged a glance before getting on their horses.

Erin blinked and fiddled with the reins in her hand, not sure how to feel with Hugo beside her and Marc's parents there as well. They began their ride in the brisk quiet of the morning, with the only noises the birdsong and the rustle of the trees around them as they took the path through the forest. The horses slowed as they approached the clearing where Erin's wedding had fallen apart, and Lady Clairmaud stifled a sob when the trees fell away to show the gently rolling hills of the meadow where their son and many of their family and friends had died, only weeks ago.

"Is this where -" Hugo broke off and grimaced as Lord Clairmaud rode up next to his wife to clasp her hand in his.

"Yes," said Erin.

They rode slowly through the grass until they reached the churned up earth where the battle had taken place. A lone bird flitted down to land on a broken spear sticking out of the ground, and Erin watched it hop from side to side along the splintered wooden handle and chirrup. She felt her heart clench with loneliness as she looked at the place where Marc would have stood in all his finery, waiting for her to come to him. She had not come to him in time, not to save his life or to spend the last few moments of his life together with him. Blinking rapidly, she rode on a little ahead to where her wedding procession would have begun, and then up to where the aisle would have been. Tears fell down her numb face. She stopped her horse and wiped her eyes dry before turning back to where Lord and Lady Clairmaud rode on with haggard faces, Lady Clairmaud glancing at Erin with a pained expression every few moments, and Lord Clairmaud squinting stoically into the distance with a trembling frown. Liana trailed behind them with a worried expression, and Hugo broke from the group to join Erin.

"Marc died here," Erin said once Hugo drew close. She turned in her seat to point to the spot where he had lain and found that she couldn't remember where that was. "I don't remember exactly where."

"That's all right," said Hugo.

"Is it?" Erin bit out, trying to hold back tears. "Shouldn't I remember exactly where he stood, and exactly where he lay when he took his last breath? Is that not one of my duties as his intended wife? Has my memory failed him along with everything else?"

"I think, if you could ask him what he would prefer between you dying with him or you here, alive and well and not quite remembering where he died, he would chose the latter in a heartbeat," said Hugo.

"Perhaps." Erin stared at the ground, but the rains had washed away the bloodstains, and only the unsettled earth remained to hint at the violence that had torn apart the hope for a good marriage and peaceful life that Erin had held in her heart. She pressed her lips together and lifted her chin. "I still must do my duty by Marc, as much as I can. I must secure the alliance between the Harts and Clairmauds, now more than ever." She turned her horse around and rode to join Lord and Lady Clairmaud with worry and sorrow tightening her shoulders and churning her stomach.

18
Love and Loss

FREDERICK WAITED TO greet them at the front steps of Clairmaud House when they rode into the courtyard, and Lady Clairmaud jumped down from her horse and ran to hug her son with a choked off gasp. Lord Clairmaud rode up at a steadier pace, and was slow getting down from his horse, only gripping his son tightly on the shoulder while Lady Clairmaud continued to hug him. "Mother, I'm all right," Erin could hear Frederick saying when she rode up and dismounted. Frederick gently broke free from his mother to hold Liana's reins while she dismounted, and then he nodded a greeting to Liana and Erin. "Lady Erin, Lady Liana. I'm glad to see you safe and well," he said.

Erin looked at Frederick's tall, wiry form, the slight dishevelment of his clothing, his flyaway blond hair, and the round glasses perched at a slight slant on his nose and found comfort in the familiarity of his distracted, scholarly air. "I'm glad to find you the same," said Erin.

"I, too, am glad to see you," said Liana. "How do you fare?"

"I'm well, Lady Liana." He gestured to the house and began to lead them up the steps. "Please, make yourselves at home."

"What's the situation with the council?" Lord Clairmaud asked.

"Captain Stoutney is in fine form," said Frederick. "More than that, I have yet to ascertain. I'm just back from the collegium myself and have only had the time to sit in on one meeting thus far."

"Call them together, for time is of the essence. We have much to discuss."

"As you say, Father," said Frederick. "The council has already gathered in anticipation of your arrival."

"Good," said Lord Clairmaud, and he took the lead past the potted plants and white benches that decorated the atrium. They walked into the main living room, where light shone down through the glass ceiling and warmed the earth tones of the reddish brown tile floor and the white, gauzy curtains that framed the archways leading to the central garden.

Two men and one woman awaited them, and one of the men in fighting leathers with close shaved hair and a scarred, hachet-like face stepped forward the moment they entered. "Lord and Lady Clairmaud, welcome back," he said.

"Thank you, Captain Stoutney," said Lady Clairmaud before she took a seat on a light blue divan.

"Please accept my apologies for failing to protect you," said Captain Stoutney.

"There's no need for you to apologize," said Lord Clairmaud. "None of us expected what happened, and how could we blame you when we were just as surprised."

"Nevertheless, I will be diligent in my efforts to keep you and your remaining family safe from this moment forward," said Captain Stoutney. "Starting with this fight between the Harts and the Mortons, which I assume you have some news about?"

"We were held captive in Morton Manor and heard of Ardent Morton's plan to force Lady Erin here into marriage," said Lord Clairmaud. "We bring with us a new compatriot who aided us in the fight against the Mortons, named Lord Hugo."

"My sources tell me he is more than a compatriot to Lady Erin," said Captain Stoutney. "Is it true, Lady Erin, that Lord Hugo has asked permission to court you?"

Erin blinked. "He has."

"So quick to find a new suitor after Lord Marc's death!" Captain Stoutney bellowed. "Our numbers are already more than halved by the attack on the wedding, and now Lady Erin wants our continued support while she breaks the rules of mourning. What will we get out of a renewed promise to help her, save more bloodshed?"

"Captain Stoutney, the Harts have been good friends to us for generations. They deserve more consideration," said Lord Clairmaud.

"Indeed they have been good friends," Captain Stoutney said, "which is why I propose a new match, made between Lady Erin and Lord Frederick, who is now the heir of the estate in Lord Marc's stead. Lady Erin is entertaining suitors again, so what trouble would one more be? We would have the assurance of a marriage and a renewal of the promise held by Lord Marc and Lady Erin to revitalize ties between our families."

Liana gripped Erin's hand in surprise, and they shared a glance while Frederick pushed his glasses up his nose and looked out the window. Lord Clairmaud tilted his head to the side. "It's unusual for you to concern yourself with marriages, Captain."

"With our numbers reduced so sharply, can you blame me for turning my attention to the fate of the next generation?" Captain Stoutney asked.

"Let there be another wedding," said a woman dressed in a light purple silk gown. She smiled encouragingly at Erin and Frederick, who avoided Erin's eyes when Erin looked at him to gauge his reaction. "It will bring joy to our grieving people and give resolve to our forces, so terribly reduced in the attack."

"Madame Verdegris makes an excellent point. It would raise morale to have a wedding," said a man in a black doublet and leggings with a sharp goatee on his chin. "Lord Frederick and Lady Erin know each other well enough that we can skip most of the steps for courting, and with Lord Frederick's studies almost done, he would soon be at a point where he would be looking for a wife anyway."

"Before we go rushing to put on another wedding, Sir Noyer," said Lady Clairmaud, "perhaps it would behoove us to learn what Erin and Frederick think of the idea."

Frederick stared fixedly out the window. "I will respect the council's decision." He gave Erin a sideways glance. "Provided Erin has no objections."

"There you have it, the boy doesn't mind," Sir Noyer said.

Lady Clairmaud raised an eyebrow, looking amused. "But what does Erin think?"

All eyes turned to Erin, and when Erin looked to Liana for support, Liana only stared back at her, looking as shocked by the proceedings as Erin felt. "I need time," Erin blurted out. She took a steadying breath, then said, "I have to think about this."

"It's a wise decision to take time for thought, and one that more people, perhaps, should make," said Lady Clairmaud. "I propose we take a break for dinner and come back to this issue with rested minds and full stomachs tomorrow."

Captain Stoutney bowed. "As my lady wishes."

Lord and Lady Clairmaud led the way into the dining room and sat on opposite ends of the table, with Frederick, Liana, and Hugo sitting in between. Erin sat next to Frederick in the only empty chair left and tried to catch his eye, but he avoided her gaze and focused on the food that the servants began to bring out.

"Thank you for the meal," Erin said to break the silence. She noticed Liana looking strangely sad as she watched Erin and Frederick. "You're truly gracious hosts."

Lord Clairmaud smiled, and Lady Clairmaud said, "Thank you, Erin. We're glad to see you whole and healthy. You've always been like a daughter to us."

"Not that we wish to pressure you into deciding one way or another about this proposal the council has dreamed up," said Lord Clairmaud.

"Excuse me," said Liana. "I find our travels have worn me out excessively." She rose from her chair. "I must take my rest." She put her napkin down on the table next to her still full plate and left the room.

Erin caught Hugo's eye. "That was strange of her, wasn't it?"

"You'd know better than me," said Hugo.

Erin nodded thoughtfully. "What do you think of the council's proposal?"

Hugo sighed and looked off into the distance. "I think you have a weighty decision lying ahead of you, one that none can make for you." His lips twitched into a shadow of a smile. "As far as prospects go, you could do worse." He looked at Erin and seemed to shake off the gloom that had passed over his features. "Forgive me for the maudlin cast to my thoughts. I find I, too, am weary from our journey and am not fit for company. May you find the answers that you seek as you take your rest tonight."

Frederick rose from his chair. "I, too, would like to retire for the night."

"Sleep well, son. We're glad to have you back here," said Lady Clairmaud.

He smiled absently at his mother. "I'm glad to be back." He walked out of the room, too, and left only silence behind. The rest of dinner went quickly, with Lady Clairmaud making generally benign comments about the weather and state of the farmlands. Lord Clairmaud and Hugo focused intently on their food while Erin did her best to keep the conversation going. It was with relief that she left the table for her room, and she cut through the central garden on her way to sleep, walking the winding pathway and trying to decide what to say to the council the next day. Her thoughts were interrupted by the sound of footsteps around a turn in the path.

"Stop following me!" She heard someone say in a harsh whisper, and she stopped, confused.

"Liana -" Erin recognized Frederick's gentle baritone.

"Nothing you can say can change the fact that you threw what we had away with barely a pause for thought today."

"Please understand that I'm trying to fulfill my duty as the Clairmaud heir. That doesn't mean I love you any less."

"No. If you truly loved me, you wouldn't have given up on us so easily. I'm no fool. Don't treat me like one."

Erin stepped back as Liana's voice grew louder, but it was too late to hide as Liana rounded the corner, closely followed by Frederick.

Liana fell silent and came to a stop, and Erin caught the gleam of tears on her cheeks.

"Liana, I didn't know-" Erin began, only to stop at Liana's raised hand.

"I'm not angry with you, but please don't blame me for not wanting to speak with you just now, Erin," said Liana before rushing past Erin.

"Liana -!" Frederick reached out as if to stop her, but it was too late. He looked at Erin, and his hand fell to rest at his side. "Now you know.

I suppose it's something of a relief for someone besides us to know of our feelings for each other."

"Why did you hide it for so long?" Erin asked.

"Liana felt self-conscious about dating a lord, even one as lowly as I was until my station rose to heir, and I wanted to avoid the pressure to break off the relationship that I could predict the council might apply. You have some sense of how overbearing they can be, now, with the meeting today." Frederick smiled self-consciously. "It seemed easier to keep it to ourselves."

Erin smiled back. "I understand."

Frederick's smile faded. "Though I'm glad to have our secret out, I would've spared you the knowledge of it if I could. It will only make your decision harder, and for that I'm sorry. Now you must consider the well-being of your people, your own heart, and Liana's happiness, too."

"Yes." Erin sighed. "What do you think we should do?"

"I meant what I said, earlier. I'll marry you, if that's what my people need."

"But you love Liana."

"I do." Frederick smiled at the ground. "I suspect I'll love her all my life."

"Then you condemn us both to a loveless match, for no love will grow where it is not cultivated."

"Perhaps, but I don't find you objectionable, and I believe we could be great friends. I pledge to treat you well, should you choose to marry me," said Frederick.

"You are kind and dutiful," said Erin. She thought of Frederick as a child, following in the wake of Marc with an eager smile or sitting in the lounge with his nose stuck in a book while Erin and Marc ran outside. Liana had stayed inside on those occasions, Erin remembered. She looked at Frederick, now a grown man with some of the same characteristics that she had so loved in Marc including, most importantly, a kind heart. She wondered if that would be enough. "I have much to think on," she said.

"Indeed you do. I'll leave you to it," Frederick said, and he walked off in the opposite direction to the one Liana had taken. Erin sat on a nearby bench and thought long into the night, until she had to retire to her room, eyes drooping and steps heavy.

The next morning, Erin woke from a restless sleep and went downstairs to take one more walk in the gardens, her mind still turning over what she had discovered the night before. She felt undecided about what route to take, and the ever-turning garden path mirrored her thoughts as she turned over and over her warring desires to both serve her people well and follow her heart. After the passing of some time, she saw Hugo turn a corner and come into her view. They both startled at the sight of each other.

Erin curtsied, not sure where she stood with Hugo anymore. "Lord Hugo."

Hugo bowed deeply. "Lady Erin." He rose from his bow with a determined expression. "Have you made your decision?"

"I have not," said Erin. "I find myself as conflicted this morning as I was last night."

Hugo stepped forward slightly. "I thought about your situation all night, and I have something to say, if you will hear me out."

Erin nodded. "Please, go ahead."

"Don't marry Lord Frederick," said Hugo.

Erin blinked. "I beg your pardon?"

"Not that I would presume to tell you what to do," Hugo said, "but you clearly don't love him in the way that you would need to in order to have a successful marriage."

"And I suppose you think I feel these things for you?"

"I don't know what you do or do not feel for me, but I do know that there is something growing between us. Don't you feel it, too?"

Erin's eyes widened. "I hardly know what to say, except that I'm much too busy attempting to protect my people and allies to contemplate such things as love between a man and woman."

"So you do think there might be love between us?"

"As I said before, I hardly know what to think."

"But you did mention love," said Hugo.

"What is love when there are armies to lead and lives to protect?"

"I would argue that love is the most important at times when lives are in danger." Hugo's face took on a grave cast. "I have fought a great many fights, and have seen the power love holds to strengthen hearts, bolster courage, and change the tide of battle. So I am begging you." Hugo stooped down to kneel on one bended knee to Erin's surprise and consternation. "Please. Don't marry Lord Frederick."

"Lord Hugo," Erin said, feeling curiously faint and hard of breath. "You don't fight fair."

"I find, when it comes to you, Lady Erin, that there is little I won't do to secure your affections." Hugo looked up at her with piercing dark eyes. "Please give what we have growing between us the chance to bloom."

Erin stared at the man kneeling before her and could think of nothing to say in return to his heartfelt plea except, "Please rise, Lord Hugo. You don't need to kneel before me to get me to consider your words."

"Perhaps not, but it's no great trouble for me to do so," Hugo said as he rose to his feet. "Will you consider what I've said, then?"

Erin nodded. "I can make no promises except to say that I'll think on your words. There is much at stake." She turned away. "Please leave me to contemplate what my decision will be."

"As you wish," said Hugo, and Erin heard his footsteps recede down the path, leaving her with a heavy heart and conflicted mind.

19

The People's Heart

WITH THE TIME until the next council meeting growing shorter, Erin felt as though the walls of Clairmaud House were closing in on her. Itching to be free of the worries that plagued her, she walked outside into the expansive grounds. She couldn't make up her mind about what to do, and her lack of decisiveness wore at her. In search of a distraction from her quandary, she turned her steps to the training grounds behind the house, and came upon one of the fighting rings soon enough. Two young men fought each other in the center of a small circle with wooden swords and thick leather armor. Erin leaned against the fence ringing the grounds and watched them hit at each other until one fell to his knee and yielded. The watching men applauded the victor, who raised his fist into the air before stepping forward to help his opponent back to his feet.

"They're good boys," a voice came from behind her, and Erin turned to find Captain Stoutney walking up to join her. "Green, perhaps, but their hearts are in the right place. That's the important thing. The experience will come, like it or not, but a good heart is not something that can be replaced with battles fought, no matter how many."

"That's true," Erin said, and they watched a new pair of soldiers square off and begin fighting.

Captain Stoutney leaned on the fence and gave Erin a considering stare. "Where does your heart lie, these days, Lady Erin?"

"It lies with my people, my family, and my friends, of course," Erin said.

Captain Stoutney raised an eyebrow. "Some friends more than others, perhaps?"

"What are you implying?"

"Only that you seem to have replaced the Clairmauds in your affections with a man that may not deserve your regard. A former mercenary, I hear."

"But his heart is in the right place, and as you have just said, that's the important thing, isn't it?" Erin looked out over the fighting youths. "And we all have parts of our lives we don't wish to have define us."

"Those moments when we are brought low by circumstance are when our true colors shine. Lord Hugo may have felt he had to sell his sword, but there were other choices he could have made."

Erin watched as one of the youths fell back beneath an onslaught of blows. She could muster no reply in Hugo's defense. In lieu of talking, she walked closer to the fight, with Captain Stoutney following close behind.

"Lady Hart!" She heard one of the soldiers whisper, and then a rush of whispers followed her progress through the training fields. Soldiers abandoned their practice fights to cluster around her, and all watched her as though waiting for her to do something. Erin found she could sympathize with them, as she was waiting for herself to do something, make some decision, too.

"Hello," she said to the crowd that had gathered, and an anticipatory quiet fell upon the men. She looked from face to face. Many looked either too old or too young for battle, and her heart clenched with sorrow at the many faces that were missing from the crowd, lost in the fight with the Mortons.

"Hello," one of the soldiers standing near the front said in reply, and his fellows shoved him as a chuckle ran through the crowd.

"Why have you come?" She heard someone near the back say.

"I'm here to gather an army to fight the Mortons," she said.

"Good!" A man in the back shouted, to scattered cheers from the crowd.

"I'm also here to decide something that has been weighing on my mind," Erin said, and she looked from inquiring young face to old and back again. "Perhaps you can help me."

"Help how?" one man asked.

Another asked, "What are you trying to decide?"

"The members of Lord Clairmaud's council tell me that your numbers have been greatly reduced," Erin said.

"Aye, they have," said an old man standing near the front. "Those Mortons took no quarter." He spat on the ground. "No mercy left in their black hearts, I suppose."

"I suppose so," said Erin. "The council also tells me your spirits have been low because of it."

"I reckon so," said one of the men, but then another said, "Low spirits, pah! The Mortons would have to be a much greater foe to dampen my spirits!" A ragged cheer rose from the gathered men.

Erin smiled. "You disagree with the council's view on things?"

"Begging your lady's forgiveness, but I think we'd be better authorities on our own spirits than anyone else," said the old man in the front.

"True enough," said Erin. "Perhaps you could tell me, then. What would you need to prove the strength of the alliance between the Harts and Clairmauds before you would fight by our side against the Mortons?"

"Nothing!" a man shouted.

"Less than nothing!" one of the younger boys shouted.

"Down with the Mortons!" a man shouted, and his cry was taken up with the crowd. "Down with the Mortons!" they all repeated, some waving their fists in the air.

Erin looked at Captain Stoutney with a smile. "Down with the Mortons, indeed," she said. Captain Stoutney tipped his chin at her as the chant grew louder and more men raised their fists.

"All right, all right, back to work with you!" Captain Stoutney stepped forward and shouted over the hubbub. "You won't be defeating the Mortons without practice, and lots of it." He turned to Erin. "Lady Erin, I stand corrected."

"Thank you, Captain Stoutney." She turned to leave, then paused and looked back. "And you're wrong about Lord Hugo. Once he was in a position where he could afford to stop selling his sword, he did.

And he sacrificed his principles to support his people until that day came. He put his people first." She made her way back to the house. "People first," she murmured to herself, and her way forward became clear once more.

When Erin walked into the atrium, she found Frederick sitting with a book, his glasses perched precariously on his nose. He looked up at the sound of her footsteps, used a scrap of ribbon to mark his place, and stood to greet her. "Lady Erin. I hope you had a good tour of the grounds?"

"I did," said Erin.

Frederick held out a hand in a half-hearted gesture to the central gardens before letting it drop once more. "Shall we take our lunch in the garden?"

"All right," Erin said. She felt curious to learn more of Marc's little brother who used to keep to his room or the library on the days she visited, before he went away to school. "How are your studies progressing?"

"Well enough," said Frederick. He stopped to speak to a servant passing by them. "Please notify the kitchens that Lady Erin and I will take our lunch in the central garden."

"Yes, my lord." The servant hurried away.

Frederick and Erin walked down the winding cobblestone path in awkward silence until they reached a gazebo with a cast iron table and set of chairs, decorated with metal vines winding up the table and chair legs. Frederick pulled out a chair for Erin. "Thank you," Erin said, and they sat facing each other. She watched Frederick look around absently as a bird chirruped. "What exactly are you studying, these days?"

"The stars," said Frederick, pointing up at the roof of the gazebo. "We use telescopes to map the night sky and work to discover what the planets and stars are made of, to shine so brightly." Frederick's manner became easier as he discussed his studies, and his flyaway hair waved to and fro as he gestured excitedly. "There's so much out there that we know so little about," he said. "Enough to fill countless lifetimes with work."

"I'm sorry that these tragic circumstances have pulled you away from such interesting work."

"It's more important to be here for my family and my people," said Frederick. "May I thank you once more, Lady Erin, for finding and freeing my parents? It was brave of you to do it."

"I didn't do it alone," Erin said. "Liana was there, too, you know, along with Jax and Duke Bavencian and Lord Hugo."

Frederick pushed his glasses up his nose and blinked. "I shall have to remember to thank them as well."

Erin struggled to find a polite way to bring up Frederick's attachment to Liana, but they were interrupted by servants bringing them lunch. Erin didn't speak further until the servants were gone, hoping to prevent gossip from spreading. It was unusual enough that they were eating together in the garden. Erin saw no need to add to the spectacle.

Frederick studied her over their lunch, and his gaze was sharp and observant now that it had fixed upon her. "You want to know about me and Liana, don't you?"

"Yes." Erin kept her answer short and simple out of respect for his straightforwardness.

"You and Marc were so often in your own world when you visited each other. Liana was left to her own devices." Frederick shrugged. "She liked to explore. One day, she found me. I was so glad to be found." He smiled. "That was it for me. I can't speak for Liana as to why she decided to put up with me."

"I see," Erin said.

Frederick's smile faded. "But now I'm the heir, in Marc's place, and I'm ready to carry that responsibility. I will marry you, if the situation calls for it, and it seems that the situation does. I must ask you," Frederick paused and got out of his chair to kneel before her. "Lady Erin, will you marry me?"

Erin stared down at Frederick's earnest face and thought, what a horrible waste of a perfectly good heart. She thought of the soldiers she had met, of Hugo's impassioned plea for her not to marry Frederick, and of Liana's fallen expression, when she had looked from Frederick to Erin at dinner, when she thought Erin wasn't looking. "We don't need to marry," she blurted out. She reached down to Frederick. "Please, get up."

Frederick rose and returned to his chair with a perplexed expression. "Why do you think so?"

"We don't have to do all that our advisors ask of us," Erin said. "That's something you learn with time, when you're heir. You're new to this, and haven't had to deal with the focused attentions of a council before. We can find another way forward. There are other things that can improve morale, and the Clairmauds and Harts are already good friends. The people have plenty of reason to want to fight off the Mortons, Hart and Clairmaud alike. Many of your people died in the attack side by side with Hart family and friends. Besides," Erin smiled gently at Frederick. "I can't bring myself to ruin your happiness. There must be another way. Will you help me to find it?"

Frederick sat back in his chair and let out his breath in one big whoosh. "I'm relieved to hear you say that." He scrubbed a hand through his hair. "I don't know what other way we'll find, but I'll do my best to help you find it."

They finished their lunch with an easy conversation over Frederick's research and Erin's morning with Captain Stoutney. After they were done, Frederick offered her his arm, which she took, and they walked back into the house. In the hall, they came upon Hugo walking in the opposite direction. He stopped when he saw them.

"Lord Hugo," Frederick said, while Erin stared up at Hugo, at a loss for how to act around him after his impassioned speech.

Hugo nodded solemnly. "Lord Frederick." He met Erin's gaze with sombre brown eyes but didn't say anything beyond, "Lady Erin."

"I must be going." Frederick looked between them. "I have happy news that needs sharing." He smiled at Erin, who smiled back, and walked away. Erin looked back at Hugo, and his expression was darker than before.

"Why do you frown so, my lord?" Erin asked, worried.

"Forgive me, Lady Erin." Hugo bowed his head. "I see that you're happy, and I don't want to ruin your good mood. I am, perhaps, not fit for company at present."

"That's unfortunate, because I dearly enjoy your company," Erin said.

"You're kind to say so," Hugo said. He looked down the hall in the direction Frederick had walked. "I trust you have resolved matters to your satisfaction?"

"I have." Erin grinned. "I am more sure of my present path than ever, and I look forward to our council meeting later today, where I can share the news with everyone."

"Then I shall endeavor to be glad for you," Hugo said with a downcast look. "Please excuse me, so that I may gather my thoughts before the meeting."

"Certainly." Erin watched Hugo stride away and felt a little uncertain all over again. She walked back to the garden and wandered the winding paths, lost in thought, until it was time for the council to meet.

When they had all assembled, Captain Stoutney cleared his throat and said, "I see no point in beating around the bush. Lady Erin, what have you decided?"

All heads in the room turned to Erin. She took a breath and said, "I have decided not to marry Frederick." Captain Stoutney and Sir Noyer looked disappointed.

"Why?" Asked Captain Stoutney.

"You say I must marry for the benefit of the people's morale and to strengthen the bonds between the Harts and Clairmauds, but we're already linked by the great tragedy brought upon us. Today I saw people already rallying around a central purpose to seek justice."

Frederick looked up from his contemplation of his feet, fresh hope rising in his eyes. "Additionally, remember that I've been away at the collegium for many years, and the people don't know me well enough to identify with me as strongly as they had with Marc. A wedding with me may not affect their hearts very deeply at all."

Captain Stoutney scratched his chin. "Good point."

Hugo broke out into a rare, beaming grin, and Erin smiled back at him. She had not seen Hugo looking so joyful before, and the sight lifted her heart.

Madame Verdegris looked between them, and a secretive smile flitted across her face. "The lady has spoken," she said.

"I suppose," said Sir Noyer. "What say you, Captain Stoutney, you were the greatest proponent for the match."

Captain Stoutney crossed his arms and gave Erin a look of grudging respect. "It remains to be seen if Lady Erin can inspire my troops all on her own on the eve of battle when it truly counts, but I'm willing to be convinced."

Lord Clairmaud gave a decisive nod. "Now that we've settled that issue, let us discuss battle plans."

"The day approaches when Ardent Morton will retaliate against me for my refusal to marry him, and I heard the prince say that an army is coming from the north," Erin said.

"There have been reports of an increase in criminal activity, no doubt supported by the Mortons and therefore the prince," said Liana. "We saw evidence of this increase on Duke Bavencian's lands during our visit there."

"The rise in thievery has adversely affected profitability in our lands, as well," said Madame Verdegris.

"This harassment must be stopped," said Sir Noyer.

"What is the state of the troops?" Lord Clairmaud asked Captain Stoutney.

"They're a motley bunch," Captain Stoutney said. "They're a mixture of wet behind the ears boys, aged veterans, and the ne'er do wells who avoided service back before our numbers were so greatly reduced."

Lord Clairmaud turned to Erin. "We can no longer offer the best of us, but what we can offer is yours, Lady Erin."

Erin inclined her head. "My thanks to you and your people."

"I myself must remain here to protect our home," said Lord Clairmaud, "but Frederick can go with you, to offer the aid of his bright young mind." Lord Clairmaud smiled proudly at his son, while Lady Clairmaud grasped Frederick's hand tightly with a worried expression on her face.

"But Frederick is so-" Lady Clairmaud began, only to be cut off by Frederick.

"Mother, I must. For Marc." He looked around at the council members. "I will do my best."

"I'll send for a good portion of my men, too," said Hugo.

"Mercenaries," grumbled Captain Stoutney. "How much will you charge, I wonder?"

"You're mistaken, Captain," said Hugo. "This, we will do for free."

"I can't argue with that price," murmured Sir Noyer.

"Your help will be most appreciated, Lord Hugo," said Erin.

"My men may not have had the luxury of being as morally upright as some in the room," Hugo gave Captain Stoutney a sidelong glance, "but they're loyal, experienced fighters who conduct themselves with valor."

"No one doubts the valor of your men," Lord Clairmaud said. Captain Stoutney harrumphed, but after a quelling glance from Lord Clairmaud, said no more.

"All that remains is to rally the troops," Erin said.

Lord and Lady Clairmaud rose from their seats, and the council rose with them. "Let us prepare the men to leave, then, for swiftness is providence when lives are on the line," said Lord Clairmaud.

20
The March

ERIN RODE AT the front of the group of soldiers with Hugo, Liana, and Frederick at her side. The soldiers followed in ragged lines with some muttering among the ranks. They traveled slowly through the day, with those on foot needing more time to get from one place to another. Whenever Erin looked behind her, she saw a mixture of disgruntled, uncertain, and weary faces. She tried not to let the general mood of unease affect her, but it slid into the back of her mind and stayed there despite her conscious efforts to dislodge it.

When the sun hung low in the sky, Erin began to look for a place to make camp and found one when the trees opened up into a meadow. She brought her horse to a halt, raised her hand, and turned to face her men. They stumbled to an untidy stop behind her.

"We'll sleep for the night here," she called out. "Make your preparations." The soldiers broke ranks and began setting up tents.

Erin watched with some trepidation. "There's no order to what they're doing," she said to Liana, who had rode up next to her.

"We'll have to go among them and direct them to do a better job," Liana said.

"Yes, we will." Erin turned to Hugo and Frederick. "Will you help?"

"I have some experience making camp." Hugo dismounted. "I'll take that area." He pointed to where a group of young men were beginning to dig a firepit near the center of the meadow.

"I have less experience, but I suppose I can ride around the perimeter to set up watch stations," Frederick said. "We'll need those."

"I'll take that side, then." Liana pointed to the right. "Will you go to the left?" she asked Erin.

"All right." Erin got off her horse and began directing men to set up tents in orderly rows. She was walking along the aisle that was beginning to form between two rows of tents when she heard shouting coming from the direction of the center of camp. She ran toward the noise to find an enraged youth throwing punches at a grizzled older man in worn leathers with a crooked smirk on his face. A circle of men had formed, and they were shouting encouragement and making wagers. Erin shoved her way through the crowd and shouted over the uproar, "What's the meaning of this?!" The two men didn't stop fighting.

Erin waded between them and tried to push them apart, but they kept leaning around her to try and take shots at each other. "Stop!" she yelled. She saw Hugo appear at the edge of the crowd. "Hugo, help me!"

Hugo ran forward and pulled the older man away, while Erin managed to get the younger man into a hold to keep him from following.

"Let me at him!" the younger man shouted. "I'll show him how well I can fight!"

"You?" The grizzled man scoffed. "You're nothing but a farmer's son with a pitchfork! You wouldn't know the business end of a sword if it stabbed you!" The onlookers guffawed and elbowed each other in the ribs.

"Enough!" Erin yelled. "We're all equally valuable in the fight against the Mortons and the prince!"

"Beggin' yer pardon, your righteousness, but what do you know about it?" The older man sneered. "You're little more than a girl yourself!" The men laughed. Erin looked around at the faces filled with mirth and felt something inside of herself snap. She had enough of her own doubts without anyone else adding more, and she had been through more than enough to earn her place among these soldiers. Anger flared to life within her.

"What did you say?" Erin let go of the younger man and pushed him aside. Her voice had gone quiet, and so had the crowd. She advanced on the grizzled man, a hand on the hilt of one of her knives.

"How dare you question the honor of your Lady and Commander. I challenge you-" Hugo began.

Erin raised a hand and stepped in front of Hugo, enraged by the entire situation. "I don't want your protection, Lord Hugo. I'm just as capable of taking care of myself as you are," Erin snapped.

"My Lady," Hugo began to say, but Erin interrupted.

"I'm not your lady. I am not anyone's lady but my own, and if someone is going to be defending my honor, it will be *me*." Erin snarled the last word as she focused her attention on the soldier who had insulted her. "Duel me, or are you not man enough to face me in a fair fight?"

The onlookers looked increasingly uneasy. One soldier clapped her opponent on the shoulder and muttered, "Win or lose, Silas, you're going to look bad. Good luck." The older soldier's face fell into unease.

"A thousand apologies, Lady Hart. I spoke out of turn." Silas bowed deeply at the waist, and Erin grew apoplectic with frustrated rage.

"Why are you apologizing to me when you would fight me if I were a man? I face as much danger and fight as well as any of you. Let's have it out, once and for all! I'm tired of this! Am I or am I not your leader! Are you or are you not loyal to my family and to Norcliff?! I won't tolerate your disrespect!" Erin began to pace and drew her knives to point them at the soldier, who flinched back. "No more! If you're going to fight my authority, then fight me!"

"Enough." Hugo grabbed her around the waist and bore her away from the growing crowd of onlookers. "Enough, Lady Erin. Your people are loyal to you."

"No, it's not enough! It's never enough! I'm never enough, and I've had it!" She raised a knife, and Hugo grabbed her arm while pushing her into the nearest tent.

"Calm yourself."

"Oh, that's rich, coming from you. Who was it, who spoke of duels? Don't tell me how to act. Don't tell me how to feel. My feelings and actions are mine and mine alone. We will speak as equals or not at all!"

Hugo released her and held his hands out in supplication. "Peace, lady. I mean you no insult."

Erin stalked away from him and stared angrily at the cloth wall of the tent, breathing deeply. "No, never mind. I know. There's no winning with some people. Fighting won't change their minds." She sank down to sit on a rickety folding stool made of cloth and wood, one of the few pieces of furniture available.

"I disagree." Hugo's voice softened. "I think you changed a great many minds today."

"Thank you for saying that."

"I'm not just saying it. I also believe it to be true."

Erin looked up into Hugo's deep brown eyes and noted the line of his jaw, hardened with resolve. She smiled slightly. "Thank you for your faith in me, then."

Outside the tent, they heard the Liana's faint voice. "What are you all lallygagging about here for? Get back to work. Go on, go!"

Hugo smiled gently at Erin. "Your friends want to help you, if you'll let them."

"I suppose so." Erin stood and sheathed her knives. "I'll have to deal with this insubordination, though."

"May I suggest you not go too harshly on the men just yet. They're as new to this as you are."

Erin laughed. "Is it so obvious that this is my first command?"

Hugo stepped forward to lay a hand on her shoulder. "No. I only recognize the signs because I experienced them myself."

Erin quieted and looked up at Hugo's earnest face. He was dear to her, she realized with a swelling of emotion that she didn't know what to do about. She stared and leaned closer as if drawn to him like a magnet, only to pull back sharply at the sound of footsteps outside. Hugo's hand fell back to his side, and he watched her intently as she stepped away. Liana parted the cloth of the tent door and walked inside with a huff. "What was that all about?" she asked.

"The men are uncertain." Erin threw her hands up. "Everything is uncertain!"

"They're untested," Liana said. "Of course they're uncertain. Don't despair." She smiled. "Frederick and I are beginning to cook dinner. Would you join us?"

"Yes, let's join them," Hugo said. "We accomplish nothing worrying about things we can't change."

"But what if we can change them?" Erin asked.

Hugo smiled. "Then we can change them in the morning." Erin sighed and nodded, and they went to have dinner.

The morning dawned cold and wet, and Erin joined Hugo at the campfire near their tents with a crick in her neck and the beginnings of a headache. Hugo grunted at her in greeting and offered her a mug of tea, which she took with gratitude. All around, she heard the sounds of the camp slowly stirring to life with the rustle of movement, the clanking of cookware, and the soft murmuring of voices. Erin and Hugo sipped at their tea in companionable silence until suddenly a great clanging sounded from the outskirts of camp. Erin sprang to her feet as Hugo reached for his sword.

"What's that?" Erin asked.

"Intruders!" someone yelled.

"Bandits!" another shouted.

"Fighting," Hugo said, his face grim, and then there was no more time for talking as cries of alarm rose from the camp. Erin and Hugo ran toward the source of the commotion.

Liana and Frederick intercepted them, and Frederick shouted over the rising noise, "An ambush!"

"Courtesy of the Mortons, most likely," Liana said.

"How did they know we were here?" Erin asked.

Hugo scowled. "They must be tracking you."

"We can address that later," Frederick said. "First, we must face the challenge in front of us."

"You're right," Erin said. "Frederick, you gather some men and scout the extent of the attack. Liana, look after him."

Liana nodded with a serious expression, and they ran off to disappear into the general hubbub of soldiers rushing out of their tents, buckling on their armor and weapons.

"Hugo, come with me," Erin said. "Let's show these bandits why nobody attacks the Harts or their allies and gets away with it."

"As my lady commands." Hugo gave a sharp smile, and they waded into battle.

As Erin traded blows with a heavyset bandit, she began to notice that some soldiers tumbling out of their tents were running away from the fight. Erin dispatched the bandit with a swipe of her knife to his throat and ran back, yelling to Hugo, "Hold the line!"

She grabbed at the shoulder of a fleeing young man, shoved his sword into his hand, and said, "Turn and fight!" She ran from man to man, turning them and shoving them toward the bandits, yelling, "Stand and face them! They want to take everything that you have! Fight back!" She ran until she could find no more deserters and looked to find Hugo near the center of an unbroken line of her fighters. They were defending the camp from what looked in the morning light to be a veritable army of bandits.

Erin rejoined Hugo, and soon they fell into a rhythm of watching each other's backs. One particularly enterprising bandit rushed at Erin from the side, and Erin yelled, "Hugo!" He looked toward her and beyond at the bandit, nodded, and held out his arm. Erin linked her arm in his as if joining a dance, and he hoisted her up along his side to give her added momentum for a devastating kick that Erin delivered to the bandit's head. Hugo set her back down and offered her a fell grin, which she returned.

Erin fought and fought until her arms ached and her blades ran with blood. She blinked sweat out of her eyes and looked to her left and right. The bandits were still coming. "Where are they all coming from?" she breathed.

"Milady! Milady!" A young man ran up to her, and Erin stepped behind Hugo, who moved to cover her space in the line. "Message from Lord Frederick. He wants to speak with you. He has an idea."

Erin gestured to where Hugo fought. "Take my place. Where's Frederick?"

The young man pointed to a gently rolling hill at the edge of the meadow, where Erin could make out a small cluster of soldiers. She nodded and ran toward the hill.

"Erin!" Frederick waved from his spot next to Liana at the center of the cluster. Erin joined them.

"What news?" she asked.

"We have a plan," Liana said. "It's like this. The bandits are relentless."

"Yes," Erin said.

"If it keeps going like this, they'll tire our soldiers out," Frederick continued.

"Indeed," Erin said.

"We need a way to force them into retreat," Liana said.

"I know," Erin said.

"I'm always in favor of collecting as much knowledge as possible, so as to make an informed decision," Frederick said.

Erin shifted her weight impatiently. "Go on, what's your point?"

"Frederick wants to send these men behind enemy lines to look for weaknesses," Liana said.

"We found a weak spot at their side where we can sneak through," Frederick said.

Erin looked at the men grouped before her. She recognized Silas, the man who was in the fight the day before, and frowned. "What secrets do you think these bandits possess? I'm loathe to send men away from the front, where they are needed."

"They may do you more good gathering information," Liana said. "It's worth a try. Things can't continue on as they are for much longer."

Erin looked at the fighting only to see one of her men fall beneath a bandit's axe. The line moved sluggishly to stop up the gap the fallen man created. "No, you're right," she said. "I'll go with them."

"Excellent!" Frederick clapped his hands together. "Now we can - wait, what?" He looked at Erin, who was walking toward Silas. "Lady Erin! You can't be spared!"

"You have things well in hand here," Erin said. "I'll join the search for a way to victory." She turned to Liana and clasped a hand on her shoulder. "Watch him well. We can't have the last Clairmaud heir fall on our watch."

"All right," Liana said.

Frederick huffed. "If you insist." He turned to Liana. "I can very well watch after myself, you know."

Liana smiled wryly. "Humor us."

Erin looked at the soldiers. "Who knows the way through the bandits' line of attack?"

Silas stepped forward. "I do, yer ladyship."

"Where do we go?" Erin asked.

"There's a river that runs right through the main area where the bandits are gathered. They ain't watching it. We though maybe we could swim up it, right into the center of them, and see what's what." Silas said.

"Show me," Erin said.

Silas led them to a river that was a few yards wide and many yards deep. It was overhung with tangles of branches. Reeds grew along the banks by the trees, and Erin plucked one from the ground.

"We can breathe through these," she said.

Silas nodded. "And stay underwater."

"Breathe through that? Not in a million years," one man said to mutterings from the others.

"If you aren't willing to go through with it, go back to the battle. Go, all of you who can't see this mission through," Erin said.

A large contingent of the men peeled away and made their way back to where the fighting was taking place, leaving Erin with just four, including Silas.

"Silas, I know," Erin said, "but what are your names?"

"I'm Thibault," said a blond-haired man with a mustache and pointed goatee.

"Alain," said a brown-haired, brown-eyed, stocky man.

"Call me Remy," said a man with shoulder length brown hair and hazel eyes.

"Well met," said Erin. She handed them reeds, then picked up a handful of mud. "Smear this all over for camouflage." She rubbed some into her hair until it looked brown and spread it over her clothes and skin.

"Good thing I'm not particularly attached to this outfit," Thibault said with good humor as he spread mud over his woven cotton shirt. Mud trickled down his neck and clumped his goatee together.

"I'll buy you all replacement clothing," Erin said.

"Much obliged, milady," Remy said as he waded into the river behind the cover of a low-hanging willow tree.

The rest followed, and before they put their heads underwater, Erin said, "Follow my lead." She had been trained well by Jax to navigate underwater, so she began to lead them upstream.

It was a different world underwater. The sounds of battle were distant and faint, and light filtered in rays through the water to make shifting patterns on the riverbed. Erin kept close to the overgrown reeds, and every few yards, when she found a well-hidden spot, she surfaced to get a look at the shore. Soon they were behind the line of battle, and Erin searched avidly for what information she could gather. She led the men behind a large bramble and tapped their shoulders to signal that they could surface.

Once they had wiped the water from their eyes and caught their breath, they began looking around at the scant belongings the bandits had brought with them. "What do you see?" Erin asked.

"They don't have much in the way of supplies," Alain said.

"Let's move down the line and gather more information," Erin said. They rushed from tree to tree, but they almost didn't need to have been so careful. Most of the bandits were focused on the fighting, save for one or two scouts near the wagons and pack horses gathered every so often along the line. Erin signaled the men to stop by one wagon, and they all hid in a cluster of trees to talk.

"The wagons must be precious to them, if they are sparing guards," said Silas.

"They might be precious enough to distract them from the fighting, don't you think?" Erin asked.

"If something were to go wrong…" Remy trailed off, eyes sparkling.

Erin nodded. "Let's set the wagons on fire and free the horses. At the very least, it will weaken them."

"I have a flint," said Alain.

"So do I," said Silas.

"Me too," said Erin. "Silas, you and Thibault go sabotage their supplies over to the left. Remy, Alain, and I will handle this side." She gestured to the large gathering before them and to the right.

"As milady commands," said Silas, and he and Thibault began to sneak away.

"I'll handle the nearest wagon," Erin told Remy and Alain. "You two go on to the next." They crept up to the wagons when the lone scout assigned to them wandered a little ways off, and Erin took out her flint while Remy and Alain went farther. Curious, she looked inside the wagon to find it was full of gold, silver, fine clothes, and scattered belongings.

"It's their loot," she whispered. Determined now, she struck a spark, and after a few tries one caught on the cloth piled inside the wagon. While it was catching fire, she hurried on to the next, and the next, until she, Alain, and Remy had gotten to them all. With one last look at the scout, who was still turned away, they cut the pack horses loose.

"Leave them," Erin whispered when Remy moved to urge them to run. "The fire will spook them soon enough, and it will give us time to get to the next cluster of wagons." Remy smiled in understanding and lowered his hand. They crept as quickly as they could to the next gathering of wagons and horses.

About midway down the line, shouts of alarm rose over the clash of the fighting. Erin looked to Alain and Remy. "They're onto us. Quickly, now." They rushed through sabotaging the wagons before them and ran into the cover of the forest as fighters began returning from the front lines to check on the hubbub. Erin, Alain, and Remy watched as they shouted and rushed to the stream for water, but it was too late. The fire had caught quickly, and the pack horses had already run away. Bandits turned from the battle and ran in increasing numbers to search for their loot, and Erin could see, farther down the line, that those whose wagons were still intact were driving them off away from the fighting. The Clairmaud forces soon followed, pressing their advantage, with Hugo leading. Erin waited until the Clairmaud forces had reached them, and then signaled that Alain and Remy could leave cover. She stepped out from behind her tree and clapped them both on the shoulders. "Well done, both of you."

"Well done yourself, milady," Remy said, and Alain nodded.

Erin smiled. "Off with you, now, go and celebrate our victory." They walked into the fray and soon disappeared in the general press of soldiers cheering as they ran the remaining bandits out of the area. Erin walked over to where Hugo stood his ground with his hands on his hips and overlooked the action.

Hugo did a double take as she walked up to him. "What happened to you?"

Erin looked down at her muddy self and grinned sheepishly. "Don't worry, it's self-inflicted. I covered myself in mud for camouflage."

"Ah." Hugo nodded. "They didn't see you coming, I'm sure. I barely saw you coming myself."

Erin laughed. "Flattery will get you nowhere."

"I would never. Your skill at stealth speaks for itself." Hugo offered her his arm. "May I escort you back to camp?"

Erin rested her hand in the crook of his elbow. "You may."

"What did you do to drive them off so effectively?"

"We found their ill-gotten gains stashed in wagons and on pack horses behind the lines. We freed the horses and set fire to the wagons," Erin said.

Hugo grinned. "That'll teach them not to trifle with you."

"I hope so." Erin looked ahead at the camp, where cookware was still scattered about campfires and tent flaps hung open in disarray. "I can only hope that we didn't lose too many men today."

Hugo sobered. "You led them well. There are always casualties in war, but you found a way to end the fighting. You should be glad of that."

"I don't know if I can manage glad," Erin said. "I'll let you know if I can at least feel relief, once the numbers are in. We'll have to make a count of everyone still here and figure out a way to get the belongings of the fallen back to their families."

"Your sergeants will know what to do better than you, in that area," Hugo said.

"I'll write as many of the letters to the families as I have time for," Erin said.

"You must prepare yourself for the eventuality that you do not have much time for it at all, after everything is said and done," Hugo said sadly.

Erin squared her jaw. "I'll make time."

Hugo bowed his head. "I'm sure you will." They reached their campsite. "Shall we finish our breakfast?"

Erin raised her eyebrows. "Breakfast? At a time like this?"

"One thing I've learned from my years of fighting is not to waste an opportunity to eat." Hugo righted their fallen pitcher of water and stoked the fire that had burned down to coals. He rummaged in the bag he had left by the fireside and took out a package wrapped in paper and tied with string. He opened it to show her bacon with a grin. "Would you like some?"

"I suppose so." Erin sighed and sat by the fire, and they ate their abandoned breakfast while soldiers slowly trickled back into the camp. Erin felt jittery after all the action, as if there was something she had left undone, but slowly she relaxed back into herself as she sat by Hugo and ate. "What a way to start the day," she said with a wry smile.

"What a way, indeed," Hugo replied.

21

A Solemn Duty

As THE SOLDIERS set the camp to rights, Erin went in search of Silas and Thibault. She found them sitting together on a fallen log, still streaked with mud, with cups of tea in their hands. She took a seat next to them. "You did good work," she told them.

"Eh." Silas shrugged. "You were the one to think it all up."

"You were the one to discover the way behind enemy lines to begin with," Erin said.

"She's got you there," Thibault said.

Silas grunted. "I suppose."

"When we get to Norcliff, I want you both to report to Jax. Find Remy and Alain and get them to go with you. Tell him I sent you," Erin said.

"What for?" Silas asked.

"It's up to you, but if you want, you can find a place among our spies and scouts for the coming battle," Erin said. "You've proven yourselves able to do the work."

Silas and Thibault looked at each other. Thibault shrugged. "All right," Silas said.

"Good." Erin rose from her seat. "I'll be seeing more of you, then." The men gave her nods in parting, and she resumed her walk of the camp. Every once in a while, she stopped to help someone tidy up their belongings or repair a torn tent or broken weapon. Eventually, she found her way to Frederick and Liana. Frederick was hovering over a healer, who was binding a wound in Liana's upper arm.

"I told you, I'm fine," Liana said. "Sit down before you fall down."

"You should tighten that bandage a little more, I think," Frederick told the healer, and Liana sighed.

"It's just a scratch," she said.

"Scratches get infected too," Frederick said.

Erin walked up to them. "What happened?"

"Liana got hurt protecting me," Frederick said.

"I'm not that hurt," Liana said.

Erin watched them bicker with amusement. "It's just as well that I'm going to order everyone to take the day to sort themselves out before we start marching again. Can you pass on the news, Frederick?"

"Of course." Frederick looked torn.

"After Liana is all squared away," Erin added.

Frederick looked relieved. "Yes, all right, then."

"Good." Erin went back to her tent to find Hugo still sitting in the same spot, and she joined him in his contemplation of the fire. She was beginning to feel the wear and tear from the fighting as her adrenaline wore off, and she was glad of the chance to let her mind and body rest for a while. They kept each other company in amiable silence until a sergeant walked up to her.

"Beggin' yer pardon, milady, milord," he said.

Erin looked at him for a moment until her sluggish brain supplied his name. "Sergeant Cartwright."

"We've a listing of the fallen for you."

Erin closed her eyes for a moment, then stood and reached out for the list. "Thank you."

"We've got next of kin listed for those who have it," Sergeant Cartwright said.

Erin examined the list. "I see. I'll get to work on letters to the families."

"Yes, milady." The sergeant saluted and went back to his duties, and Erin slowly sat back down, not taking her eyes off the list.

"It's longer than I would have liked," she said.

"It always is," Hugo said. "Do you want me to help you with the letters?"

"No, I'll do this. They were under my command, it should come from me," Erin said. She read through the list again and hesitated, then continued, "I just don't quite know what to say. I hardly knew these men."

"Don't pretend to," Hugo said. "Just tell what you know, which is that they were brave, and that you appreciate their service and sacrifice."

"Yes, you're right," Erin said. She rose again. "I'll start doing that now."

"Let me know if you need help," Hugo said.

"I will." She strode into her tent and sat at her traveling desk to begin. The words didn't come easily, and she spent a large amount of time staring at the tent wall. An idea came to her while she was staring, and she stepped out of the tent to find a soldier walking by. "You there!"

The soldier stopped and came closer. "Yes, milady?"

"Bring me Sergeant Cartwright, please."

"As you command, milady," the soldier said and ran off.

Erin went back to her writing, and soon a knock came on her tent pole. "Enter," she called.

Sergeant Cartwright stepped inside with a curious look. "You sent for me, milady?"

"Yes, I want to organize a memorial service for tonight. Can you tell the men, and set up an area for us to remember the fallen?" Erin asked.

The sergeant smiled. "I can, milady."

"Thank you."

The sergeant began to exit the tent, then paused. "Beggin' yer pardon, but I think what your doing is the right thing. These letters, the service. It may bring peace of mind to the folks who need it most."

Erin looked up and met the sergeant's eyes. "I hope so."

The sergeant nodded and left, and Erin got back to her letters for the rest of the day. When the shadows grew long, she pushed back her chair with a sigh and got up to find her friends. Hugo was by his tent, sharpening his sword, and Frederick and Liana were resting by the edge of the clearing, Liana dozing and Frederick reading. She gathered them for the memorial service, and they went to the little area where men had begun to congregate with what candles they had scrounged from the camp supply. They all turned to look at Erin with expectant faces when she arrived.

"They want to hear from their commander," Hugo said.

"Oh dear," Erin said softly.

"Go on," Liana whispered and gave Erin a little push.

Feeling awkward and uncertain, Erin walked to the center of the group. She stood there for a moment and felt the weight of everyone's eyes upon her, and then she cleared her throat. "We have faced our first test, and we've prevailed. But this came at a terrible cost. Every day we fight, we put our lives at risk. Today, some paid the ultimate price. It could have been any of us. How we treat our fallen defines who we are as a people. Let us remember those brave men who fought and died so that we all might one day enjoy safety and prosperity once again. Let us grieve tonight, so that we can rise again to fight tomorrow. For these fallen wouldn't want us to give up. They sacrificed themselves so that we could go on." Erin looked at her feet, then out at the crowd. She was out of words. The men nodded and murmured in agreement as she stepped back to the outside of the circle where her friends stood.

"Well spoken," Hugo said. Frederick nodded, and Liana clapped Erin on the shoulder.

It was a somber walk back to her tent that night. In her mind's eye she could still see the bodies of the fallen, and as she laid down to rest, she knew their loss would linger.

The rest of the march back to Hart Keep was uneventful, and when they rounded the corner and saw the town, Erin felt an easing in her chest of tension that she hadn't noticed she was carrying. The flags with her parents' standards flew from the battlements, and Erin's heart felt light to see them. There was a general hubbub as the Clairmaud forces merged with the people of Norcliff, and Erin wouldn't have been able to keep order without the help of her friends shouting instructions to the sergeants and soldiers. They proceeded down the street to cheers from the townspeople, and Erin smiled to see the bright, newly hopeful faces of her people. At the end of the road, she found her parents waiting at the doors of the keep to greet them.

"Erin." Evelyn came forward to hug her, with Finley close behind.

"Mom, Dad," Erin said warmly.

Finley stepped back from hugging Erin to nod at Liana and Frederick and give Hugo a measuring look. "Lord Hugo, still with us, I see."

Hugo straightened under the scrutiny. "Indeed."

"Well." Finley turned back to Erin. "How did your trip go?"

"Smoothly enough, save for a battle with bandits on the way," Erin said.

"Bandits! Are you all right?" Evelyn asked.

"We're all fine, though we suffered some losses," Erin said.

"The prince's doing, I presume," Finley said.

"No doubt," said Erin.

Jax strode through the front doors with a sheaf of papers in one hand. "Good, you're back. Come in here, I have news."

The group all followed Jax back inside, and once they were safely ensconced in the library, Jax turned to speak. "Reports have come from the north of the approach of an army. They'll be here in a matter of hours. My scouts are watching their movements as we speak. Hundreds of men are on the move, and if we don't get reinforcements before they arrive, we could very easily be overwhelmed."

Hugo stepped forward. "My men won't abandon you to your fate."

"We'll see," Finley said evenly. "Duke Bavencian's forces are also on their way here."

"Where is the duke?" Erin asked.

"I believe he's still in his rooms," Evelyn said. "He didn't join us for breakfast."

"His nephew's actions have troubled him greatly," Finley said.

"We should strike out at the prince and the Mortons before the Varnallans arrive, while we have the advantage," Erin said.

"Don't be too hasty," Finley said. "We should wait until our allies have arrived. Then we'll be in the best position to attack."

"But even now they're plotting, off in Morton Manor. I know it," Erin said. "We can't keep giving them opportunities to come up with plans."

"I agree with Lord Hart," Jax said. "The keep will hold until our allies arrive, should the northerners get here before they do."

"But -" Erin began before her mother stepped forward.

"We all have much to think on, especially with this news. I'll send a page to inform the duke. Now, please, get what rest you can after your journey," Evelyn said.

"Erin, a word," Finley said as everyone filed out of the room. Evelyn hung back as well.

"What is it, Father?" Erin asked.

Finley waited until the door swung closed behind Hugo to speak. "That man, Lord Hugo, I'm not so sure you should keep spending time with him."

Erin sighed, a breath away from rolling her eyes. "Dad, he's fine."

"Who knows how he'll act, when push comes to shove. You can't trust mercenaries like that. Now, I know you've vouched for him, but -" Finley began only to be cut off by Evelyn.

"Dear, let Erin tell us why she has chosen to give this man her trust."

Erin took a moment to collect her thoughts. She didn't know how to put into words the feelings she was developing for him, especially to her parents, so she began with something simpler. "He's proven himself to be a courageous fighter. I learned that the moment I first saw him. More than that, he's seen me through thick and thin and stuck by my side through it all. I know that he'll prove himself worthy in the coming battle, and I know that soon you, too, will learn of his valor and kindness."

Finley frowned and crossed his arms. "You speak as if...as if -"

Evelyn cut him off again with a hand on his arm. "That's wonderful, dear. I'm sure your father and I will learn to trust him with time."

"Hmph." Finley looked away.

"Dear?" Evelyn asked.

"Yes, fine, I'll reserve judgement," Finley said.

Erin stood on tiptoe to kiss her father's cheek. "Thank you."

Finley smiled grudgingly. "Off with you."

Erin grinned and skipped out of the room. The hall was empty, so she went in search of her friends. Frederick and Liana had disappeared off somewhere, but Erin found Hugo in the stables brushing his horse.

"Erin," Hugo said and put down his brush.

Erin walked up to Hugo's horse and stroked his nose. "What's his name?"

"Fortitude."

Erin nodded. "A worthy name."

"For a worthy mount," Hugo said. "He's carried me through many battles." Hugo stepped out of the stall to come closer to Erin, and Erin looked up at him and giggled. Hugo's brow wrinkled in confusion. "What?"

"There's a piece of straw in your hair." Erin reached up and plucked the straw out of Hugo's hair, which brought her closer to him. He looked down at the straw in her hand, then met her eyes with a smile. His hair was a little unkempt, and his brown eyes were soft as they looked at her. Erin stopped laughing and stared, then took a step back. "Sorry," she said, and she let the straw fall to straighten her skirts.

Hugo took another step forward to capture Erin's hand in his own. "There's nothing to apologize for. If I spent the rest of my days making you laugh, I would consider it a life well lived."

Erin looked up at Hugo and wondered at how she had somehow found him, somehow found another chance at love when she had thought all her chances had run out. She reached up and pushed some of Hugo's black hair behind his ear. "If you don't take better care of your hair," she said with a grin, "you just may do that." She danced out of reach as Hugo made an offended sound and moved to brush her hand away. "Shall we go into town? Might as well do something while we wait."

"As my lady desires." Hugo offered her his arm, and she took it.

It was a relief to be wandering the town now that her parents were back. Erin no longer felt the pressure to lead, and she was allowed to meld into the hustle and bustle of people a little more, though the townspeople still recognized her as Lady Erin. "Let's see how the preparations are going," Erin suggested, and Hugo nodded. They walked to the outer walls, where a familiar man was directing people with pots of pitch. "Eliot Cooper, is that you?" Erin asked.

Eliot stopped and looked over at her before sketching an abbreviated bow. "Lady Erin, good to see you."

"So you knew it was me all along."

"Difficult not to, milady."

"Are you in charge of preparations here, again?" Erin asked.

"Some of them," Eliot said. "We're setting out the pitch so that the archers can light their arrows on fire."

"Can we help?" Erin asked.

"I couldn't impose upon you, my lord and lady," Eliot said, already turning to direct another person holding more pots.

Erin let go of Hugo's arm and straightened to her full height. "Let us help," she said.

Eliot gave Erin another glance and sighed. "Very well. You can help fill the pots over here." He pointed them to a nearby table.

Erin nodded and led an amused Hugo over. "How is your family preparing for battle?" Erin asked Eliot.

"Ma is busy stitching leather armor for those who can't afford chain mail, and Pa is working on sharpening his many knives. He's a butcher," Eliot said.

"Do you have any siblings?" Erin asked.

Eliot shook his head. "No, just me. It keeps all their attention on me. They'd rather I not have such a visible role, but I have the ability, and someone needs to do it."

"Yes," Erin said. "Someone does need to do it. You're a valuable addition to our forces. Without people like you volunteering their talents, I don't know where we'd be."

Eliot gave Erin a measuring look. "The same goes for you, you know. We all know what you did to get your parents back here. We all appreciate that you went to the capital to plead on our behalf to the king. It doesn't matter how it turned out. It matters that you did it."

Erin blinked. She had seen her ill-fated trip to the capital as something to regret, but the way Eliot put it made her see it in a different light. "I guess I'm glad, then," she said slowly. "Yes, I'm glad I did it, even though it turned out badly."

"Turned out badly how?" Hugo asked.

Erin stopped what she was doing, frozen with newfound

apprehension. How would Hugo see her, if he heard how things had really gone? What should she say to him about what the prince had done to her?

"The king refused to aid us, of course," Eliot said before Erin could speak.

Hugo sighed. "The king does not take the people's concerns to heart. My men and I have been hired many times by nobles and merchants who had nowhere else to turn for their protection. Don't feel as though you failed your people, Erin."

Erin forced a smile and nodded, and they went back to their preparations. Once things were going smoothly, Eliot left them to go back to directing others. The day passed slowly for Erin with the heavy thoughts that ran through her mind. She didn't know how to tell Hugo about her damaged reputation. She didn't know what to say or when to say it. She tried to focus all of her attention on her work, but it was no use. She stopped what she was doing and looked at Hugo. Could she trust him with this information? Could she trust him not to turn on her? The other nobles at court had changed the way they had treated her so quickly, but they hadn't been through what she and Hugo had been through together.

Hugo noticed her eyes on him and raised an eyebrow. "What is it?"

"There's something about me you should know, since you're courting me," Erin said.

Hugo set down his pot and gave her his full attention. "What?"

"When I was at the capital, I..." She trailed off, at a loss for words. It was difficult going back to that time. "Something happened between me and the prince."

Hugo frowned. "What happened?"

Erin fiddled with one of the bottles of oil. "He stole a kiss from me. No," she shook her head. "More than that." She took a breath. "He held me against the wall and forced me to kiss him." She couldn't look up, couldn't see Hugo's reaction. She forced herself to keep going. "I didn't do anything to stop it. I fear it only went no further because a maid interrupted us."

Out of the corner of her eye, she could see Hugo's feet as he stepped closer. "Have you told anyone about this? Your parents?"

"No. Jax and Liana know. And the whole court thinks I threw myself at him." Erin felt her throat clog up. "I might as well have. I didn't even put up a fight." Her eyes burned with unshed tears.

"It's not your fault." Hugo said. Erin took a breath and stole a glance at him. He held out his arms to her. "You did nothing wrong."

Erin stepped into Hugo's embrace as a great weight fell from her shoulders. She hadn't realized she had been carrying guilt from the events in the palace, but it seemed that she had. No longer, she thought, no more, and she buried her nose in between Hugo's neck and shoulder and returned his embrace.

"Milady!" Erin heard someone call, and she sprang back from Hugo, face burning.

"I wasn't - we weren't - what?" she stuttered as a page ran up to them.

"The Mortons and the prince approach!" the page said.

"Oh." Erin felt her stomach turn over with anxiety. "Thank you for the news." The page bowed and ran off again. She turned to Hugo. "They're here."

"Good," Hugo said with burning dark eyes. "I'd like to show the prince my displeasure with him and his ilk. Let them come. We're ready."

"You're right," Erin looked over to the battlements where calls were being sent from group to group and troops were running to their posts. "We're ready to face them."

22

The Starting Strike

ERIN CLIMBED TO the top of the outer wall with Hugo close behind. She watched as the first line of soldiers garbed in red and black appeared, followed by another line, and then more. Her stomach swooped down, and she felt a chill as the prince's flag appeared next to the Morton one.

"How dare they," she muttered.

"Hmm?" Hugo turned to her.

"How dare they come here so brazenly, with all their greed and corruption out in the open, flags on display, and think they can force us to bend to their will." Erin gritted her teeth. "They can think again." She whipped around and marched her way back to the keep as villagers ran to and fro around her, and Hugo strode alongside her. She met with Liana at the doors.

"I'll help you into your armor," Liana said.

Erin grasped Liana's hands and held them for a minute, as if they might stop hers from shaking. "Thank you," she said. Hugo left them to make his own preparations, while Erin and Liana went to Erin's rooms.

Erin stood before the mirror as Liana buckled her armor on and wondered at the passing of time. Was it only a few short weeks ago that she had stood in the same spot in her wedding gown? She looked herself in the eye. Her face was pale and her lips were pressed together in a stubborn, grim line. Her armor was well-polished, but that, too, might soon change. Her wedding gown had looked nice at the start, too.

"How quickly circumstances can change," she murmured. "How quickly we can change, too."

"Yes," Liana said. She tightened the last strap and stepped back. "You're ready."

"Am I?" Erin took one last look at herself in the mirror and lifted her chin defiantly. "I'll have to be."

Liana rested a hand on her shoulder. "You will be."

Erin nodded and went to help Liana into her own armor. Soon they were as prepared as they were going to get, and they went down into the main hall to meet with the others.

Finley cut a striking figure in his silver armor with the family stag engraved on the breastplate. He was near the doors, speaking with Jax. Evelyn wore leathers and chain mail instead of armor, to allow for greater movement. She had a large satchel slung over her shoulder that was full of bandages and medicinal plants.

"We have to at least try to negotiate with these people," Finley said.

"Anything they offer will come at a steep price," Jax said.

"Nevertheless," Finley said. He adjusted his underlying chain mail and strode out the door.

"Father!" Erin called and followed him.

Finley stopped by his warhorse. "What is it, Erin?"

Erin hesitated. What could she say that would be useful to him, she wondered. Did he know of what had happened to her in the capital? Had Jax told him? Should she? "Be careful," she said at last. "They can't be trusted."

Finley smiled warmly at her, though his eyes remained worried and grave. "I'll do my best for our family and our people," he said, and then he mounted his horse and rode away with his honor guard behind him.

Erin turned back to find Hugo, Liana, and Frederick waiting for her at the front doors. "Let's follow him," she said. "They don't want peace, they want dominion over us. We have to be ready to fight."

The four of them rode ahead of the rest of their party to the outermost wall of town to see the Morton army waiting there for them through the bars of the main gate. Bandits wearing garb of no particular color hung around the edges of the Morton lines. Hugo scowled. "They're as good as admitting that they've set that lawless scourge upon us," he said.

"They think they won't face consequences for their actions," Erin said, reining her horse in to look at the enemy lines. "We'll teach them differently."

Hugo grinned at her and bowed his head. "Well said."

They watched from afar as Finley met with Lord Morton and Prince Thomas in the empty field between their two armies, but it was difficult to tell how the meeting went until Finley turned his horse around and made to ride back. The prince raised his arm, and an archer aimed at Finley's back.

"Father!" Erin shouted, but she was too far away to stop the arrow that flew into Finley's side. He curled in on himself but stayed on his horse, which carried him out of range. Evelyn met him at the gate to help him from his horse and look at the wound. Erin knelt by her mother's side and tried to help while fury burned deep in her gut.

Behind her, Hugo said, "They have no honor."

Erin held out a strip of gauze to her mother and snapped, "Are you surprised?"

Hugo laid a hand on her shoulder in silent support, then said, "Not at all. We'll crush them."

"I can't fathom why they would prefer war to peace," Finley struggled to say to Evelyn as she finished cleaning his wound. "They barely listened to my offer before refusing me."

"Some people just don't understand the cost of war," Evelyn said. She began to apply a bandage.

"Don't worry, Dad. I'll look after our people, and so will Jax. You rest," Erin said.

"Be careful," Finley said to Erin before Evelyn directed some nearby guards to pick Finley up and carry him to the nearest healing tent, where a cot waited for him.

Erin got back to her feet and faced her friends. "There's no other option. We must fight." She led them to the command tent, where Jax stood looking over a map.

"Ah, there you are," he said. "The battle has begun. The outer wall doesn't have many fortifications. I fear we'll have to fall back to the second wall soon. Go and have a look and tell me what you think. Frederick, Liana, stay here and help me plan our next move. Hugo, watch out for her." Jax looked sharply at Hugo, who nodded.

Erin and Hugo climbed up the nearby watchtower to gain a view of the fighting, and Erin was dismayed at what she saw. The addition of the bandits to the Morton's forces gave them an edge over the people of Norcliff that Erin could see all too clearly. The red and black wave of the Morton army had already almost overtaken the outer wall. Even now, soldiers were attempting to climb it, and the Norcliff guard was just barely holding them at bay. Erin looked over the outer ring of town with worry. She didn't know how she could bear to see the homes of her people looted and burned.

"Take heart," Hugo said.

Erin turned and looked at him. "How?"

"My army is less than a day's march away. I received a letter from Arnau just this morning." Hugo stepped closer and laid a hand on her shoulder. "You're not alone."

Erin rested her hand over his. "Thank you for reminding me." She turned to look over the battle once more. "Let's go and plan how to hold our defenses until help arrives."

On their way back to Jax, they came across Eliot Cooper talking to a mutinous looking middle aged man. "Leave your things! You must evacuate to the second ring right now," Eliot implored, but the man wouldn't budge, and his family stood still as stones behind him. Eliot gestured at the general chaos. "Look around you! There's no time to waste." He saw Erin and Hugo in the crowd of people making their way to safety behind the second ring of walls. "Good, you're here. Order this man and his family to leave immediately."

Erin walked closer and looked at the frightened faces of the man's family. She met the man's narrowed eyes. "You must leave," she said. "Your house is made up only of things, things that can be replaced. People are priceless. Not a day goes by that I don't miss Marc, my fiancé. But he's gone, never to return, except maybe in the afterlife. If I lose my father today, I don't know what I'll do. I know what it's like to lose people, and I don't want that for you." She looked at Hugo. "I've learned to value the people I do have in my life all the more because of it." She met the eyes of the man and his wife. "Please, leave while it's still safe. Your lives are more important than any trinket or building."

The man uncrossed his arms slowly, and his face softened. "Yes, milady," he said.

"Finally!" Eliot shepherded the family toward the gate to the second ring, then came back to Erin. "Can you help us get the people to safety? Some won't listen to me, but maybe they'll listen to you."

"All right," Erin said, and the three of them went from house to house for what felt like hours. The sounds of battle kept drawing closer, and when Erin turned from one of the last houses on the street, she found an arrow fallen at her feet. "It's time to get behind the second wall," she told Eliot and Hugo. "Is there anyone left?"

Eliot consulted his map. "One last street, though they should have evacuated already, they're so close to the fighting."

"Hugo and I will go, you get to safety," Erin said. "Make sure everybody made it."

"Ok. See you there," Eliot said, and he waved and ran toward the nearest gate through the second wall.

Erin and Hugo ran in the opposite direction to the street Eliot had pointed out and found abandoned chaos. Discarded belongings lay strewn across the cobblestones, and doors hung open, swaying on their hinges in the light breeze. They walked from one house to the next to check for stragglers.

"Found one!" Hugo called to Erin at one house. She joined him to see a little girl clutching at a stuffed rabbit, hidden in a closet. Hugo crouched and held out a hand. "Where is your family, little one?" he asked in a gruff, gentle tone.

"I don't know." The girl looked up at them with round eyes.

"Shall we go find them?" Hugo asked.

The little girl appeared to think about it for a moment. "Ok," she said. She stepped forward and put her hand in Hugo's.

"That's just about the last of them," Erin said. "One last house."

The final house on the street was a little more decorated than the rest, and it had a small garden with shrubbery groomed into various shapes. Erin went ahead to check inside, with Hugo and the little girl following.

"I don't see anybody," Erin called from the kitchen, where a meal lay unfinished on the table. She went back into the hall where Hugo and the girl waited. She smiled at the girl. "Let's go. Your family must be worried sick. What's your na-" She broke off as a door opened behind Hugo and a bandit rushed forward with a raised sword. Hugo turned, and instead of drawing his weapon, he moved to shield the girl from attack.

"Look out!" Erin drew her sword and sprang forward to parry the blow aimed for Hugo's heart. The bandit stuttered to a halt, seeming surprised that his sneak attack had met with resistance, and Erin used the moment's confusion to slice open the bandit's throat. He bowled over, dead before he hit the ground.

Erin turned to Hugo. "Are you all right?" She raised her hand to touch Hugo's breastplate where the bandit's sword had aimed. "He didn't get you, did he?"

Hugo laid his hand over Erin's. "No. You saved me again." He looked down at the girl, who stared with a pale face at the fallen bandit. He stepped in between the girl and the corpse to block her view. "That was close, wasn't it? Lucky we had Lady Erin to protect us."

It had indeed been close, Erin thought. One misstep, and Hugo could have died. Another dead, just like Marc. Was life just full of near-misses and deadly mistakes? How could she guarantee Hugo would live long enough to build a life with her, she wondered. She couldn't, she answered herself. They only had the moment, one after the next, and if they continued to be lucky, those moments might add up to a lifetime.

"Let's get you to safety," Erin told the girl, and they walked as quickly as they could to the nearest gate. It was already closed. Erin knocked on the door.

"Who goes there?" asked a guard.

"Lady Erin, Lord Hugo, and..." Erin looked at the girl. " I never did get your name."

"Priscilla Hopkins," the girl said shyly.

"And Priscilla Hopkins," Erin told the guard.

The guard's head appeared in the little window set in the door, and his eyes widened. "Lady Erin!" He disappeared again, and Erin could hear bolts unlocking. The doors to the gate swung open, and they stepped through into the general disarray of the people on the other side.

"Thank you," Erin said to the bowing guard. "Can you tell me where we might find Eliot Cooper?"

"Last I heard, he was at the west watchtower, handing out weapons," the guard said.

Erin nodded. "Follow me," she told Hugo and the girl, and they began to pick their way through the crowded streets. Townspeople from the outer areas lined the roads with their belongings gathered about them. Erin found it difficult to meet their desperate, worried eyes, so she focused on her goal of the watchtower that rose overhead a few blocks away.

When they reached it, they found a line of men and women stretching out the door. Erin stopped by one woman, a brunette with a resolute expression on her face, to ask, "What are you waiting for?"

"A weapon," the woman said. "They've opened up the armory to anyone willing to fight."

"Ah," Erin said. She began to walk to the front of the line.

"You have the women fight in battle?" Hugo asked.

"Is it so strange? I fight. The women are in the same amount of danger as the men, and have an equal right to defend themselves," Erin said.

"Who watches the children?" Hugo asked.

"That's up to the parents. Whoever is best suited to the task, I'd imagine," Erin said.

Hugo hummed thoughtfully.

"I can watch myself," Priscilla said. "I'm old enough."

Erin smiled. "Even so, I think your family will be relieved to see you."

They reached the head of the line where Eliot stood with a list he was writing names onto. He looked up and saw them. "Lady Erin, we meet again," he said briskly.

"Eliot, have you heard of a Hopkins family looking for their daughter, Priscilla?" Erin asked.

"Yes, the mother is upstairs, waiting for news," said Eliot. He looked at Priscilla. "You found her?"

Erin nodded.

"Finally, something good to share," he said.

They went upstairs to find a woman with graying hair and a face lined with worry. The moment she caught sight of them, she shouted, "Priscilla!"

"Mommy!" Priscilla ran into her mother's open arms.

"We thought we'd lost you," Priscilla's mother sobbed. She clutched her daughter to her, then looked up at Erin and Hugo. "Thank you, Lady Erin, thank you."

Erin smiled. "You're welcome," she said. She and Hugo stood and basked for a moment in the joy and relief of the reunion, then Erin turned to Hugo and said, "We have to find Jax and get news about the state of the battle."

Hugo nodded. "Lead the way."

Erin took Hugo to the central guard tower of the second wall, where a makeshift command center was set up. Jax stood on the battlements with a spyglass. "There you are," he said.

"How goes the battle?" Erin asked.

"Badly," Jax said. "With the bandits involved, we're outnumbered. We're trying to recruit townspeople to fill the gap, but it's slow going."

"Where do you want us to go?" Erin asked. "Where can we be the greatest help?"

Jax considered her. "The soldiers are dispirited after their retreat to the second wall, no matter how strategically sound the move was. Go find a spot where the fighting is particularly bad, and join them. It may raise morale."

"Ok," Erin said.

Jax waved her over and pointed to a spot on a map. "I'd look here first. I hear they're struggling there."

"Good idea," Erin said. She turned to leave, Hugo following.

Jax was right. When they reached the spot he had pointed out to them, they found soldiers with drawn, tired faces who moved sluggishly. Without fanfare, Erin drew her sword and blocked an attack on a soldier who looked at her with surprised gratitude, then did a double take. "Lady Erin!" he exclaimed. Her name ran like wildfire through the troops.

Hugo smiled at her as he raised his own sword. "No speech?"

"No time," Erin grunted as she blocked another swing.

With renewed vigor, the soldiers were able to reclaim their section of the wall and drive back the invading force, but the sight that greeted them was not encouraging. Erin found it difficult not to despair as she looked from left to right and saw a sea of black and red interspersed with the motley assortment of colors from the bandits. She clenched her jaw and cut at a rope one such bandit was attempting to use to climb up the wall.

Hugo paused after pushing away a hastily assembled ladder. "Do you hear that?"

"Hear what?" Erin asked. She listened, but all she could hear was fighting.

"I thought I heard..." Hugo trailed off and peered into the distance.

Suddenly, far away, Erin could hear the faint blowing of a horn. "What's that?"

A grin broke through the grime from fighting that caked Hugo's face. "That would be Arnau coming to rescue us."

"Your men?" Erin felt a lightness rise within her and recognized it as hope. She searched the edge of the forest for the telltale glint of armor.

There was nothing for a few long minutes, and then a line of men in armor mounted on sturdy, rugged warhorses broke through the trees. "There they are!" Hugo exclaimed as he fought back a Morton soldier.

Hugo's army was a welcome sight coming upon the battle and breaking through the Morton lines with brutal efficiency. "We have to open the gates, or they'll be caught between the Mortons and the wall," Erin yelled, and she ran to the main gate with Hugo not far behind. "Open the gate!" she yelled to the guards stationed there. "Lord Hugo's army arrives!"

A wizened guard looked at her doubtfully, then peered through the peephole in the door. His eyes widened. "Yes, milady," he said, and the guards opened the gate just in time for Hugo's forces to reach the wall. The Castelli soldiers rode through the gate in groups. The men were battle-hardened and austere with armor that was well-made but not showy, and their gear had the little nicks and scratches that came from use. Some stayed out behind the walls, and Erin could see them driving the Morton forces back into the forest.

"Arnau!" Hugo called out, and Arnau led his horse forward from among the men.

"I see you've gotten yourself into trouble again, my lord. Though this time it's because of a lady, which I must say is new for you," Arnau said dryly.

Hugo laughed. "Thank you for getting me out of trouble once again, Arnau."

Arnau dismounted, and they clasped hands. He gave Erin a nod. "Milady."

"Hello, Arnau," Erin said. "Thank you for bringing such badly needed help to us. You can see for yourself the dire situation we're in."

Arnau smiled faintly. "You're welcome, milady. The bandits are trouble for us, too, so we're helping ourselves as much as we're helping you."

"Even so," Erin pressed.

Hugo clapped a hand on Arnau's shoulder. "Come, we must plan how to strike back at these foul men, now that reinforcements have arrived."

23
The Final Blow

EVERYONE MET AT the keep as night fell. Finley was resting in his chambers with Evelyn holding vigil over him. Erin visited the moment she returned and was encouraged to see he had regained some color in his cheeks as he slept. She then rejoined Jax, Liana, Frederick, Hugo, and Arnau in the library.

"Now is the time to strike," Erin said as Liana and Frederick helped Jax arrange his maps. "The Morton forces are discouraged and in retreat. We must drive them away from our lands once and for all."

"Patience, Erin," Jax said. "Our people are tired. Let them rest. There'll be plenty of time to drive the Mortons out in the morning, and fewer lives will be lost."

"What if something happens to rally the Morton spirits tomorrow? What of the Varnallans?" Erin asked. "We must strike while the iron is hot!"

"No, Erin!" Jax snapped. "You're not listening. You were wrong when you wanted to attack early before, and you're wrong now. If you can't contribute to the conversation, then be silent!"

Erin scowled. "I might as well not be here, then, for all that you're listening to me!" Enraged, she stormed out of the library and to her room. She fumed and paced, but once she had calmed down a little, she wondered if Jax was right. She didn't think he was, for all his wisdom and experience. She felt, deep in her gut, that they couldn't waste a second in dealing with the enemy.

Someone knocked at her door. "Erin?" It was Liana's voice. Erin walked over and let her in.

"There you are," Liana said. She went to sit in one of Erin's armchairs. "Jax went through a lot today. Don't take his scolding to heart. He just wants to be careful, you know that."

"Yes, but I also know, in the depths of my soul, that we can't take our eyes off these treacherous villains for even a moment," Erin said. She began to pace again.

"Then don't," Liana said.

"Don't what?" Erin asked.

"Don't take your eyes off them." Liana smiled slyly. "Nothing's stopping you from sneaking into their camp to learn the lay of the land."

Erin paused in her movements and thought it over. Slowly, she started to smile, too. "No, nothing's stopping me. Quick, help me into my armor."

Liana steepled her hands. "Not your armor, this time. It would be difficult to be stealthy in that."

"Yes, you're right," Erin said.

"A dress and a cloak, I think." Liana stood and went to Erin's wardrobe. "You'll be underestimated as a woman, and perhaps you might be able to go where a soldier could not." She pulled out one of Erin's plainer dresses and a cloak made of black velvet.

Erin held up the dress and nodded. As she changed into her outfit, Liana got out Erin's favorite set of knives and helped her hide them about her person. Erin looked at her reflection in the mirror. She seemed nondescript and unremarkable, perfect for sneaking about. She frowned in thought. "Wait." A fell sort of fancy took her, and from her travel bags, she found the vial of deadly lip paint and its antidote that Madame Neigely had given her. She took the antidote and carefully applied the paint to her lips. If the prince, or any other man, trespassed upon her on this night, he would learn to regret it, she thought with satisfaction. Liana put Erin's hair up with a pair of sharp pins, good for stabbing and lockpicking, and then Erin was ready.

Erin clasped Liana's hand. "Thank you."

"Happy hunting," Liana said. Erin smiled, but she couldn't get out the traditional family farewell, so she nodded instead. She took the servants' way out of the keep with her hood over her hair and her eyes averted from those she passed. She crept through the front courtyard, keeping a wary eye out for anyone who might recognize her, and got to the gate before she heard a voice come from the shadows.

"I thought I might find you here." Hugo stepped into the light.

Erin jumped in surprise, but then she squared her shoulders resolutely. "You can't stop me."

"I don't intend to," Hugo said. "I only mean to ask you to please watch out for yourself and come back to me unharmed."

Erin looked past him to the village beyond the gate. "I'll do my best," she said.

Hugo smiled grimly. "Then go, with my best wishes for success in your endeavors."

"Thank you," Erin said. She felt an urge to kiss him on the cheek, but, mindful of the lip paint she wore, she touched him on the arm instead. She would kiss him when she returned, she decided. Erin waved and walked into town before anyone else could waylay her. She sneaked her way through the side door at the outer gate while the guards napped at their posts, and then she was out in the open. She stole across the land dividing the two armies as quietly as she could and hoped the darkness of her cloak would keep anyone from seeing her.

Erin came upon the first Morton sentry at the edge of the forest and was glad for the cover the trees offered. He was alert and doing his job well, looking this way and that and listening carefully. She hid behind a large tree many paces away and thought up a plan to deal with him. She threw a rock, then another closer to her, and then she snapped some twigs and rustled some branches. The sentry's gaze whipped around to her direction, and he drew his sword. Erin picked up a large rock and climbed a little way up the tree, just in time as the sentry walked over to investigate. She waited until he was beneath her, and then she threw the rock at his head. While he was stunned from the blow, she jumped from her branch to fall upon him and swiftly knocked him unconscious.

"There," she whispered as she stepped back. She went closer to the enemy camp, on guard for more sentries, but he must have been the only one assigned to his area, because she didn't run into anyone else until she found the guards right at the edge of camp.

"Right," she whispered, "Here goes nothing." She nervously checked that her hood covered her hair. Then she walked into the torchlight, doing her best to make her stride seductive but casual instead of furtive.

"Who goes there?" one of the guards asked.

"Just a lonely lady out looking for some fun," she said playfully. She walked up to the guard who spoke and gave him a flirtatious look. "When do you get off duty?"

The guard's stance relaxed and became more open, and a hint of a smile crept across his lips. He opened his mouth to speak but was interrupted.

"Who's that?" another guard asked.

"Just some camp follower," the first guard said.

"Send her on her way, then. We're here to keep watch, not make friends!"

"Yes, sir," the first guard said. "You heard him, move along. You'll have to find your fun elsewhere. I don't get off duty until morning."

Erin made a show of pouting but was quick to move farther into camp, relieved that her disguise was working. The Morton camp was orderly and quiet. Few soldiers walked the paths between tents, and even fewer talked. Erin walked toward the center of the camp in the hopes of finding information on their plans. While she was walking, she overheard a strange dialect coming out of one of the tents. She went closer to try and make sense of it only to step back in surprise as a man burst out of the tent and began to stalk away. Erin could tell he was from Varnall by the furs he wore over his armor and the strange words he was now muttering to himself, and she could tell he was a warlord by the quality of his gear and the necklace of fangs he wore around his neck. She wondered if the Varnallans had already arrived and began to follow the warlord at a distance.

He led her to another section of the camp, removed from the Morton one. Here, the tents were in worse repair, but the same sense of order reigned. Erin stopped in shock at the outskirts of this new section of camp, and her stomach sank. How had they arrived without anyone from her side noticing, she wondered. She saw that many of the tents were still in the process of being put up. They must have arrived as night fell, or shortly thereafter.

Erin ventured into the Varnallan section of camp, intent on getting a count of how many there were. She wandered from row to row, taking care to appear aimless, and counted an ever growing number of soldiers. As the night and her count wore on, she grew more and more worried. There were so many of them. She had to get this news to Jax, she thought as she finally stood at the outskirts of the northerners' camp. First, she decided, she would go back to the command center of the Morton area of the camp and find out what she could of their plans. They would need every advantage they could get.

She went to where the tents were larger and nicer looking and stood in indecision for a moment. The tent with the prince's flag would likely hold the most valuable information, but it might also hold the prince. The Morton tent next to it might have information, too, but she wasn't particularly interested in running into Ardent Morton either. She looked to the sky. Dawn was breaking. She had to make a decision, fast. She sighed. She supposed the most valuable information would be with the prince. She raised her chin in determination. She'd have to enter the tent like she belonged or risk looking suspicious. Her head held high, she strode through the entrance, her heart in her throat.

The tent was empty. Erin sighed in relief and walked over to the camp desk in one corner. She was about to start going through the letters piled on top of it when she heard a noise behind her. She spun around, and her hood fell from her face to reveal her tell-tale red hair. Her hands flew up, but it was too late to disguise herself.

"Well, well, well," the prince said from the entrance. "Lady Erin, we meet again." He strode forward, and Erin backed up against the desk. "I knew you couldn't resist me," he said. "This time, we won't be interrupted."

"No -" Erin began to say, but the prince wrapped his hand around her neck and crushed his lips to hers. Disgusted, she pushed him away. "I said no!"

The prince stumbled back and almost tripped on one of the velvet cushions strewn across the floor. He scowled. "What is it, what...

what…" he raised a hand to clumsily wipe at his mouth and looked at her with dawning horror. "Your lipstick…"

"Do you like it?" Erin said with barely leashed fury. "I wore it just for you."

The prince staggered and fell, and he began to convulse. Erin watched, first with righteous anger, but as the convulsions became more grotesque, she looked away, feeling a little sick to her stomach.

Once the prince stopped thrashing and gurgling about on his cushions, it took Erin a long time to check if he was dead. After a lengthy hesitation, she gathered her courage and reached out to feel for a pulse or breath from his mouth or nose. Nothing. She stared, overcome with relief and joy. The fight was done. Nobody else had to die. She climbed to her feet, wobbly with excitement, and ran out onto the dirt path where soldiers traveled to and fro in the soft light of dawn. "The prince is dead! The prince is dead! Stop fighting, the prince is dead!" She screamed as loudly as she could, but nobody reacted except to give her quelling and disdainful looks. "Didn't you hear me?! The prince is DEAD!"

"Cease your wailing, woman, and get back inside!" A passing soldier shoved her back into the tent she'd left. "No one has time for your hysteria!"

Erin tripped over her feet and fell onto her hands. Abruptly furious, she regained her footing and began to pace from one side of the tent to the other. They wouldn't listen. All that work, she thought. All that pain and suffering and death, and still nobody would believe her! She looked at the prince where he lay face down among the cushions.

She would make them listen. She would give them so much proof, they wouldn't be able to ignore it. She'd find someone else to spread the message if she must. Duke Bavencian, she thought. The duke would listen to her, and the rest of the world would listen to the duke.

First, she'd have to bring him proof. She grabbed at the prince's shoulders and tried to drag him, but he was too heavy for her to move him more than a few feet. Panting, she dropped him to the ground and bent over her knees to catch her breath. She stared down at his dead weight and sighed, exhausted. He weighed her down even in death. It was hard for her to look at him, harder to deal with his death than the deaths of the many she had killed in battle. She felt different without the urgency of a fight carrying her along. The ground swam before her, but she steadied herself with determination. It was time to end her struggle with the prince once and for all.

She took out one of her knives and knelt at the prince's head. His glassy eyes stared up at the tent ceiling, and she turned away to gag and heave. There was no food left in her stomach, so it didn't take long before she could wipe the bile from her lips. Her nose was so clogged with the stench of blood rising anew from the battlefield that she could barely smell the vomit on the ground. She rolled the prince away from the mess and onto his stomach. It was easier, when she couldn't see his face. She grabbed at his hair and cut at the back of his neck. The knife didn't go very deep before it struck bone. She grunted and leaned into the next slice, but her knife wasn't made for beheading, and it was gruesome and sweaty work. Blood and fluid oozed onto her hands and up her arms, sometimes spurting onto her clothes and face. She continued to saw away, convinced that if she stopped, she wouldn't be able to start again.

Finally she cut through the last bits of tendon and skin, and the prince's head came away in her hand. Shivering with nausea, she turned away from the head and body to dry heave, her stomach desperately trying to empty her of the taste and smell of death. The acrid stench of sick burned into her nostrils. She coughed and raised a hand to wipe her mouth clean, forgetting that her hand was dirty and smearing her face with the prince's blood. Disgusted, she spat furiously and crawled to the cushions on the floor to wipe her face and hands on the silk. The fine fabric was little help, and her hands came away still caked with blood. She crouched there and steadied herself before grabbing at a finely woven blanket and rolling the head into it. She fashioned the ends of the blanket into impromptu handles and hoisted the bundle up to hip level. It was heavier than she expected. Trying not to look at the empty space between the prince's shoulders, she yanked his signet ring off his finger and put it in her pocket. She wiped her knife on the prince's clothes before sheathing it, tested that the blanket was well wrapped and secure within her grasp, and crept out of the back of the tent, eager to rid herself of her burden.

Her journey was easier on the way back. The battle had started fresh with the morning light, and she was able to slip past soldiers in the chaos with ease. She dimly noted that the duke's men had arrived, marked as they were by their flags and shining armor. The bag she had fashioned out of a blanket held up well, with only a small, brownish red spot hinting at what might be inside. As long as she didn't look at that spot or the stains on her clothes, she could almost pretend she was walking back from the market with a bag of grain or a chicken for roasting. She clung to that illusion to calm herself whenever horror and disgust threatened to overwhelm her. Once she reached the outer wall of the keep, she looked for directions.

"Where's the duke?" Erin asked a passing guard, but all he did was give her a strange look on his way by her. She supposed she must be a sight with her skin and clothes smeared with blood and dirt.

Erin ran in front of him and blocked his way. "Where is the duke?!"

"The eastern guard tower," the guard grumbled and shoved her out of his way. Erin almost lost her grip on the blanket, her stomach lurching with revulsion, but she held onto it. She broke into a run toward the guard tower. Her blanket-bag jostled with each step, sometimes hitting her thigh. Each time it bumped against her, she shuddered and had to remind herself she would be done soon. Soldiers and medics walking the streets eyed her with suspicion, but none stopped her progress. Soon, she reached the tower and went up to the entrance, only to be stopped by a guard grabbing at her arm.

"Whoa there, young lady! Where do you think you're going?"

She pulled herself out of his grasp and raised her chin. "I've come with proof of the prince's death. You must let me in!"

"The prince's death? What are you talking about? I haven't heard anything about the prince dying, have you, Marcus?"

The guard at the other side of the entrance shook his head. "Nah."

"I don't have time for this! Will you just tell the duke that Lady Erin is out here?!"

"A lady? You?" The guard leaned on his spear and looked over her stained dress. "You'll have to do better than that to get past me, sweetheart."

Erin had never hated a complete stranger so much before in her life. She held her bag out and pulled it open far enough to show the contents. "I have proof of the prince's death," she ground out through clenched teeth. "Now tell his grace that I must speak with him."

The guard stared, transfixed, at the grotesque mess she showed him before he nodded and disappeared inside the tent. The other guard, Marcus, leaned closer to have a peek, but Erin shut the bag again and glared. She wasn't here to gossip with a guard. He held up his hands and went back to his post, muttering, "All right, you don't have to be such a bitch about it."

The door opened before she could reply, and the guard motioned her in, his posture straight and formal once more. She rushed to the duke where he stood over a large map of the battlefield. A messenger stood at attention by his side.

"What do you have for me?" The duke didn't look up from his contemplation of the battle markers.

"I bear news of the prince's death, your grace." She set the bag on the ground and rolled the head out for him to see. The duke turned to stare at the familiar features for a moment, and then he looked to his messenger. "Alert the generals." The messenger ran out with a hasty salute, and the duke came over to clap a hand on her shoulder. "Well done, Lady Erin."

"Thank you, your grace. You should spread the news to the enemy camp as well. It would strike a major blow to their morale."

The Duke inclined his head. "I agree." He led her outside and snapped his fingers. "Marcus!"

"Yes, your grace?"

"Hold out your spear." Marcus tilted the spear to the duke, who picked up the prince's head by the hair and impaled it. He then took the spear and held it aloft to consider the sight of the prince, glassy eyed and with jaw hanging open, hair matted and stringy at the ends. Despite the distortion of his face in death, his features were still clearly recognizable. Duke Bavencian nodded. "This should do nicely." He turned to Marcus. "Ready my guard. I wish to ride into battle."

"Yes, your grace."

The duke looked back up at the prince's head. "Well, nephew. It seems I have outlived you after all." He grinned. "You never could learn how to treat a lady."

24
A New Adventure

THE DUKE RODE out with the prince's head on a spear, and the Norcliff forces rallied behind him with loud cheers. Erin watched from her vantage point atop the eastern tower as little by little, the soldiers in the Morton colors peeled away from the fighting and began to retreat. Her heart didn't lighten, though, because the bandits and Varnallans stayed and continued fighting.

"They must be desperate," Erin muttered as she watched the fighting continue. It seemed to be centered around the duke, as if in vengeance for his victory. "He needs help!" she said to herself, and she ran to get her armor on. She mounted her horse and rode to the duke's aid, and the next few hours blurred together in a mass of suffering and gore. Erin grimly fought on all the while wondering how much she would have to go through before her family and her people could rest. It was a long and bloody battle, but finally, in the late afternoon, a cry of victory went up.

"They're retreating!" a boy yelled near her, and she looked up, wiping the blood from her face, to see the tide of the Varnallans turn and move back in the direction of the border. She blew out a breath and almost staggered with exhaustion. It was over. It was done. She could rest now, except her mind wouldn't let her rest. She kept seeing the severed head of the prince in her mind's eye. He wouldn't leave her alone.

She sheathed her sword and slowly walked away from the jubilant soldiers. She just needed to find a quiet place, she thought, and then she would find peace. Erin walked through the crowds of cheering soldiers, which changed to cheering villagers as she made her way into town. She found herself in the old chapel by the keep where she was baptized as a baby. She sat in the sturdy wooden pew nearest the front and stared at her hands. Lines of red decorated her palms and cracked in the creases where her fingers bent. She could use another baptism, she thought, to wash away the blood on her hands, her clothes, her armor, and her face. It was even matting her hair. She tried to run her fingers through the bloody strands, but they caught in the tangles.

So much death, she thought. How could she ever be free of it? Even if she never saw another day of battle in her life, she had more than a lifetime's worth of memories of killing now, and images of soldiers' faces as they died ran through her mind. It was all she could think of, until the image of the prince's face appeared, and then that was all she could think of. She rubbed her hand across her face wearily, heedless of the blood and grime.

"You sit like a stone when you should be celebrating our victory. Why?"

Erin turned around to find Hugo standing in the doorway to the chapel. She watched as he walked closer to stand next to her. "I've worn the memory of the prince's body pressed against mine every day since he stole what wasn't his to take. Now his blood stains my skin, and no amount of scrubbing will stop my eyes from seeing it."

The wood of the pew creaked as Hugo sat next to her. "Blood stains all who fight. It's the price we pay to make each other safe. This burden binds us together, just like the victory we wrought on this battlefield."

"Binds us together?" Erin raised an eyebrow at Lord Hugo. "After the chaos from this battle clears, and the celebrations are over, we shall part ways, likely never to see each other again."

This statement gave Hugo pause, and his eyebrows lowered to shadow his eyes as he looked down at his clasped hands in thought. "Tell me." Hugo looked intently at her. "Tell me what you feel for me."

Erin turned her head to the side, suddenly feeling shy. "No."

Hugo growled with frustration. "I'm tired of leaving things unsaid with you. We part ways soon, and I want to know how you feel about me before then."

"Fine!" Erin grasped his hand. "Fine. Just don't talk about leaving anymore." She didn't want to hear about another loved one leaving her.

Hugo's shoulders rose and fell with a sigh, and his hands covered hers to press them against his chest. She released a shuddering breath, and his hands tightened around hers before loosening again. His voice dropped to a soft rumble. "Very well. I beg of you, Lady Erin. Tell me what you feel for me."

Erin felt the sting of an old, familiar shame. "You'll laugh," she whispered.

"I won't laugh."

Heat rose up her neck, and she turned her face away. "You will make me cry," she murmured to the empty chapel.

Hugo stroked her cheek with his thumb. "For every tear, a kiss, until you smile once more."

Erin sighed. "Oh, isn't it obvious?" She closed her eyes. "I love you. How could I not?"

She felt Hugo's fingers twitch against her skin, and then he slid his hands into her hair to press his lips against hers. Her heart fluttered in time to the sensation of his lips and the prickle of his scruff against her skin. Erin curled an arm around his neck to pull herself closer in search of more heat, more fuel to add to the blaze of passion growing within her. She slid her other arm around his back, anchoring herself to him as he shifted unbearably closer until there was no space left between them. She pulled her lips from his to gasp for air, and he rested his forehead against hers, holding her tight against him.

"I feel-" Hugo's voice rasped. He cleared his throat and tried again. "I feel as though I would love you from beyond the grave." His rough, unsteady words rumbled in his chest, and she could feel the vibrations. He brushed a soft kiss to her temple. "I will love you every day for the rest of my life, I can tell you that much for sure." Hugo slid from his seat to kneel on the floor before her. Capturing her hands where they had risen to her mouth, he pulled them down toward him and bent to kiss one palm, then the other. "Lady Erin, I would like to bind us together by more than war, if you would do me the honor."

"Hugo," Erin said, breathless. "What are you asking?"

"I cannot wash you clean of blood, my love, for I am covered in it." He looked up at her with eyes dark as coal, and the candlelight only exaggerated the dirt on his cheeks and scratches gouged in his armor. "But I love you more fiercely than I have ever fought. May I, that is, would you," he pressed his lips together and furrowed his brows. "If you would gift me with a lifetime of your company, you would bestow upon me a greater honor than any I have won in battle. Please marry me."

Erin stared. "But this is so fast. I've known you for a matter of days!"

"We'll make it a long engagement, then. But please, give me your word you intend to live your life at my side, as I intend to live at yours."

Erin considered Hugo. He had become dear to her as he had proven himself to her. He'd stuck by her side through the troubles that plagued her and accepted her as she was, mistakes, weaknesses, and all. She loved him for it, and for who he was. She loved him so very much. She hadn't thought it possible to feel so much, so quickly.

Erin cupped his face in her hands and smoothed the creases on his forehead with her thumbs. "Very well." He continued to kneel, frozen, at her feet, eyes fixed upon her face. Erin laughed and leaned down to kiss him. "Yes, I'll marry you. Don't look so surprised!"

He rose with a hearty laugh and picked her up to twirl her in his arms. "I can't help it!" He settled her on her feet and met her eyes with solemn fervor. "I shall make you shine with such joy that you will drive the shadows from the room. You won't regret choosing me."

Looking up at him, Erin had no doubt that he would love her every day with the same thoughtful tenacity that he applied to all tasks that mattered to him. That knowledge was enough to make her rejoice, and she knew it always would be. "I have no doubt," she murmured, "I have no doubt at all."

They embraced again, and Erin had finally found her peace within another's arms. She might have death and sorrow in her life, she thought, but she had love and joy, too.

She would make the most of it.

Acknowledgements

THANK YOU TO my family, my friends, and all who helped shepherd me along this long and winding path to the completion of my second novel. My husband is a constant support to me day in, day out, and he is my number one cheerleader. My parents, brother, and sister-in-law also cheered me on along the way. Thank you also to Chris, who helped with the back cover. And who could forget Dash and Scrambles, who keep me company and remind me to sit back, relax, and take a nap every so often. There is little that cannot be made better by a quick rest.

A Note to the Reader

IF YOU ENJOYED reading this novel, please consider leaving a review on your favored website or social media. Your support is invaluable to me as an independent author. Thank you for picking up this book.

www.ingramcontent.com/pod-product-compliance
Lightning Source LLC
Chambersburg PA
CBHW050839180626
46814CB00007B/2529